FALL OF MAN

THE MANX DETECTIVE BOOK 1

PAUL FORSTER

For Eleanor and the girls, and for my dad.

CHAPTER 1

I T WAS A WET and windy evening. Anyone brave enough to face the weather soon sought shelter. The Nelson was as good a place to do this as any. It was an old pub that sat facing Ramsey harbour. The cream painted render and racing green finish might have made it stand out in most towns. But on the Isle of Man, in Ramsey, it was just another old pub full of its regular customers. It didn't look like much on the inside, but the friendly staff and customers made it a home from home for many a visitor. Jim Walsh had made it his second home ever since he returned to the island. A tall man with broad shoulders in his early forties, Jim was an imposing figure and stood out in most crowds. He would often be spotted on a Saturday afternoon watching the horse racing or rugby, or on a weekday enjoying a few drinks after work, or maybe just popping in for a quick pint when visiting town to run an errand. As his marriage had become more strained, rather than working on the problems, Jim took refuge in the Nelson. The usual faces and friendly conversations soothed his tired soul.

Jim had been in the pub for several hours, arriving before the weather drove in most of his fellow patrons. He had been drinking at a pace that was unusual, even for him, and was becoming increasingly inebriated. Anyone unlucky enough to stray too close had their ear bent, to the point now even in the crowded bar. He had space on either side of him as he drank alone. Long after last orders were called, the last of the patrons were leaving. Jim wasn't ready to go home and face his wife. His drunken stupor would do little to help avoid an argument. "Anyone heading anywhere?" Jim slurred at nobody in particular. A wall of silence greeted him, and even in his state, he could take the hint. He knocked back the rest of his cider and stumbled outside. Several regulars stood on the narrow path, making use of the break in the weather to enjoy one last hit of nicotine as they finished their chats before venturing back to their homes and beds. Jim looked around, hopeful of an invitation for another drink, but nobody was foolish enough to make eye contact. A shrug of his shoulders and Jim decided he'd head home, hopeful of passing another pub that may still be serving.

Jim stumbled down the narrow, uneven alleyway that led from the harbour to Parliament Street. He was halfway through when he knew he was being followed. An icy shiver went down his spine as he spun around, his fist clenched and raised, ready to defend himself. Rather than an attacker, there was an attractive girl with dark hair in her twenties, dressed for a night out rather than a violent crime spree.

"What the hell! Are you okay, mate?" the girl said, stopping dead in her tracks before taking a small step back.

"Sorry, I thought you were a mugger or something," Jim sheepishly replied. He lowered his fist and gave an awkward smile.

"I'm looking for my friend's house. They're having a party. I'm afraid I don't really know where I am. I'm just over from the mainland for a few days visiting," she told him, smiling.

Jim straightened himself up and put all his effort into not appearing as if he was half as drunk as he actually was. "What's the address?" Jim asked.

The girl produced her mobile phone and showed the screen to Jim. He recognised the street; it wasn't too far from his own home. "That's on my way. I can show you."

"How do I know you're not a mugger?" she asked, as she looked the drunk man up and down.

"This is the Isle of Man. You can trust almost all of us. And I'm especially trustworthy." Jim slurred as he replied, any thin veil of sobriety slipping.

"Just so we're clear, I know karate and I'm not interested in shagging you," she warned Jim, pulling a repulsed face.

"Good to know. This way," Jim replied. He was a little offended at the unsolicited rejection, but amused by the idea of this girl even thinking of him that way, even if only to discount it. He led them out of the alley and through Ramsey.

***

Jim had been sitting on the edge of the dirty, unmade bed for nearly five minutes, hunched over, resting his head in his hands. The room was freshly decorated, the scent of paint still obvious, but it was extremely basic. The furniture was cheap laminated chipboard, hastily bodged together by someone who didn't care. A few cheap prints and a large mirror on two of the walls added a slight level of decoration. It wasn't hard to believe that he was the first to wake up there with regrets. His head throbbed and body ached. He had endured many hangovers in his life, but this one topped the lot. His rugby player build often shielded him from the effects of a heavy night, but this was different. He was still dressed in his suit and raincoat; both were ruffled, but his belt was unbuckled, and his trousers were down to just above his knees. He reached into his jacket pocket and pulled out his phone. It irritated him to notice a crack on the screen; it was his work phone. He'd catch shit for that when they found out. There was no mobile reception; that probably accounted for the lack of missed calls.

Nothing felt right. This wasn't a normal hangover. Jim had barely opened his eyes for the pain the light caused him, but he couldn't sit there with his eyes shut forever. He knew that. He could figure out what had happened later. For now, he just needed some fresh air and as much water as possible to throw on his face and down his throat. Gingerly, he rose to his feet, swaying as he attempted to steady himself before tumbling to the floor. His head spun, and his legs were like jelly. He would have to take this slower. Jim climbed to his knees and pulled his trousers up and fumbled with the belt. He shuffled into the middle of the room and sat himself down. He looked around and noticed her. Asleep in the bed, a dark-haired woman. Her body was covered with the duvet, just her head poking out but facing away.

Shit. Jim didn't think it was possible to feel worse than he did, but what had he done? He was married, and he'd gone out and picked up some girl and cheated. He'd never cheated on Ella, despite all of their issues and how bad it had become. *Why now?*

"Are you okay?" Jim asked, his voice hoarse. He cleared his throat and tried again. "Hello, are you okay?"

He waited a moment, and there was no response or movement. Slowly, he edged around the bed and then shook her shoulder. Nothing. He pulled back the duvet and recognised her. *The girl from the alley.* She was partially clothed, but fully dead. After they had met, he remembered nothing. He couldn't recall the party or even arriving there. The sight of the corpse should have shocked him, but it didn't.

A single gunshot wound on her forehead didn't look too gruesome. A small trickle of blood down her temple and on the pillow was the only thing obviously wrong. There was no exit wound to match the small entry one. The pistol was on the floor beside the bed, a shell casing sitting close by it. Without thinking, Jim picked up the handgun. He held it in his hand and it looked like a toy. It was stamped with markings showing it was made in Czechoslovakia and had 6.35 marked inside a small circle. It didn't look that intimidating, but was apparently more than capable of ending a life. His sense regained, and he dropped the gun on to the bed, angry he'd even touched the damn thing. He knew better than that.

Jim wanted to run, but he could barely stand. He felt like screaming, but his throat was raw and wouldn't allow it. Maybe he had killed the girl, maybe not, but he couldn't stay here spreading his DNA around further. *What the hell had happened?* His mind suddenly focused, and his body surged with adrenaline. He patted himself down. His wallet and watch were present, his wedding ring still firmly on his finger. He stopped and stared at the small pistol. At best, it just had his prints on it. At worst, it had enough of his DNA on it to put him in prison for the rest of his life. *Fuck it.* He knew it was coming with him. He'd dispose of it in the first river or pool of water he passed, but it wasn't staying here to be discovered by the police.

With the pistol shoved into his trouser pocket, Jim walked in front of the large mirror. He looked as bad as he felt. He straightened himself up as best he could, but his ruffled hair wouldn't cooperate. His face was sweaty and discoloured. He couldn't do much more. It was time to leave. Slowly, he opened the door and carefully slipped out of the room.

What the hell? Jim couldn't believe his eyes. He expected an equally dated and rundown hallway to match the room. He didn't expect a large and mostly empty warehouse.

The fake room was just a set. Sitting in the middle of the warehouse, large wooden struts supported the walls. The unpainted MDF boards were strewn with wires and duct tape. On the wall where the mirror would have been in the room, a large sheet of glass allowed him a perfect view into the room. A two-way mirror. His heart skipped a beat. He stepped back and looked at the structure. It looked barely capable of standing upright, but the job had been impressively effective.

Jim looked around the warehouse. Was he still being watched? He looked for anything that resembled a way out of this damned place. A fire exit at the far end of the warehouse would do, and he headed towards it. Jim walked as fast as he could, trying hard not to fall to the floor or vomit. He made it in one piece and with the contents of his stomach in the right place. He pushed the bar; the door popped open, and the alarm sounded. Jim slipped through the exit and slammed it shut behind him in the forlorn hope that the alarm might stop. It didn't.

Even the dull light from the overcast skies was too much for his eyes. He didn't feel any less confused as he stood outside the brand new warehouse. Another near identical one stood next to it in the freshly constructed compound, all surrounded by a tall mesh wire fence. Beyond that, trees and the green slopes of the valley surrounded a single road in front of the gates. Jim adjusted his vision and scanned the site. It appeared to be deserted. He headed straight to the gates. A chain secured them, but gave him just enough room to squeeze through, out onto the road in front.

He did not know where he was. He looked at his phone, and still, it had no signal. Even the GPS was refusing to help him. He could climb out of the valley and use the higher ground to look out and try to identify where he was, or maybe get something on his phone. He pondered that for the briefest moment. In his condition, he could just as easily slip down the damp slopes and break his neck. He decided the island wasn't big enough for him to be lost for long. He headed off down the road, hoping he was going the right way.

For ten minutes, he'd still seen little more than trees and hill. Not a single car had passed, which was a relief. Jim didn't relish diving into the undergrowth to escape witnessing eyes. With every step, his head cleared a little. He ached, but he could move freely as the stiffness eased. The fresh air filled his lungs, and it felt good. Compared to the stench of death and disaster from that sordid little room of murder, anything would have felt good. The weight of the small pistol in his pocket reminded him of its incriminating presence. Even from the road, he could launch it into the woods, and they would surely never find it. He held it in his hand and felt the weight. *No.* He told himself. *Don't get even sloppier than you already have been.* Jim stepped off the road and headed into the woods. The trees were dense, but autumn had stripped nearly all of them of their leaves. He looked up, the overcast sky barely broken by the branches above. He was now twenty feet away from the road, and he could no longer see the tarmac. The ground was full of debris from the trees. The loose dirt, twigs, and leaves would provide good concealment. Jim crouched down, eager not to add mud to the miscellaneous stains and marks soiling his suit. He scraped away the loose covering to get to the ground beneath, and with his hands, he dug out a small hole, just a few inches deep. But it would do. He wiped the pistol with his coat, with a vague hope it might remove his prints in the unlikely event it would ever be discovered. Satisfied he'd done something, he dropped the gun in the hole and replaced the dirt before carefully covering it with a few leaves and twigs. He looked around, then up again before taking a step back and nodding to himself, satisfied that the pistol would not be easily found.

Jim headed back to the road and carried on walking. He'd have to think of a story to tell Ella. He rarely worked late. She wouldn't buy that. A lock-in at the Nelson? Just what every wife dreamed of hearing. '*Sorry I didn't make it home last night, love. I stayed in the pub, got battered and passed out in the bog.*' No, he'd have to think of something better. He could blame his absence on Daz, a man always one step away from throwing himself in front of a bus. Suddenly, his concentration was broken as his pocket vibrated aggressively. He reached in and pulled out his phone. Mobile service at last. He answered the call and pressed the phone to his ear. "DS Walsh," Jim answered and stopped walking as he concentrated on the call. "I'll be in at midday," he looked at his watch. "Maybe a little later." He ended the call and launched the map app. He was nearly a mile north of Laxey. At least from there, he could get the tram back home. He didn't know how he would have gotten to this place from Ramsey. Thoughts rushed

8

through his mind of who had brought him there and why. Did he come willingly with the girl, or did something else happen?

His pace slowed as he remembered the dead girl's face. Jim wasn't the best copper anymore, he wasn't the best husband, but he'd never been a bad one of either. And in one night, he appeared to have become the worst of both. His natural belief in justice had driven him to join the police service, and now he was hiding from his potential crimes.

When he left the Isle of Man to go to university in Liverpool, he had everything planned out. He'd get his degree in criminology, apply to Merseyside police and stay in Liverpool, working in the famous city where he'd progress in his policing career. He met his wife, Ella, at the University of Liverpool. She was a girl from a good middle-class family in the south; she was beautiful, funny and the life and soul of the party. Shacking up with a Manx kid who didn't want to be a barrister or hedge fund manager wound her parents up. Exactly the reaction she had desired. After two years as a beat bobby, he moved into CID, where he was a decent detective constable. Ambition, or perhaps a thirst for action, sent him towards the drug squad. It was busy work in a place like Liverpool, what many saw as the deprived north. Cannabis was popular, but amphetamines were the drug of choice. The work was unrewarding; if they took one dealer down, another two would rise in their place. It was demoralising. As the years went by, he became less fun. Less full of life. He drank and cared less about everything and everyone. His work and wife suffered. Then one day, staggering out of the pub shortly after 2am, a familiar face followed.

Leo Johnson had been a low-level drug dealer, and not a successful one. Jim was the arresting officer and testified at Leo's trial. The 100g of amphetamines and 30 wraps of cannabis were a problem for Leo, but when he swung the machete at Jim, he had doomed himself to a custodial sentence. Leo was short and skinny; the bigger and stronger Jim had little trouble avoiding the wayward blade and putting the little prick face-first on the ground before applying the handcuffs. The judge sentenced Leo to four years in prison. With just over two served, that night Leo found himself in a pub barely ten feet away from the man who had put him away. When they last met, Jim had bested him. Not today. Pursuing the drunk for a little over a minute, Leo followed him down a side street. As Jim relieved himself in the shadows, he felt the first impact. And then the next. Someone had stolen the air from his lungs. He turned to see Leo, a small blade dripping with blood, glistening in the dull light. The next thing Jim had known, he was being wheeled into surgery at Whiston Hospital.

His body would eventually heal, but his mind didn't.

Within the year, he had transferred to the Isle of Man Constabulary to work in the CID department, earning a promotion to Detective Sergeant in the process. Where he was now no longer in a big city with big crime. The Isle of Man still had criminals who needed apprehending, of course, but fewer murderers. Instead, more thieves of farming equipment or brawlers who went too far in a drunken fight. He was Manx; this place was his home. Here he felt confident that he'd get back to his old self and maybe reignite his love of the job and his wife.

If only Ella had felt the same way about the island.

CHAPTER 2

T HE TRAM PULLED INTO Ramsey station as a light drizzle and strong winds drove into the open carriage that Jim had sat himself in. When he had eventually found his way to Laxey, he had to wait in the cold for over an hour for the first tram to Ramsey of the day. It gave him time to sober up and get his head straight. The tram was still reasonably popular with tourists and used regularly by remotely based locals who depended on its service. At this time of the morning, with less than clear weather, there were few passengers; only those who needed to get to a job braved it. Jim spent the forty-five-minute journey keeping his head down and avoiding eye contact with any of the other scant passengers who looked at him from the relative, dry comfort of the enclosed carriages. He spent the time practising in his head the story for Ella. He had gone simple. Blame it on Daz, the renowned waster who jumped from one crisis to another. For all his faults, Daz was a good, loyal friend. He'd cover for him. Only Jim, the conductor, and two other passengers hopped off the tram once he came to a stop at its final destination.

His stomach rumbled for most of the short walk to his home, a small detached bungalow on the edge of the town. As it came into view, he stared, eager to see if the cars were in the driveway. Neither car was visible. *Shit*. She may have gone to work already or left hers in town, but where the hell was his car? A problem for later. The house enjoyed a small private garden and only a neighbour on one side; it was a far cry from the luxury apartment they had in Liverpool. The only thing Ella enjoyed about the house was the cosy garden, which she tended to with a passion. What Jim loved about it was the same thing Ella hated. It wasn't Liverpool. She had grown used to having a thriving city on her doorstep. The top restaurants, the bars and her friends. Ella had given up her career to move to the island for Jim. She had left the finance world behind and now ran her own shop in Douglas, selling overpriced lamps and small pieces of furniture to those with more money than sense. She thought that had been her dream, and it was. Just not on the Isle of Man.

Jim opened the door, hoping Ella had already left for the shop. The lack of worried or angry voice or text messages had surprised him. That was either very good or extremely bad news. The post was on the doormat with the newspaper. Jim sighed with relief. She must have left early that morning.

He set about the task of making himself human once more. A shower and shave made him look presentable. A round of toast, a bowl of cornflakes and an entire pot of tea made him feet the part. He had nearly forgotten about that poor girl. He became distracted and nearly missed the note stuck to the door. Unfolding it, he could see the printed text. That was impersonal, even for Ella.

'Gone to my parents on the redeye. I can't stay on this shithole of an island anymore. You changed before I did, and I can't deal with you. Don't call. I need to sort my head out.'

The bitch. Jim knew things had been tough; he knew she wasn't happy, but this? Leaving him with using a printed note; why didn't she just cut out the middleman and email him? He grabbed his phone and found her number, ready to hit call. He thought better of it. She wanted a reaction. He decided that she needed to get it out of her system, and once she came back, they could enjoy a temporary reset of their relationship. She always came back, no matter how fed up she was, and then things were better, for a little while. At least he didn't have to face her. That was one less thing to worry about.

Dressed and fed, Jim locked up the house and went outside. He paused for a moment in thought. He went over to the garage and swung open the large metal door. There was Ella's car; a light blue Mini. It didn't take him long to figure out that as a final 'fuck you,' she had taken the Mercedes. He'd swing by the airport to recover it at some point, but for now, the Mini would do. Retrieving the keys from the house, he set off to Douglas.

***

The Isle of Man Constabulary wasn't as busy or high profile as a city in England. It did, however, offer its own unique challenges. The TT and Manx Grand Prix brought tens of thousands of visitors to the island for several weeks a year. All whilst having nearly 40 miles of road closed, practically slicing the island in half. DC Kerry Hughes was the unlucky occupant of the desk opposite DS Jim Walsh. She was in her late twenties, athletic, and not afraid to be one of the boys. Something that had made her popular when she had been in uniform and had carried through to

CID. Trustworthy and hardworking would be the opinion of anyone who had worked with her, the near opposite of Detective Sergeant Jim Walsh. As a sergeant, he outranked her, but since he had transferred, he had done little to impress his colleagues. His record had been impeccable, and they had afforded him some leeway for the injury he had sustained, prompting his return to the Isle of Man. Coming in at a rank many junior colleagues felt they were entitled to have a crack at hadn't helped his cause. Kerry and her colleagues suspected Jim was an alcoholic, highly functioning, but still a problem that made this once heralded detective a shadow of his former self. Unlike her colleagues, she could still see what he could offer when the mood took him, and she had little doubt she had still learned much from him.

Jim being late wasn't a rare occurrence, and normally he looked worse for wear. When Kerry called Jim, it surprised her he had answered. They were due to visit Nobles hospital to interview a victim of a hit and run. The elderly gentleman had suffered a broken hip and had been in surgery the previous evening, the medical staff advising he should be fit for visitors in the morning. Jim had made the call himself, so the fact he hadn't bothered to turn up at the station on time was doubly frustrating. Kerry hadn't been back long from the hospital. The statement she had taken from the victim wouldn't lead to an arrest, so there was no obvious chance of a conviction unless the guilty party came forward or another witness presented themselves. The victim hadn't seen the car that struck them, insisting only that it sounded like a diesel. Or possibly an old petrol engine car.

"No Walsh yet? Bloody waster." DC Billy Mulligan dropped a small padded envelope on Jim's desk. He was in his late twenties, good looking, tall and skinny, but had never really grown up. He'd watched a few too many cop films as a kid, and the pedestrian nature of island policing hadn't provided him with the level of excitement he'd hoped for. As a local lad who loved the island, he didn't wish to leave to seek his exciting law enforcement career elsewhere. Instead, he made the best of what he had and he was comfortable.

"That's Sergeant waster, constable," Kerry corrected her colleague with a knowing smile.

"Of course, our precious sarge." Billy sat in Jim's chair and gave it a spin.

"You doing the mail round now, Billy? You finally got your promotion?" Kerry's smile widened as Billy answered back with a stretched grin and a middle finger salute.

"They left it at the front desk this morning. Feels like one of those small pocket dildos, a special-order type of thing." Billy said, mimicking the rude actions of inserting the object into his bottom.

"Billy, you can't talk to a female colleague like that. HR will put you on another course," Kerry said, in a mock stern and offended voice.

"Sorry Kerry, I forgot you were a female. Must be the fact you've got bigger balls than most of us."

Jim entered the office, prompting Billy to jump out of Jim's chair. "Good morning, constable. Keeping it warm?"

"Good afternoon, Sergeant," Billy responded, correcting his superior.

Jim's icy stare prompted Billy to head back to his own desk, much to Kerry's amusement.

"I went to Nobles to talk with the hit and run. Nothing useful," Kerry updated him. She knew he didn't care, but wanted to remind Jim that he'd missed the visit.

"Okay, very good. Get it typed up and we'll get uniform to knock on a few more doors before we put it back in the pile," Jim told her, his eyes fixed on the padded envelope with his name written on it.

"He's okay. They think he'll make a full recovery," Kerry told Jim. He didn't ask; he probably didn't care.

"Where did this come from?" Jim asked, holding up the jiffy bag.

"Billy grabbed it from the front desk. Someone dropped it in this morning," Kerry confirmed.

His name was handwritten on the front with a red marker pen. Jim opened up the envelope and slid the contents onto his desk. A USB memory stick with a sticky note attached, with just two words. 'WATCH ALONE!'

Jim's heart skipped a beat as he slowly picked up the memory stick and slid it into his suit pocket.

"You okay, Jim?" Kerry asked, noticing his face drop.

"Just some holiday snaps from my uncle and aunt. You know how it is. Family," Jim replied, placing the padded envelope into his drawer, away from prying eyes. "I've got an errand to run. I'll be back in an hour," he undocked his laptop from his desk, stood up and walked out with it under his arm,

"Unbelievable," Kerry stated, exasperated.

***

Jim used to frequent the Kings for a quick lunch when he could get away from the station. The large, dark wood panels helped give it an old-fashioned feeling that Jim enjoyed. The friendly service and the fact it was a little over ten minutes' walk away from the station sealed the deal. Despite its proximity to the Police headquarters, he'd rarely see another officer in there during the day. Most officers these days were far too professional to have a drink during the day. Jim wasn't an old man, but he felt old school compared to many of his colleagues.

"Alright Jim, the usual?" the barmaid asked as he approached the bar.

"Yeah, please," Jim responded as he looked around the pub. There were several free tables available, and he picked a couple of candidates.

The barmaid handed over the lager-shandy and Jim passed across a ten-pound note. "Get one for yourself."

The barmaid smiled politely as Jim moved to his preferred table. It was at the back of the bar and allowed him to have his back against the wall to maintain his privacy. He took several large gulps of the pint as he opened up the laptop. The computer slowly booted up, and he examined the memory stick. It was absolutely nothing special. The stick was dark blue with '16GB' etched into it. They could have purchased it anywhere. He logged in to the operating system. His desktop was full of files and folders, a mess of icons, each making the others even harder to distinguish. He popped in the memory stick and the contents instantly showed. A single video file, 'DRONE_0117'. Jim's eyes flicked around the mostly empty bar, satisfied he wasn't being observed.

Jim opened the file, and his eyes widened. A figure walking down the side of the road in the middle of nowhere. They were so far away; they were barely a blur in the picture, but Jim was certain. The figure moved suddenly and disappeared into the wooded area at the side of the road, and the camera gained height and sped quickly to the location, the camera shifting downwards, looking through the leafless trees. The figure was crouched down, wiping off a small pistol with their coat. *Shit.* They placed the pistol into a small hole and covered it. They stood up and looked around, then straight into the sky. Jim knew it was him long before he saw his face, and that glance upwards would confirm it to anyone who watched the video. The rest of the video didn't matter. They had him.

Jim quickly took the memory stick out of the laptop and shoved it into his pocket before closing the computer. He finished the rest of the shandy, but the lager and lemonade mix weren't strong enough. He picked up the laptop and moved to the bar. "A double vodka, no ice," Jim barked at the surprised barmaid. She quickly poured him the clear drink, and he pushed another ten-pound note in her direction. He knocked back the drink and left without saying another word.

His phone started vibrating in his pocket. *Did they already know?* He took the phone, and it was Kerry. "Yes," he answered curtly. "A body? Laxey?" Jim answered quietly, his face turning white as a sheet. "I'm on the promenade, just coming out of the sweet shop," Jim lied. It was the closest shop he could think of near to the pub. "Okay, I'll see you in two." Jim hurried his pace to make sure he was where he said he'd be. He got there just as Kerry's car rounded the corner and pulled up.

"Getting a stick of rock?" Kerry questioned sarcastically through the open passenger side window.

Jim got into the car and shoved his laptop under the seat. "I had to get some cash out. What's going on?" Jim asked, still not convinced he wasn't about to be arrested.

Kerry pulled the car away at speed. "They found a girl in the Laxey River, not sure of much else other than she was naked. Could be a suicide or an accident. Probably a mannequin," Kerry confirmed. The call had only just come in and no one had been onsite yet. Even the ambulance was still on its way. She sniffed and could smell the alcohol on Jim's breath, but thought better of asking him about it.

Jim couldn't work out how she had got to the river. Someone was obviously playing with him, but why take the risk of putting her somewhere so public in broad daylight? Jim wanted to jump out of the car and just run, but he had to play it cool; he wasn't done yet. Maybe if he was leading the investigation, he could steer it away from himself. This wasn't bad news. The fact she was in the river would suggest a lot of the evidence could have been washed away. They had moved the body, so that horrible crime scene, rich with forensic evidence, was still unknown and would hopefully never be found. Jim knew he'd find out sooner rather than later. Somebody was going after him and had already collected the evidence. Just what did they want from him?

CHAPTER 3

L AXEY WAS AN IDYLLIC setting; quintessential Isle of Man. It was steeped in history and now happily traded on its heritage. Few tourists to the island would pass up the opportunity to visit the water wheel, ride the tram, or delve into the mines. For the locals, Laxey was just a nice place to live. A body washing up in the river was huge news, and despite the emergency services only now arriving on the scene, a small crowd had already gathered nearby, watching the scene as it developed.

A solitary police car arrived first, closely followed by an ambulance a few minutes later, and then another marked car appeared at the scene at the same time Kerry and Jim pulled up. Slowly, the vehicles passed through the crowd, gently pushing through as those gathered in attendance eased to the side to let them pass. Two uniformed officers emerged from a police car and immediately began shouting orders to the crowd but were helpless to hold back those eager to catch a glimpse. The body of the naked woman was still in the middle of the shallow river, face down, the water washing over her.

Kerry was the first to approach the two constables. "Jesus, has nobody tried to fish her out?" Kerry looked incredulously at the graphic scene.

"We just got here. Didn't think we should touch the body, anyway. But feel free. I'll look after your shoes whilst you go for a little paddle," one officer answered sarcastically.

"She can't bloody stay in there all day. Hughes, get some photos, and when Mulligan pitches up, he and I will assist the uniformed officers in retrieving her," Jim ordered. He had little concern about contaminating the crime scene. An excuse to get his DNA on the corpse might help him if the river hadn't already washed her clean.

"What about the coroner's office, sarge?" Kerry replied, now unsure if Jim was right, but surprised by his willingness to help with the unpleasant recovery.

"Get the photos and we'll get the girl on dry ground and covered for some dignity, shall we? I'll worry about DC Doolan. You just get the pictures, okay?" Jim snapped back.

Kerry returned to the car to retrieve the camera like a scolded child.

More uniformed officers turned up, and they quickly moved the crowd back, putting up a cordon far enough away that the eager eyes wouldn't be able to spectate any longer. Jim looked down at the girl. They had obviously dumped her further up the river. The cuts and broken limbs confirmed that. The poor girl must have hit every rock, branch, and piece of debris on her brief trip through the shallow waterway. No amount of damage would hide that bullet wound forever. If her head and face were as beaten as the rest of her body, it might take the autopsy to discover the true nature of her death.

Jim's phone rang, and he answered it eagerly. "Yes, guv, I'm here with Hughes. The body hasn't been recovered yet; it's still in the river. We'll get some pictures, then get her to dry land and wait for Doolan. Will do. Thank you, sir." Jim ended the call, pleased with his performance for his superior. He watched his fellow officers set about their tasks. None had seen anything like this before. They were well trained, capable. Some, like Kerry, were even exceptional. Jim knew that an officer of her standard could go as far as she wanted, anywhere she wanted. The Isle of Man Constabulary was fortunate to have her. None of these officers had dealt with a murder like this before. They almost all would have been around dead bodies at some point, but a two-day-old corpse of an OAP having passed away in their sleep was a different proposition to this. This was violence. This was graphic. It wasn't just a fight that had gone too far between two drunks. This was a bullet to the head, the head of a young woman. This was her broken, naked body, smashed to pieces.

Kerry positioned herself as close to the water's edge as she could, being careful not to slip in. She took a series of pictures of the body, manoeuvring up and down the riverbank to get a few different angles. As she moved, she observed what she could of the gawkers, looking for anyone who didn't fit. The Isle of Man had plenty of characters, oddballs, who led their own life in their own way. None looked especially suspicious, but she snapped a few subtle photographs to view later. DC Mulligan tapped Kerry on the shoulder and she snapped round.

"Jesus, Billy, what's wrong with you?" Kerry scolded.

"Sorry, Kerry. How's Walsh? Was he in the pub?" Billy looked around to make sure Jim wasn't in earshot.

"It doesn't matter. He's in charge. Did you bring your wellies?"

"Mulligan, you're with me!" Jim shouted as he walked past the two DCs. He already had a set of long wellington boots in his hands. Billy followed and quickened his pace to catch up.

"Sarge, where do you want me?" Billy said, eager to be a part of this investigation.

"Got any boots in your car?" Jim asked, looking back at Billy.

"No," Billy replied with a sense of dread.

Jim looked down at Billy's shoes. They looked expensive. "That's bad luck," Jim said, sitting himself down on the riverbank as he removed his own shoes. "Ask a uniform if they can help you. Don't bother with the tall one, Jenkins, these are his," Jim told him, as he began slipping on the long, dark green wellingtons.

Billy looked around in a near panic and darted it off in search of something suitable.

"Was that really necessary, sarge?" Kerry asked.

"Maybe," Jim replied with a tone. Billy didn't impress him. Maybe he was jealous, but maybe it was because Jim felt Billy was just a bang average copper with nice teeth.

"I can go in; I've got something in the boot," Kerry offered, eager to save her friend's expensive shoes and get stuck in.

"No, it won't be pleasant. Billy is looking for adventure. Here it is," Jim said. Billy had often moaned about the boring life of a detective on the island. Now it was time to get involved and see the other real side of the job.

"With all due respect, sergeant, fuck off. I'm as capable as any man, especially DC Mulligan. This job isn't always pleasant, and it's not your job to hold me back!" Kerry all but shouted at her superior.

"Kerry, I know exactly how capable you are," Jim said, his tone easing.

"Well, I'll get ready then," Kerry announced as she headed back to her car. She passed Billy, who was begging another officer for help. "Don't worry, Billy, that lovely Italian leather will live to pull again another day." She reached her car and popped open the boot. She fished around and produced a pair of purple Crocs and removed her shoes, socks and rolled up her trouser legs before slipping them on, propped up against the car.

Jim watched from the riverbank, unimpressed with her choice of footwear. Billy approached glumly. "Since she's going to be doing the heavy lifting, why don't you talk to witnesses? I want to know if that girl has been there all night and nobody bothered to report it, or she washed down," Jim spat the words out.

Billy nodded and was happy to get away. Passing Kerry, he mouthed 'thank-you' with an appreciative and subtle thumbs up. "Sarge, ready?" Kerry asked.

"What the bloody hell are you wearing? Do you think that's professional?" Jim said as he stared at the purple Crocs.

"Sorry, Sarge, that's all I had in the car. Are you sure we should move her?" Kerry asked, handing Jim a pair of latex gloves. Her first instinct had been to move the body away from public view, but now that seemed like that horse had already bolted, and preserving the scene felt more important.

"Yes, I'm sure," Jim snarled. He'd have to work hard to get his DNA on the body.

They both waded in carefully; the water barely passed their shins. The rocky riverbed ensured they moved cautiously. Two uniformed constables followed, only one having boots. The other, Jenkins, looked longingly at his boots on Jim's feet. As they approached the body, it was hard not to notice the lack of bruising. Her right wrist was badly broken, a small section of bone pushing through the skin. Other large cuts and scratches were present, but the river had expertly cleaned them. No blood, just opened flesh on display. It was still gruesome, maybe even more so for the bloodless wounds and her pale grey appearance.

"How are we going to do this, Sarge?" Kerry asked, looking at the other three, hoping someone would have an idea.

"We could take a limb each and gently lift her over," PC Jenkins suggested.

"I don't know, with that wrist, it looks like that hand could separate completely," the other PC stated.

"You two grab her ankles. Kerry, we'll lift her under the arms. Take it slowly. I don't want anyone falling on her or worse, letting go of so she gets washed out to sea," Jim ordered them, gently putting his hands under her arms. He felt around underneath. *Bingo.* The rock wasn't sharp, but it had a jagged point and that would do. He didn't let himself think about it. He pushed down firmly on the rock and slid his right index finger across it. The pain was instant. "Shit!" Jim cursed as he pulled his finger from the water. The latex was ripped, and blood was already pouring from the wound.

"Bloody hell, are you alright, Jim?" Kerry looked at the blood as it dripped into the water.

Jim held his hand close and nodded. "Can you three manage without me? I can't risk contaminating the body more than I already have. You lads take the top, Kerry, her legs. Watch your fingers. There's something sharp down there," Jim warned, content with his work. The other three rearranged themselves, and Jim moved a few paces back to keep out of their way. Gently, the three lifted the body. She wasn't a big girl, but weight wasn't the problem. Handling her with care and respect was one thing, but nobody had woken up that morning wishing to be carrying a human corpse out of a river. Up close, the wounds were obvious and disconcerting. Each was uneasy handling the body. It wasn't pleasant, and it wasn't their job.

"I don't think we should be doing this," PC Jenkins protested, but didn't stop.

"It's too late now. Let's get her to the bank. Then it's done, and we can scrub every inch of our skin with a Brillo pad," Kerry replied, wishing she had let Billy get wet feet.

Jim stood back and watched. As the body was being moved, the small crowd had crept forward. Many now had a view once again, and several using their camera phones to record the grim activity. "Can we get the crowd back, please!" Jim shouted to the officers on dry land. They, too, had been captivated by the recovery and had momentarily allowed their fascination to impede their job. They quickly shuffled the crowd back. A single person stood firm, in dark blue racing leathers and wearing their motorcycle helmet with the visor down. Jim stared at the figure, who gave a slow and deliberate wave back before holding up a small padded envelope. Jim's heart raced, and he scrambled out of the river. His foot slipped underneath him, and he plunged downwards. Only landing on his knees and outstretched hands stopped him from being completely soaked in the cold water. "Fuck!" Jim screamed as he stood back up.

Quickly he climbed the bank and jogged to the assembled crowd, searching for the rider amongst the many spectators. Barging through them, he caught sight of the rider astride of a powerful motorcycle. The rider watched in their mirror as the dripping wet detective struggled to reach them. They revved the engine, and this was enough to force Jim to find an extra bit of pace. The rider held up the padded envelope, as if taunting his victim before riding slowly down the road. Jim's breath had already left him, but he pushed further forward as the bike pulled away. It was tantalisingly close, but the bike was too fast and too cruel for Jim to catch it. They dropped the padded envelope to the floor and sped up. The motorbike was out of sight within seconds.

Jim slowed to a walk. He looked around, but everyone was too interested in the dead girl to notice just another motorbike on an island full of them, and picked up the envelope, leaving a bloody smudge from his injured finger. They had written his name on the front with the same red marker. Again, Jim looked around. A single constable looked over at him before resuming his crowd control duties. Satisfied he had some privacy, Jim opened the envelope and looked inside. He couldn't clearly make out the contents, so he reached in. He pulled out a small, sealed plastic bag. The bag was smeared with blood. Jim cursed himself for not being more careful and reached into his pocket, pulling out a wet handkerchief which he wrapped around the injured digit. Examining the bag, his face dropped. Most of the blood was inside the small bag; only a small smear of his own blood stained the outside of the plastic. A female human finger. He quickly placed the bag back into the envelope and was about to close it when a glint caught his eye. Again, he looked around and felt confident he wasn't being observed, and reached back into the envelope. A single 6.35mm pistol cartridge, unfired.

Jim dropped the round back into the envelope and shoved the whole thing into his pocket and briskly returned to the riverbank.

"You need to get that looked at, mate," a man shouted at Jim and signalled to his blood-drenched finger.

Jim could only muster a silent stare at the individual as he carried on back towards the dead girl.

"Doolan is here Sarge, and he's not happy," Billy helpfully informed Jim.

Another silent stare sent Billy stepping backwards. Jim approached DC Ken Doolan, the coroner's officer. A strict man who was in his sixties, with a shock of brilliant white hair and red cheeks. He'd spent his life on the island as a doctor before joining the constabulary in his late forties. The appointment to the position of coroner's officer seemed a perfect mix of his unique skill base. And he knew it.

"What the fuck did you think you were doing? Moving the bloody body, Jesus Christ. Do you know how much extra paperwork you've just created? Even DCI Ingham is going to lose the plot on this one. Did you do that in there?" Doolan demanded an answer as he grabbed Jim's arm to hold up his hand with the blood-covered handkerchief.

Jim snatched his arm back. Any doubt or fear he had of his current predicament was replaced with anger at this red-faced fool. "DC Doolan, I've informed DCI Ingham we were going to move the body. It was in the middle of the damn river. What were you hoping to find? And look at her, look at that girl. Then look at each of those rubber-necking bastards up there, eager to catch sight of something grisly. It was the right thing to do. And I'm sorry if me slicing my finger open in the grim recovery of that girl is an inconvenience for you. Do what you need to do and then let's get her out of here," Jim all but shouted at Doolan. He spun away and towards Kerry. "Hughes, I think I'm going to need my own trip to Nobles. Can you do the honours?" Jim spoke much more softly to her than he had to Doolan.

"Sarge, what about the crime scene?" Kerry asked. She didn't want to pass up the opportunity of working on a potential murder. Chances like this wouldn't come up often on the island.

"This isn't the crime scene. Someone has dumped her upriver within the last forty-eight hours. We'll find more tracking back that way rather than paddling about down here where she washed up. I'll arrange extra personnel on the way to the hospital, and we'll be back within the hour. Tell Billy to hold the fort and not to take any shit from Doolan. I'll be in the car," Jim ordered. He walked back towards Kerry's car, but it was locked. Rather than call out, he waited. He again started racking his brains. Why him? Jim gave himself a moment and tried to compose himself before he got worked up. He thought of Ella and still couldn't decide if her leaving him was good or bad luck. Jim pulled his phone from his pocket. The crack again reminded him of his predicament. He found Ella's number and hovered over the call button. He thought better of it and put the phone back away in his pocket. Jim couldn't trust anyone; he was on his own.

CHAPTER 4

N OBLE'S HOSPITAL HAD BEEN constructed nearly twenty years ago. Even today, it still enjoyed both a modern and a classic hospital feel. It was the main hospital on the island, located outside of Douglas on a large site. It catered to most of the islanders' needs and could provide a good level of care during the TT races. Often, unfortunate riders and spectators alike would be treated at Noble's and, if needed, transported over to Liverpool once stabilised. Kerry had been instructed to wait in the car by Jim whilst he had his wound seen to in the emergency department. That was nearly an hour ago. Kerry often resented being treated as little more than a chauffeur or personal assistant by Jim. She would much rather still be ankle-deep in the water, searching for evidence, rather than sitting in her car hoping the emergency waiting room wasn't packed. She had called Billy twice already to see if he had found anything. He hadn't.

Apart from the girl's body, there was no evidence of foul play. None of the gathered crowd had seen anything or even knew how long the body had been there for. The body would have been at the hospital too now, but would be unlikely to be examined that day. She knew that Doolan would cause a fuss about something; he normally did if given a chance. He didn't like many of his fellow officers; it just so happened that he hated Jim. Kerry wasn't sure why Jim was worthy of extra special ire, but Jim had a habit of rubbing people the wrong way. There was no question he had problems, but she could understand why he had become the way he had. The stress of big city policing was one thing, but being stabbed was something she didn't even like thinking about. She feared a blade more than any gun. It was much more personal, more violent, and more likely. Any kid or drunk could carry a knife grabbed from a kitchen drawer. Guns were hard to get hold of and difficult for most novices to be effective with, but give an angry attacker a blade, and they don't need any great skill to stab and slash at a victim. Even the most uncoordinated individual could score gruesome hits and wounds. At least when Jim had been stabbed, he was apparently so wasted he knew little about it.

A tap on the window drew Kerry back from her daydream. Jim stood by the passenger window and held up his bandaged finger, and signalled for her to unlock the car. She obliged, and he slid in.

"They didn't have to amputate then, Sarge?" Kerry asked mockingly.

"Just the five stitches. They said I was very brave."

Kerry started the car and began driving off. "Laxey?"

"Do you have your walking boots?" Jim countered.

"Are the Crocs not suitable?"

A dozen police officers and volunteers slowly swept down either side of the river, searching for anything that may be related to the dead girl. Two specialists walked down the river that was little more than a stream this far away from the sea. Whilst Jim had been waiting for treatment on his finger, he had organised his resources. He had considered how he could delay the investigation, but it would have been pointless. He knew he didn't enjoy the best reputation, and if he wanted to stay in charge, he had to be seen to be taking charge. The team had already covered a quarter of a mile of the river and found little more than an old soft drink can, a dead longtail and a used condom. The can and the condom were bagged for potential evidence, but neither was the potential breakthrough in solving what had happened to the girl.

"Kerry, is your phone off?" Billy shouted across the line of searchers.

Kerry pulled her phone from her pocket and looked at the screen. "No reception," she shouted back.

"Doolan is trying to get you or Jim." Billy jogged across to Kerry and handed her his phone. He already had the number dialled in.

Kerry pressed the phone to her ear as it rang. "Hi Ken, it's Kerry. Sorry, no reception out here. Okay. A gunshot? How did we miss that?" Kerry looked at Billy, who perked up at the word gunshot. "Just a twenty-two? Okay, when will they know for sure? I'll tell Jim. No, I won't tell him that." Kerry handed the phone back to Billy. "It's official. This isn't some girl just falling in the river."

"Murder?" Billy replied, unable to hide his inappropriate excitement.

"Small calibre gunshot wound to the head," Kerry answered in a calm, professional tone.

"Could it be a suicide?" Billy asked, changing his tone to match that of Kerry.

"Very unlikely."

Billy struggled to hide the enthusiasm coursing through him. He had hoped this was something special. Billy and a few colleagues had speculated about what had happened to the girl, but none had dreamed of something as exotic as a murder involving a firearm. He was surprised they hadn't noticed it. The girl was pretty beaten up, but he would have thought a bullet to the head would have been more obvious.

"Sarge!" Kerry shouted and signalled for Jim to come over. He approached with a grim look on his face.

"What, DC Hughes?"

"It's only a bloody murder," Billy blurted out with a poorly hidden smile before Kerry responded.

Jim's blood ran cold. He knew it was a murder, but suddenly it felt official. "Jesus Christ Mulligan. A woman is dead. You've not won the pissing lottery. Calm down and try to remember you're a professional copper, not a professional twat."

The lines of searchers carried on sweeping along the river, drawing closer to Laxey and where the body had been discovered. As the Laxey Wheel came into sight, a brief flurry of excitement and a voice from a member of the search party called Jim over. The searchers had broken position and crowded around the discovery as Jim gently moved them aside to get through.

"What is it?" Jim asked.

"Some women's clothes, Sarge," PC Jenkins responded, pointing to them.

The clothes had been neatly folded and placed in a pile. They were damp but otherwise remained in the same state as they had been when they were placed. There was a smear of blood that was barely noticeable, but it drew Jim's eye straight to it. "Photograph them, bag them and carry on. Come on!" Jim snapped, and the gathered searchers resumed their positions, with Billy following Jim's command.

Jim didn't know what these people wanted. They hadn't been considerate enough to tell him yet. But the body, the clothes, these were very public shows of their leverage. Not directly implicating him, but a demonstration of their control. The jiffy bags were a statement of their ownership of him. They either wanted to ruin him or use him, and he wasn't sure what was the more favourable outcome. The Isle of Man was a small rock. Secrets didn't stay secret for long, and a murderous policeman would be one hell of a story that would spread back to the UK. Ella's family would at least be delighted to have finally been proven right.

"Sarge, I've got something," a uniformed police officer announced loudly. Those nearest crept over to look, with others holding their position.

Jim focused in on the officer and proceeded towards them.

"There, amongst the grass. It's a bullet," he announced proudly and pointed towards a clump of turf.

Billy rushed in and started taking pictures before Jim nudged him gently to one side and awkwardly stuffed his hand into a latex glove. Jim picked up the small shell casing and examined it in the light. "It's the case. The bullet is the metal bit that shoots out of the end." Billy was already holding an open evidence bag for Jim to drop the case into.

"Is that a .22?" Billy asked.

"Could be," Jim replied as he stared at the case through the plastic.

"So that belongs to our murderer? The one he used to kill the girl?" Billy pushed, hoping to solve the murder before teatime.

"Maybe. Could just be from a local farmer taking a rabbit for the pot. It's a common cartridge, and this is a field. Let's not get too excited." Jim knew it differed from a .22 and matched the unfired cartridge they had sent him. It could have his fingerprints on it. Jim panicked internally, but only for a moment. If they wanted him caught, they had better evidence than an empty cartridge case. Billy handed the bag to Jim to log. As a detective, he only had bits of information available to him, but he wasn't just a detective in this case. His colleagues were unaware that he was a suspect and a witness. He had information the police couldn't possibly know, and he had a choice. He could wait to see what happens, or take the initiative and go after these bastards. If he had killed that girl, they were as guilty as him and he would take them down with him if he had to.

CHAPTER 5

T HE LOCAL PRESS HAD sent their best journalists to the police headquarters for the briefing. Patrick McNeil was a rising star at the Manx Times. His writing style, hard work and determination added flair to a normally dull read. He could write about the arrival of a new squirrel monkey at the wildlife park and engage the reader as if the story was a failed assassination attempt on the President of the United States of America. Such was his growing reputation, the Manx Times had agreed to lend his services to one of the broadsheets on the England who wanted to cover the story but didn't see the need to send one of their own to do it. As big a story as the murder was on the island, in the UK, it would muster little more than a few lines buried deep inside the paper. That didn't bother Patrick. For him, it was exposure, and for the Manx Times, they would enjoy a little extra money to float the struggling paper.

The press and photographers had made themselves comfortable in the hastily assembled conference room as they waited for the Chief Constable to emerge and stand at the small podium. They laughed and joked amongst themselves as various police admin staff and officers added the finishing touches to the stage.

In the hallway, a selection of senior officers were getting themselves ready to face the assembled press.

"Do we have a name yet?" asked the Chief Constable.

"No sir, we've had no missing persons reported, and so far, no luck with a positive ID," DCI Ingham answered.

The Chief Constable looked at his watch, straightened his tie, and adjusted his collar. "No name, suspected murder, victim in her early twenties, enquiries ongoing."

"Sounds about it for the moment, I'm afraid," Ingham glumly confirmed.

"That's fine for now, but tomorrow we will need more. I'll deal with the questions. Tomorrow, I'll need you and a detective to join me," the Chief Constable responded, allowing himself a last check of his appearance to make sure everything was in place.

"I've authorised the overtime, and everyone is going at it with both barrels," Ingham replied confidently.

The Chief Constable looked at the DCI Ingham and shook his head at the choice of words. "I guess we should get this over with."

Jim had already sneaked into the back of the room, unseen by the small number of attendees whose attention was focused on the podium and stage, waiting for the briefing to start. Kerry entered quietly and stood next to Jim without him noticing.

"You didn't fancy answering a few questions?" she whispered.

"Hell no. I'm sure we'll all be dragged up there in the coming days or weeks. Best stay out of it, Kerry. You don't want your face on the local news at teatime or plastered across the local rag at breakfast. Let the brass do that bollocks," Jim answered, backed up by experience.

The Chief Constable and DCI Ingham appeared on the stage, illuminated by the flash of the photographers' cameras. The journalists all jumped into life and started shouting their questions to those on stage in the vain hope that protocol may be broken and answers provided.

"Thank you for joining us tonight for this briefing. I'll take questions at the end, but we will provide a statement now about what we know and what we're doing with our investigation," the Chief Constable started confidently.

Kerry looked at Jim and was almost surprised there wasn't a hint of alcohol coming from him. "Well, it doesn't hurt getting yourself out there if you want to boost your chances of progression."

"Progression isn't everything. You still work the same cases; you just work longer hours and feel the weight on your shoulders that little more," Jim replied solemnly, speaking from experience.

"And more money. We don't all have the means you do, Jim. Some of us would actually appreciate a Detective Sergeant's salary," Kerry stated defensively. The press conference continued on, with both of them looking at the stage but not really paying attention. They knew there was little information to release. The press conference was just a means to appease the journalists and allow them to ask questions they would unlikely receive satisfactory answers to.

"Don't tell me that money motivates you. You're too good a copper for that and too smart. If you wanted money, you could have become one of those finance pricks. I'm sure you would have done very well." Jim smirked, satisfied with his little dig.

"We need to head over to Nobles first thing. Look at the pathologist's preliminary report and the body." Kerry's whisper remained, but was enforced with a sterner tone.

"We've already seen the body," Jim responded quietly. "We can get the report emailed over."

"Well, now's our chance to ask a few questions and look at the findings."

"You go. Take that shagwit Billy with you."

"Sarge, you should be there," Kerry pleaded. Displeased, he was obviously planning a bender and would shirk his responsibilities once again come the morning.

"I've got a few lines of investigation I want to follow up. Probably a waste of time, but I trust you, and I can read the report later." Jim tried to remain calm, but didn't appreciate his junior trying to force the point.

"Should I come with you?"

"No. You teach Billy a thing or two about being a detective. No point in wasting your time and mine." Jim didn't look at Kerry or say anything further as he left the conference room.

Kerry remained and looked around the room. It was far from full, but every news outlet on the island was represented, and even a few unfamiliar faces had decided to attend.

"Any questions?" the Chief Constable asked.

"Pat McNeil, Manx Times and Daily Journal."

"Daily Journal? Congratulations, Pat. I'm sure Fleet Street must be thrilled to have snagged you," the Chief Constable replied with a forced smile.

"Thank you, sir. At the moment, you have no suspects, no motive and no idea. Will you be requesting help from any UK police services?" Pat asked confidently.

"No, not at this time. We have an experienced and extremely capable team. We are lucky we don't have to deal with many violent crimes on the island, but we are more than equipped to deal with this case. Our officers are working hard and we have already seen results."

"John Stevens, Isle of Man News. When will you be releasing further details of the victim?"

"I'm sure you understand that we're in the process of confirming the identification of the woman, and our detectives are working extremely hard. At the moment, the details I have briefed you with are the only ones we're able to release."

Kerry looked at her phone. It was nearly 10pm, and she was shattered. Unless they caught a break, she knew this would be the norm for the next few weeks. She wasn't complaining. This kind of case could really help her career. She shuddered with shame at the thought of using this young girl's death to progress within the force, but knew that if she did well, it's because she helped the victim find some justice.

"You're keen to tell us that your team is working hard, extremely hard, I believe you said, but is it true that detective Jim Walsh is leading this investigation?" a female voice with a thick Scouse accent questioned harshly from the back of the room.

"Yes," the Chief Constable replied, unsure where the question was leading to.

"The same detective that is a renowned drunk, thrown out of the Merseyside Police force for being a liability and bent?" the woman asked with venom in her voice.

The entire room turned to look at the woman. Kerry moved to try to get a better look at her superiors' accuser. She was in her early thirties, attractive but hard looking.

"Excuse me, who am I addressing?" The question pissed the Chief Constable off, both the attitude and the lack of etiquette striking a nerve.

"Linda Jones, Mersey Post."

"Well, Ms. Jones, I think you are out of line. I do not discuss my officers in public forums except to say every one of them is a trusted and respected member of a fantastic team. If they weren't, they wouldn't be one of my officers."

The room switched its focus back to the podium. All except for Kerry. She didn't know how this woman knew Jim, but she wasn't far off with her summary of him. As the questions continued, Linda Jones stood up and made her exit. Kerry opened the door for her on the way out, followed her into the corridor, and observed her walking towards the exit. Linda wasn't out of the station before she had her mobile pressed against her ear and was talking as she departed into the darkness.

Kerry didn't know why a Liverpool paper would bother sending a journalist to the Isle of Man for a murder with little to no details available. Maybe she was working as a freelancer and trying to sell a few stories to some of the nationals. The woman could even have been on a break and had written a few lines to send back to her editor.

"She doesn't like your boss, does she, Kerry?" Patrick McNeil had quietly approached Kerry as she concentrated on Jones.

"Jesus Pat, are you trying to give me a heart attack?" Kerry scorned him and gave him a light shove in the chest.

"Sorry Kez," Patrick responded sheepishly.

"The Daily Journal? Are they paying well?"

"You'd have to ask the owner of the Manx Times. He's taking the fee." Patrick answered with a smile.

"So, why are you doing it?"

"It's the same work, but I get my name out and around the big papers. It won't do me any harm."

"Didn't fancy staying for the rest of the conference?"

"I doubt the Chief is going suddenly give any juicy details now I've left the room. That's what I've come to you for." He smiled and raised his eyebrows.

"You can piss off."

"Come on, there must be something you can tell me, something not critical but exclusive?" Patrick begged.

Kerry looked at Patrick. She had known him since school. They had always been friendly, but not friends, having moved in different social circles. She certainly didn't feel close enough to him to risk a reprimand and perhaps even being thrown off the case. "You want an exclusive?" she said in hushed tones as she moved in closer to whisper into his ear. "The Manx Times is a rag, and the Daily Journal is better for wrapping chips than reporting the news." With that, she walked out of the station, eager to catch a few hours' sleep before an early start.

Patrick smiled. It had been worth a shot. With no ground-breaking details of the murder, maybe he could look at the angle the reporter from the Post was working. He could add a little of his flair to a disgraced cop story, and with the background of a shocking murder to prop it up with, it would certainly be more interesting than any of his other local colleagues would come up with.

CHAPTER 6

I T WAS STILL DARK outside as Kerry entered the hospital, she had given Billy an opportunity to miss out on the trip. Despite wanting Jim there, she knew it didn't require two detectives, but it would have been nice to see Jim engaged in such an important case. The significance of it could be just what he needed to pick his career back up. It wasn't to be, and Kerry was feeling tired. She hadn't slept well. There was far too much going on in her head to rest, and she hated herself for it. Coffee would be an important element of her day if she was planning on functioning at all. The friends of Noble's cafe and shop wouldn't be open for a few more hours, so she hoped that the team in the mortuary might take pity on her and offer a cup of instant coffee and maybe a few biscuits to keep her going. Hospitals were funny places when they weren't packed with visitors and worried family members. Never truly quiet, there was always a nurse, porter or doctor busily hustling from one ward to another, but such a large place with so few people walking around felt very lonely. Maybe it was the lack of sleep, but today the hospital felt even more lonely than normal.

Kerry arrived at the mortuary. The pathologist was fast asleep at their desk. His head rested on his arms and he had made an effort to move his keyboard back and take off his spectacles. Kerry was jealous and didn't blame the man one bit. Kerry had spoken to Jake Shimmin the previous day. He had been eager to get the report ready as soon as possible and do his part. Not just for Kerry, but for DC Doolan, who had also been very keen to get everything moving. Doolan put the fear of God into Jake, so any chance to stay in his good graces was worth taking. Although both ultimately reported to whichever one of the island's coroners the case fell under, Doolan liked to take charge, and Jake wasn't about to try to assert himself.

"Jake," Kerry whispered quietly, trying to wake him up at the same time as not disturbing him. "Jake. Jake!"

Jake sat up, a small trail of drool running down his chin and impressions from his shirt sleeves and buttons marking his face. "Sorry Kerry, I must have dozed off."

Kerry smiled and looked around, hoping to see a pot of coffee, or at least a kettle, ready to boil. "How's the report looking?"

Jake responded with an unsure smile. "The preliminary report is finished, but I'm not sure it's what you're hoping for." Jake pulled his keyboard and mouse closer and began typing away before hitting print. A small printer at the end of the desk started screeching into action. "Coffee?"

"Black with four sugars." Kerry nodded and started pulling out the printed sheets and reading them. She scanned through the report, hoping for a DNA sample, maybe semen or skin under the fingernails. Nothing. She began reading faster and flicking through the pages until she got to the last one. She looked at the printer, hoping for something else. "There's nothing here?"

"I'm sorry," Jake confessed.

"So she died the night before, but because of the cold river water, you can't be sure when. No DNA because the river washed any potential trace away. Jim pissed blood from a cut all over her. Did that not even show up?"

"I'm sorry, there was nothing. The river washed anything useful away. It was the gunshot wound that killed her. The rest of the wounds, broken bones, cuts and scrapes occurred postmortem. I couldn't find any marks on her that I could attribute to being inflicted before death."

"It was a .22, right?" Kerry scanned the report but asked anyway.

"No, actually, it was a .25 or a 6.35mm depending on where in the world you are." Jake perked up, keen to discuss the naming practices for cartridges around the world, but sure that wasn't Kerry's interest.

"A .25? Would that be from a rifle?"

"No, I don't think there are many rifles in the world for that calibre. It's an old pistol round. Used in small pocket pistols, typically for self-defence, it's over one hundred years old and would probably be used in an older firearm. Obviously, as we can see, it's lethal, but not something that is known for its effectiveness," Jake replied, eager to elaborate further if Kerry gave him the opportunity.

Kerry pondered this news. The Isle of Man had little in the way of a gun problem. If it was a .22 rifle, that would widen the suspect base, but at least give them a list of gun owners who might be the killer. With a pistol, it would be an illegal firearm, and unless they found the murderer with the gun, they had no way of tracking it down. "Any sexual activity?" she moved on.

"Inconclusive. There was an absence of any tearing or bruising, making rape unlikely."

"Unlikely, but not impossible?"

"Correct." Jake replied.

"Is there anything you think might be worth highlighting?" Kerry asked, frustrated, as she tossed the pages of the report onto the desk.

"There was a tattoo. A distinctive one," Jake offered, hoping to satisfy Kerry's desire for something useful.

Kerry had seen the girl naked but hadn't noticed a tattoo. When she had seen the brutalised body of the girl in the river as she helped fish it out, she hadn't been keen to stare. It had been a grim job and would not have been made any more pleasant by memorising every inch of her pale, dead flesh. "What of? Where?"

"It was on the inside of her arm, close to her armpit." Jake handed a cup of coffee to Kerry and sat himself back at his desk in front of the computer. He searched through his files and pulled up the picture, enlarging it to make it clearer to see.

Two red football shirts, one either side of a name and a year with a halo above. "Barry Thompson – 2015," Kerry whispered, "Liverpool fan?"

"Or a Manc," Jake added, with a touch of disdain for having to mention the rivals of his own club.

"That is something. A memorial to a fallen love. When is Doolan coming?"

"I'm expecting him before 9am. Once he's had me rerun some tests and perform another examination, I'll confirm to you guys that the preliminary report is correct." Jake was used to having to redo work to meet Doolan's expectations. He didn't even fight it anymore, instead taking satisfaction when his initial report of an elderly man dying of a heart attack was once again proven correct.

Kerry took several large gulps of the scorching hot coffee. Her need for a caffeine boost was greater than the desire to not scold her throat. "Thanks, Jake. I'll look forward to you finding a stray hair on your second examination that blows the case wide open."

Jake stretched back in his chair and took a small, timid sip of his hot coffee.

***

Kerry had found an extra energy boost. She wasn't sure if the caffeine had done its trick or whether it was the name. *Barry Thompson*. The name repeatedly spun around her head. They could easily track the name down if they had lived on the island. It was just as likely that this man had been from the UK and may have no ties to the island at all. She smiled to herself. It seemed like the perfect job for Billy. Spending all day on the phone trying to trace the person who probably died back in 2015. It certainly wouldn't be easy, but she was confident they'd have tracked down the correct Barry by the end of the day.

Kerry walked towards her car and dialled Jim's number. It rang several times before she hung up as the voicemail kicked in. She wasn't surprised that Jim hadn't answered. It was early, after all. She could wait to tell him the news. If he couldn't be bothered to get out of bed and down to the hospital himself, he could wait.

As she approached her car, she slowed. Something didn't feel right. She looked around the large but mostly empty car park and saw a single figure standing fifty metres away watching her. Dressed in blue racing leathers, they stood beside a powerful motorbike and just seemed to stare at her. The riders' build and stance suggested they were a man. She felt uneasy as she turned to face the rider. It was the Isle of Man, motorbikes were far more common than the UK, so it was hardly unusual. Even so, why was he watching her? Even if they were a grieving relative, a doctor coming off a night shift or just a local out for an early morning ride, it felt off, so she confronted them. Nothing illegal had happened, but Kerry decided you can't just have a man intimidating a lone female like this. Even if they hadn't realised, this would be a learning opportunity for them.

Kerry began walking towards the figure, slowly at first, but after the first ten metres, he quickly mounted his bike. Kelly picked up the pace as the engine revved to life, and the rider accelerated away before she could get close enough to see the plate, and was gone. She carried on to the spot where the rider and bike had been. There was nothing there. No discarded cigarette butt or used chewing gum. She pulled her phone out of her pocket and called Billy. After a few short rings, he answered. "Billy, are you at your desk? Bed? Jesus, Billy, get your arse into gear, and I'll see you in the office within the hour." She rolled her eyes as she listened to his excuses. "Look, it's probably nothing, maybe even a reporter from the UK being nosy, but I'm fairly certain there was a guy on a motorbike watching me. I know it's the Isle of Man and there are motorbikes everywhere, but he acted weirdly. No, I didn't get a plate. He rode off before I had the chance. Blue leathers, or maybe black or a dark colour. It was hard to tell in the light. Okay, cheers." She began walking back to her car. Billy could wait until he got to the office before she gave him the good news of how he'd be spending his day.

CHAPTER 7

S TANDING OUTSIDE OF THE Nelson, it was difficult for Jim to not slip into autopilot and go inside for a quick drink or three. The pub hadn't opened yet, and maybe that's all that stopped him trying, but it wouldn't have been the first time he had invited himself in and forced the landlord to offer a breakfast pint. Today, he was determined to find out what had happened. He'd been blackout drunk several times in his life, but rarely did he remember so little for so long. He had expected to see flashes of memories hit him throughout the previous day, but nothing had come to him. If his brain would not offer up the information to fill in the gaps, he'd have to give it a helping hand.

Jim lit up a cigarette outside of the pub and took a long draw on it before starting his journey. He rarely smoked these days. Jim had enough vices, and nicotine was the one he was willing to drop, but today he was going to stay off the alcohol and a pack of twenty from the local shop would give him some kind of crutch to lean on. He walked down the alley where he had met the girl. Jim remembered that clearly enough. He walked along Parliament Street.

Many of the shops and businesses were getting ready to open for the day and paid him no attention as they arranged displays and performed a spot of last-minute cleaning. So far, he believed he remembered the walk to this point, but didn't trust that his brain wasn't deceiving him. Mixing details of an area he is so familiar with, along with that drunken night, the memories could easily have been false. He could only continue and see how far he could make it.

As he reached the Post Office, he slowed. Unsure of where to go next. He crossed the road and walked past two more closed pubs, putting the thought of a drink into his head, but he pushed on. Stopping only at the petrol station to get himself another packet of cigarettes and a weak coffee dispensed from a machine. Walking along Lezayre Road, he looked around, eager to see any detail that would provoke a memory. He stopped for a moment as he walked past the school. *Vodka.* He remembered the girl had a small bottle of vodka that she offered him. He had taken several swigs from it before handing it back to her. She had dropped it and the bottle had smashed on the concrete path. Jim remembered telling her some kid would hurt themselves on the broken glass, and the girl had laughed at him. He looked around for the bottle, but it wasn't there, but a glint of light gave him hope. He walked towards a railing by the crossing, and at its base, several shards of broken glass. One still had a trace of the red label attached. It would have been just his luck had the pieces of glass been cleared more thoroughly, but at least now he knew he was on the right track. His memory wasn't trying to trick him and perhaps he could trust it, just a little.

The further away from town he got, the more mundane the landscape. The houses were all of a similar build and vintage, a render applied to a structure and then painted, often magnolia or another shade of off-white, and most of the structures were single-storey. Each had a similar patch of grass, a small tarmacked driveway, and the addition of a simple hedge proved a popular choice. Any hope Jim had of a house standing out from the crowd and jogging a memory was becoming increasingly unlikely.

He'd been walking for nearly half an hour, and his legs were protesting their enforced early morning exercise. The houses became sparser and Jim more downbeat. He was about to give up, turn around and head back to town and demand a pint from the first pub that would be foolish enough to open its doors when he saw it. Another fifty metres down the road, a small house, the render a faded pink and the garden overgrown with the front lawn nearly knee height. As he walked closer, he remembered falling into the grass and struggling to get back to his feet. Two men had helped him up and sat him down, either on a car or in one.

Jim walked up the narrow path at the front of the property to the front door. The house had been vacant for some time and had received little love. The render was blown in places, the pink paint discoloured with age, and piles of rubbish stacked against the side of the house, creating an inviting home for any nearby rodent. Jim tried the doorbell, but it was mushy and unresponsive. He instead knocked on the door loudly and waited for a moment. There was no sign of movement or even life from inside. He cupped his eyes and tried to look through one of the small frosted panes of glass, but it was too dark inside to see anything.

Taking a step back, Jim looked at the house, then behind him to see if anyone was passing by. Jim opened up the wooden back gate with the lightest of shoves, causing the rotten wood to succumb and the metal brackets to break free. The back garden was much like the front, overgrown and abandoned. He spotted the large kitchen window and peered inside. Like the outside, it was a mess. Some kitchen units had been ripped out, tiles smashed, the ceiling had partially collapsed and wallpaper was peeling off. He knew he hadn't been in this house. No one had for quite some time.

Jim walked back to the front and looked at the spot where he had remembered falling. He wasn't normally one to lose his balance, but he had been intoxicated and obviously drunker than even he was used to. When the men had helped him up, what happened? He closed his eyes and desperately tried to recall. They sat him down and told him to take it easy. Then they both sat next to him and the girl sat in the front passenger seat with another older man in the driver's seat. He rubbed his leg and then he remembered the last detail. They had injected him with something. Without a care in the world, Jim dropped his trousers and examined his thigh. The tiniest red mark was present, and a small yellow bruise. "The bastards," he whispered to himself. He hadn't killed the girl, he was out cold. It had been a setup from the beginning, but if he hadn't killed the girl; why were they trying to set him up? What had they seen or recorded that they hoped to use against him?

CHAPTER 8

T HE CID DEPARTMENT WAS nearly empty. The on-shift detectives were all out trying to crack the girls' murder, each eager to be the one who solved the case. All except Kerry and Billy. Despite his many flaws, DC Billy Mulligan excelled in one area. Dealing with other police forces. His local boy charm worked wonders on the officers of the UK police services. He loved playing down their expectations, making them think he was a simple little island idiot, and making them feel sorry for him. In no time at all, the office administrator with the Merseyside police had found three records for a Barry Thompson. The first was an elderly man who lived in a care home. Second was for another elderly man, but this one was very much deceased, and had been for nearly twenty years. Finally, a record for a one-year-old boy who had sadly died.

Billy didn't see the need to rule out any of his Barrys. He had found three likely candidates who may have been honoured in ink by the dead girl. As far as he was concerned, he'd done his job and now he was happy to hand the baton back to Kerry. "Kerry, mission accomplished."

"You found Barry?" Kerry perked up, ready to be impressed.

"Yes, times three," Billy replied, smiling.

"I don't want three Barrys. I want just the one. The right one." Kerry replied, unsatisfied.

"Two are old, one of them is dead. The other was young. Very young, he's also dead," Billy stated, hoping to avoid doing any more of the legwork on his own.

"Cause of death?"

"Drugs overdose. He got into his mother's stash of amphetamines and that was that."

"Jesus." Kerry stopped for a second, as the thought of the child's tragic end struck her. "Anything interesting with the others?"

"Nope, just a pair of old farts."

"Who was the kids' mother? She must have a record?"

"Cassie McLean. Lots of drug charges and petty theft. She did a little time for possession with intent to supply but got out last year. She's twenty-two years old." Billy handed over a fistful of printouts to Kerry.

She quickly thumbed through them, looking for anything that stuck out. "Can you get a picture and a set of prints?"

"I can ask." Billy responded.

"Do it. Report back as soon as you're off the phone."

"Yes guv," Billy replied with a smile.

"Piss off," Kerry responded curtly.

"You're the closest thing we have most of the time. You're just missing the pay bump." Billy was sincere with his comment and looked to Kerry for approval.

Kerry sat down at her desk. The morning paper was in front of her. She wouldn't normally read the local papers at work, but with the murder case, she believed it wouldn't hurt, so she had requested a copy. The headline stated, 'GIRL MURDERED IN HORROR SHOOTING'. Kerry wasn't sure what made this shooting any more horrific than another that may cause the loss of life. Pat might have done well to stick to the end of the briefing. She read his report, and it was unusually tame and boring. Admittedly, he hadn't been given much to go on, but this wasn't up to his usual quality of work. Fleet Street would be disappointed if they had run the same report in their papers. She tossed the paper back down; she had little doubt it would start heating up in the days to come.

She picked back up the printouts that Billy had provided. The two older gentlemen seemed less likely to inspire a lasting tribute on a young girl's body. The kid though, a mother's love, no matter how brief the life, the love would last a lifetime. Cassie McLean, an unfortunate life. In care from seven years old, pregnant when she was just fifteen, her child, Barry, was dead at fifteen months. They locked Cassie up at eighteen, released her at twenty, and now she was possibly dead a few years later. Not a long or glorious life. Kerry could only imagine the hardship Cassie had gone through in the few years she had. If she was their girl, what was she doing on the Isle of Man? Was she living here or on a short break? The island remained a popular budget friendly destination for those from England, Scotland and Wales. She could have flown in, but from Liverpool, the ferry would have been more likely.

"Billy, whilst you're waiting for the Merseyside police to get those records sent over. Run a check with the ferry port; I want to see if they have a record of Cassie arriving. If she came by boat, I want the date, time, and see if they can get any CCTV footage of her that we can compare once we have a picture."

"Yes, guv," Billy replied, this time without the smile.

***

Jim didn't want to return to the warehouse, the scene of the crime. But if he was going to work out who was doing this to him, he had to work with the little information he had. The light blue mini was hardly the first choice for a surveillance vehicle. In the dark green and brown countryside, the light blue car stuck out like a sore thumb. He couldn't clearly remember where it was. Everything had been a blur. He put it down to the shock of what happened that his memory was so unreliable. When he had tracked it down, he drove past the warehouse entrance twice, both times he noticed and was noticed by a single security guard sitting in the small booth behind the locked gate. An old transit van and a small lorry were being unloaded into one building. The cargo being unloaded was a mixture of boxes and small crates. They could have contained absolutely anything. He noticed the guys doing the work. These guys were brutes. Shaven heads, large builds and even from the distance he could tell they weren't to be messed with.

After his second drive by, Jim pulled up further down the road. The warehouse was barely visible, but he could tell if one of the vehicles left. There would be no getting into the site during the day, and at night he'd be putting himself at risk. These people were capable of anything. His best bet would be to follow one of the vehicles and find out where it was going. It might be delivering tins of sweetcorn for all he knew, but the people who were playing with him could have built their little hotel room charade anywhere. They needed a place they had control over, somewhere that they wouldn't be disturbed. A location that allowed them to create and dismantle their scene whenever they wanted. It wouldn't matter that he knew where it was. They believed they owned him. They could put him away for the rest of his life, they had the evidence, probably more than he knew. He just had his own word. Maybe the vehicle would lead him to another location of interest. Maybe he'd just beat the driver to a bloody pulp and force a confession. Just as likely, one of the large lads unloading the boxes would beat him senseless instead. For a second, he wished he'd kept the gun. That would have evened the odds. But he knew that carrying a murder weapon would have been a stupid idea.

Jim had been waiting outside of the warehouse for nearly an hour. His phone had buzzed several times, but he had ignored it, only once sending a message to Kerry informing her he was following a lead and he'd check in later. He knew what his reputation was. Kerry would probably assume he was in the pub and not question it any further. Being a crap person with a poor work ethic had its advantages. Without warning, a small drone suddenly dropped down in front of his car windscreen and hovered in place, facing him. The small camera lens twitched as it focused in on him. Instinctively, Jim covered his face and started the engine. He threw the car into gear and put his foot down. The drone rose gracefully out of the way of the small car as it swung around in the road and drove off at speed.

Jim cursed himself for being seen. No doubt another video would be on its way to him. It probably wouldn't have been so bad if he hadn't been so close to where he had buried the damned pistol.

CHAPTER 9

THE FERRY TERMINAL IN Douglas wasn't much to look at. Perched one end of the town, the area itself had been undergoing a constant spell of regeneration. The older buildings were now refitted as pleasant restaurants or small bars rather than the dark and unloved derelicts that they once were. Tired office blocks replaced with impressively shiny buildings, tall and modern, they wouldn't look out of place in any major city's financial district. The terminal itself had changed little. It was functional and well used, but no one had deemed it necessary to spend a large sum of money on improving it.

Merseyside police had been quick in sending over a photo of a young Cassie, and her prints that soon confirmed she was their victim, but that news was yet to be released to the public. Kerry had spoken with the terminal manager and agreed to be granted access to the CCTV footage from the day that Cassie had arrived. Jim accompanied Kerry. He was still unsure of what his next move should be, so he decided to at least try to do his day job.

They pulled up in Kerry's car at the terminal and parked in the crowded car park. The near-full car park suggested they had planned their visit poorly and that a ferry was due to arrive or depart. Without a ship in view, it was probably the former. The pair exited and moved into the terminal.

"This Cassie girl, we should keep that from the press until we've got a full background. When the bosses want it out, it goes out. Not before." Jim stated, his tone accusatory.

"Of course," Kerry replied.

"Your friend Patrick, don't be tempted to give him an exclusive. I don't care what he promises you."

"Piss off, Jim. You're a fine one to talk about professionalism. How was the hangover this morning?" Kerry accused.

Jim shot her a look, and they both left it as that as they approached a member of staff in the terminal. He flashed his warrant card and asked for directions to the Harbour Control Unit. The man happily accompanied them into the secure area and up the stairs. The terminal manager was waiting for them with a wide smile and a firm handshake. Jim and Kerry quickly showed their identification, but the manager was too excited to scrutinize it.

"Detectives, welcome. I'm Bob Jones. My team and I are happy to assist you in any way we can," he excitedly led the detectives through the area. "It's all very exciting, isn't it?"

"Sir, a woman has been killed," Jim replied coldly.

"Sorry, I know. Sorry. We're here to help. Oscar is in our security office. He will be able to help you with the camera footage." The terminal manager began leading the two detectives to the small office just at the other end of the Harbour Control Unit. "So, is it the girl you're looking for? The victim?"

"No, we're trying to track down a witness who may have information relating to the events that evening," Jim lied. This guy was obviously enjoying being part of the spectacle, and they didn't want to risk the identity of the girl being confirmed on the evening news before they had more information.

"Right this way." The manager opened up the door to the office.

Oscar was a young guy wearing thickly rimmed glasses. He looked like he was fresh out of school and possibly was. He quickly rose to his feet nervously as they entered.

"Oscar, this is Detective..." the terminal manager began but realised he did not know their names.

"DS Jim Walsh and DC Kerry Hughes," Jim interrupted. Eager to not waste any more time.

"Help the detectives with anything they need, okay?" the terminal manager told Oscar.

"Yes, sir," Oscar replied.

"Take us back to the fourteenth. We're looking for the ferry from Liverpool that was scheduled to arrive at around 10pm," Kerry requested.

Oscar began searching a computer screen for the relevant video.

"No tapes or DVDs?" Jim asked, knowing there wouldn't be.

"No, it's a completely digital system. Everything is recorded locally and backed up to the cloud every hour. We hold two weeks' worth of footage onsite. Anything older than that, we have to download it. But it's pretty quick."

"How far does it go back?" Kerry asked. She couldn't see how it would help them today, but good to know next time they had a case involving the terminal.

"About two years. That's when the system came in. I'm sure as storage costs become apparent to Bob, he'll reduce that considerably. Here you go, got it," Oscar said, satisfied with his quick work. He pulled the folder over to a large 65-inch screen mounted on the wall. He looked for the correlating time stamp that matched what had been requested and opened it up. The video was divided into eight smaller screens, each showing the feed from a different camera.

"Which one is covering the disembarking passengers?" Kerry asked, a little overwhelmed by the amount of information from the videos all playing at once.

"All of them. These are the main cameras that cover where the ferries come in and the passengers and vehicles exit. This is for the foot passengers only. The cars and other vehicles will be in a different video. We can look at that next if you need to."

All three of them gazed at the screen as the crowd started departing the ferry. A large number of passengers carried with them hand luggage, large rucksacks and even full suitcases. It felt next to impossible to spot a single face amongst the crowd and identify them. The quality of the footage was great, but trying to spot one individual from hundreds was difficult. It was made all the harder by having only seen that face on a pale corpse and from photos that were years old. Only Jim had seen the girl recently before her death and he couldn't remember a single detail of her face.

"Can we start again and play the footage from a single camera at a time?" Kerry asked, knowing full well that Jim would be pissed, but she didn't want to miss seeing the girl arrive and who she may have arrived with.

Jim shot Kerry a disapproving look, but didn't say a word.

"Sure. Here you go." Oscar zoomed in to the first window and rewound it to the start.

After thirty minutes, they eventually spotted Cassie. She was alone, carrying only a handbag, a backpack and a small hold-all. As soon as she stepped off the boat, she was looking around as if she was searching for someone or something. With Oscar's help, they could follow her from each camera as she made her way through the terminal and out to the car park. Oscar had to load several more videos to follow her outside until she stood alone and waited. There were twenty minutes of footage of her waiting. She never stopped looking around and smoked three cigarettes in that time, eagerly sucking down the nicotine from each one.

Just as she was about to light a fourth cigarette, a car pulled up. It parked ten metres away, but the darkness obscured the make, model and plate. A figure left the driver's seat and approached Cassie. They were female with a slender build, tall and able to move with an uncommon elegance. As the woman walked closer to Cassie, the light hit her face.

It was Ella.

Jim recognised her instantly and was in shock. His own wife was setting him up. He asked himself if she could have been so foolish and desperate to get rid of him and leave the island that she could murder an innocent girl? Jim looked at Kerry. She had only met Ella a few times; maybe she wouldn't recognise her. She carried on watching the video as Ella led Cassie back to the car and helped her with her bags before driving off.

"Are you able to get a copy to us following the girl until she leaves in the car?" Kerry asked.

"Sure, I can cut it together and put it on a memory stick. It might take an hour or two."

"That's fine. We'll send somebody over to pick it up later on. In the meantime, could you get a still image of the girl and the person she met with and email it to me?" Kerry handed Oscar her card with her contact details on it.

"Of course!" Oscar beamed.

"That's great, thanks for your help." Kerry looked at Jim, who was silent, his face ashen. "After you, guv."

The pair left the security office and made their way to the stairs. Bob, the manager, was on the phone. He signalled for them to wait, but Kerry just waved back and carried on walking. Jim remained silent all the way to the car, not even looking at Kerry or acknowledging her. They arrived at the car and both entered, closing the doors behind them.

"So, do you want to tell me what the fuck your wife was doing picking up our murder victim the day she arrived on the island?" Kerry asked sternly.

Chapter 10

KERRY HAD BEEN AS shocked as Jim when she saw Ella accompanying their murder victim on the CCTV footage from the ferry terminal. Back in the car, he explained he hadn't seen her for a few days as she'd gone back to see her parents and that things weren't great in their relationship. He did not know what her link might be to Cassie. Even when they were living in Liverpool, she wouldn't have had many opportunities to cross paths with a drug-addicted offender. Jim had pleaded with Kerry for some time so that he could talk to Ella and find out what was happening. Kerry agreed, but only until the CCTV footage was delivered back to the station. Once they had the footage logged as evidence, she couldn't deny recognising the wife of her DS.

Jim had been grateful. If Kerry had known the full facts, she would have slapped the cuffs on him there and then. But now the clock was well and truly ticking. Once they identified Ella on the video, they would remove him from the case and he would come under suspicion of having some involvement. As soon as he saw Ella on the screen, he knew he had to talk to her. Jim had driven straight back to Ramsey and to his home. He tried to call Ella from his mobile as he drove, but it just rang out. He would have to contact her parents, in itself, an ordeal, but it didn't compare to what was coming.

As soon as he burst through the front door, he went straight to the small table in the hallway. He opened its two small drawers and began quickly searching through them until he found it. A small red notebook. It was worn; the corners were curled and discoloured through time and spills. Jim searched through until he found the number and quickly dialled it on the landline phone.

"Roger, it's Jim. I need to speak to Ella." He was out of breath and blurted out his words. "I know she's there, Rodger. This is important!" Jim was panicking. If he couldn't talk to her, he had no chance of getting ahead of the trouble that was about to come down on them both. "Don't give me that shit. I know she's there!" He listened intently as he caught an earful of abuse before his father-in-law hung up the phone. Jim slammed the phone down, nearly smashing it to pieces. He hunched over the table and tried to think, to catch his breath and regain control. All he could think about was the betrayal, the hatred she must feel to do this to him.

His breathing slowed, and he stood up straight. He casually walked into the kitchen and opened up a cupboard. An open bottle of rum was on the shelf, ready for him. Jim slowly picked the bottle up and opened it. The scent of the rum caught his nostrils. He so desperately wanted to take a swig and neck the whole thing, but he would not drink. Jim couldn't. Without a chance to change his mind, Jim walked towards the kitchen sink and poured the contents of the bottle down the plughole. A small wave of relief and a hint of pride in himself for not giving in to his urges. Jim looked out of the window and he saw a sight that sent shivers down his spine. The blue leather-clad motorcyclist was outside of the house, parked up on the road, staring at him.

Anger coursed through Jim once again as he ran outside as fast as he could. As the front door swung open, the bike sped forward fifty metres, then stopped as Jim ran into the road. The rider turned around and waved, taunting his victim. Jim ran back and jumped into the small mini and slammed his foot down, sending the car into the road, narrowly avoiding a transit van who had to hit his brakes to avoid a collision. This was a terrible idea. The motorbike didn't look far off the standard used to compete in the TT. The mini was a bog standard entry-level model. It would have no chance of keeping up with the bike, but that didn't stop Jim in his rage.

The rider led them both out of the town towards the mountain road. Jim was just about keeping up, but that was only because the bike allowed him to. Whenever he dropped back, the bike slowed just enough to not discourage its pursuer. The conditions were good on the mountains. Visibility was fine, no rain or cloud. It would have been perfect for the rider to disappear from view whenever he wanted to. Both vehicles were now going over seventy mile-per-hour, barely any effort for the bike whilst the small car's engine sounded like it might explode. The bike suddenly slowed, inviting Jim to close the distance until there were barely five metres between them. On a straight patch of road, the rider turned and raised his middle finger at Jim.

Jim screamed obscenities as he physically urged the car to go faster as the bike remained tantalisingly close. He now had only eyes for the bike. His tunnel vision couldn't see the bend in the road ahead until he was on it. Jim overcompensated the steering in a desperate move to avoid flying off the side of the road and down the steep hillside. The car swerved wildly and travelled sideways, the momentum still carrying it forward and off of the road. He didn't feel or hear the car breaking through the small wood and wire fence that caused the car to flip over. The second or two that the car was airborne felt like minutes as the car cleared the sudden drop and fell a metre downward before hitting the grassy bank on its roof. Still, it carried on flipping once more and airborne for just under a second. The sloop eased off, this being a far less steep section of the mountain road. The car came to a stop nearly forty metres away, on its side. Broken glass and mud were all over the inside of the car. As bad as the crash felt, it would have been far worse on many other parts of the mountain.

Jim wasn't sure if he had been unconscious or not. His head hurt and he felt the unmistakable sensation of blood dripping across his face from a wound on the side of his head. The sound of the blood drops landing on the shattered glass beside him was like a small drum beating constantly. A small puddle had developed and was continuing to grow as more blood added to it. He checked for any other wounds, but he seemed okay. There were no bones sticking out or limbs bent the wrong way. Jim tried to move, but he was still strapped in, and the seatbelt had tightened, allowing him little room to manoeuvre. His body tensed as he tried to brace himself and unbuckled the strap. Jim flopped onto his side, onto the smashed door. He awkwardly positioned himself to stand up and could open the passenger door that was now above him. He gave it all he could to swing it open, but it only wanted to close as soon as he removed his hands and gravity took over. Desperate to get out of the car, he allowed it to rest on him as he scrambled out between the door and the frame. Lacking all dignity, he slid down the side of the car and landed on his shoulder, causing him to wince with pain. With a moment to catch his breath and examine the trail of destruction the out-of-control car had caused, Jim staggered to his feet and took a few steps back to look at the vehicle. If his wife didn't hate him before, she would after she saw the mess he'd made of her little mini.

The road was only forty metres away, but it was much higher than his current position. A glint of blue caught Jim's eye. It was the damned bike rider. He had doubled back and stopped at the hole in the fence that Jim had made. The rider gave a little wave, then rode off at speed. Jim walked towards the road. His ankle was sore, but he was sure it wasn't broken. His head was still dripping blood, and he felt dizzy. As he walked, his legs felt like jelly and he swayed heavily until he fell to his knees and crawled towards the road.

He was only ten metres away now, but would have been completely invisible to any cars passing on the road above.

Now just five metres to go. The pain was going, but his vision now blurred, and he felt like he was about to vomit.

Jim reached the smashed fence and used every bit of energy he had to haul himself up onto the tarmac at the side of the road. He couldn't see or hear anything now. He stopped and waited, hoping someone would see him. As he drifted off, the last thought on his mind was the one that continued to haunt him. Why was this happening? What did he do to deserve any of this?

CHAPTER 11

A PASSING MOTORIST HAD spotted Jim only a few minutes after he had passed out on the side of the road. An ambulance had taken him to the hospital, where he had drifted in and out of consciousness. The accident had caused him to lose well over a pint of blood by the time the ambulance had arrived and began treating him. At the hospital, they gave him blood and checked over his mainly superficial injuries. Besides the wound on his head, a few bruised ribs, a sprained ankle, and a few small shards of glass having penetrated his skin, he was okay. The doctors were worried about a probable concussion and had insisted he stay in overnight so he could continue to be monitored. Jim had argued with them, but soon gave in, realising they wouldn't take no for an answer. He also realised that the overworked night shift wouldn't put up as much of a fight if he left.

Kerry and Billy had been the first to visit him. Whilst Kerry brought him a bar of chocolate and an energy drink, Billy had enquired with the doctors regarding the state of

Jim when he had arrived. He thanked them for their help and joined his two colleagues.

"How are you feeling, Sarge? Looks like a bit of a nasty one? Is the wife here?" Billy asked, admiring the bandage on Jim's head.

"I'm fine, thanks. No, she isn't. She's back in England."

"Do you remember what happened?" Kerry asked kindly.

"I was driving back towards Douglas on the mountain road, and something ran out in front of me. I think it was a sheep. It was on the road. I swerved to avoid it, but I lost control. It's fine, it was just an accident." Jim became more defensive as he spoke. Kerry was judging him, and he didn't want to give anything away. "I hadn't been drinking. It was just an accident." Jim added, keen to remove all doubt.

Kerry didn't say a word as she stared at him. She nearly believed him. She wanted to, but she knew about Ella. Just before they had been called about the crash, Oscar from the ferry terminal had called to tell her the CCTV footage was ready to be collected. Maybe Jim had tried to top himself; maybe he had tried to drink his problems away and lost control. Either way, he had bought himself a little more time until his wife's involvement became public knowledge. "It's okay, Sarge. We have to get back to the case. Do you need a lift tomorrow if they release you?"

"When they release me? I'm not staying here for more than one night," Jim stated forcibly.

"Of course. So do you want that lift?" Kerry asked again.

"I'll call you."

"Can we get you anything, some clothes from your house? Does your wife know? I can call her," Kerry offered, doubting Jim would allow it.

"Ella knows, and my friend Daz is going to bring me some bits later." Jim hadn't spoken with Daz in a week, but the last thing he wanted was to give any of his colleagues reason to traipse around his house and find something incriminating.

"Okay, well, I guess we'll catch you tomorrow. Take it easy and get some sleep," Kerry suggested with a polite smile as she led Billy away down the long corridor. "So, was he over the limit?" she asked quietly when she believed they were well out of earshot.

"No, not even a trace of alcohol or any other substance. He was clean." Billy confirmed, surprised.

"I'm not sure that I believe the one day he was sober was the day he drove his car off the side of a mountain." Kerry knew Jim too well to believe alcohol hadn't played even a small part in the accident. Despite her smiles, she was angry with Jim. She had left herself vulnerable by not reporting Ella's mysterious appearance on the CCTV footage as soon as she had seen it. She would have to rectify that before he spiralled completely out of control and dragged her down with him.

"Maybe that's why he crashed. He probably depends on the stuff now. Without it, I bet he can barely function like a normal person," Billy openly hypothesised.

"We need to swing by the ferry terminal for the copy of the CCTV footage. We'll see in the morning what state he's in."

Jim hobbled out of his bed and poked his head around the corner of his bed space, and looked down the corridor. Satisfied, his colleagues had departed. He closed the curtain around his bed and sat himself down, stretching out his legs. Jim picked up his mobile. It was smeared with his own blood, and another small crack on the screen had appeared. He searched through his contacts and found Daz. He rang the number and held the phone to his ear and waited. After several rings, the voicemail service kicked in. He waited as the personalised message played, growing more frustrated as it went on. When it eventually finished, he wanted to scream into the handset, but that wouldn't help him. "Daz, it's Jim. Call me as soon as you get this. I'm in the hospital and need you to get me some clothes. Tonight." Jim disconnected the call and laid back on the bed. There wasn't much he could do until his friend came back to him.

His stomach rumbled, and he picked up the chocolate bar Kerry had brought him. He snapped the bar into rows before carefully opening the wrapper and laying it flat on the bed beside him, devouring the first row in a single go.

"Mr Walsh?" a nurse meekly asked from outside the curtain.

"Yes?"

"Are you decent?" the voice asked as the curtain moved slightly, a hand clutching it, ready to swing it open.

"Yes."

The nurse opened up the curtain all around the bed. "Please try to keep the curtain open. We need to be able to see you."

Jim couldn't prevent himself from loudly huffing as he sat up.

"Also, somebody left this for you." The nurse handed over a familiar looking small padded envelope.

"Who left it?" Jim asked as he felt his heart rate rising.

"I don't know, I'm afraid. They handed it in at reception. Can I get you anything?"

Jim shook his head, and the nurse smiled and returned to his desk. Jim stared at the envelope. The familiar red marker and handwriting were on the front. It didn't feel heavy. He gave it a squeeze, unsure if it even contained anything, but he didn't want to open it to find out. He placed it in front of him and continued to stare at it. What they had put inside wasn't about to make his day any better, but leaving it to fester wouldn't solve anything, either. Maybe finally, they had given him some instructions, a sign of what they needed from him.

After a few minutes, Jim suddenly ripped it open and peered inside. A small glint caught his attention at the bottom of the envelope. Jim squeezed the sides, puffing it open, and tried to direct it under a light. It was a bracelet, or maybe even a necklace. Confident he wasn't about to pour out a few live rounds of ammunition in the middle of the ward, he spilled out the jewellery into his hand. It was a small silver necklace, nothing too fancy, but a pendant housed a single small diamond. It looked familiar. He held it up to the sickly light, then spread it out in front of him. The silver was stained with a reddish-brown liquid that had dried to a crust. It looked very similar to the one he had bought Ella many years ago. He pulled it closer to his face and inspected it.

It was Ella's.

CHAPTER 12

WHEN DAZ HAD CALLED back, Jim sounded like he was in a controlled panic. They had been friends since school, and Daz knew when his mate was in trouble. He didn't hesitate to drive as fast as he could to the hospital after picking up a few items of clothing for his friend. When he arrived, Jim looked in terrible shape. Despite having been treated and cleaned up, his skin looked pale and small bits of crusty dry blood hid in every wrinkle, fold of flesh, and along his hairline. Daz was short, a little overweight, and looked well into his fifties even though he hadn't yet turned forty-five. A lifetime of drinking had added a few extra years to him; a poor diet had thrown on a couple more. Today, when he looked at Jim, for the first time, he didn't feel like the weak link.

Daz handed over the bag of clothes as he approached. "Bloody hell. What the fuck did you do now?"

"Excuse me, visiting time is over. Please come back tomorrow at 9am," a stern nurse interrupted, having spotted the dishevelled visitor entering the ward.

"Piss off, love. He's a hero copper. If you can't give him a few minutes with his friend, you have no bloody heart," Daz protested passionately.

"It's okay. I'm leaving," Jim added, standing up and rummaging through the bag of clothes. The selection failed to impress him. Two pairs of jeans, a purple t-shirt, one of Ella's blouses, three socks, a pair of boxer shorts, and a belt. "Thanks Daz," he remarked as he held up the frilly blouse before stuffing it back into the bag.

"We have not discharged you. You need to see the consultant," the nurse barked, unhappy her night shift had taken a turn by a loon and his friend.

"I don't need to see anyone. I'll sign whatever you want, but as soon as I'm dressed, I'm gone." Jim stated.

Daz stood beside Jim and nodded his support. The nurse looked utterly fed-up before she threw her hands in the air out of frustration and walked away.

"Are you sure you should leave? You look pretty fucked." Daz whispered in case the nurse heard him.

"I'm fine. I just need some fresh air. Do you mind?" Jim gestured towards the curtain.

Daz wasn't one to go against his friend and pulled the curtain around the bed space and stood back, turning away to afford Jim the illusion of privacy. Jim chose the t-shirt and jeans. It would be nippy outside. He would have preferred a jumper had been thrown into the bag, but he would have to do without.

***

Despite the late hour, the police headquarters were still busy enough that the thought of getting 20 minutes' sleep in the corner didn't linger long with any of the tired personnel. Kerry had picked up the memory stick with the CCTV footage and had put off watching it. Kerry knew what it would do, but she also knew it was inevitable. She had it planned. She'd ask Billy to review the footage with her, then act in shock when she recognised Ella. Jim had blown his chance to get things square with his wife, to find out what she was involved with. Now it was the entire department's responsibility to get her to explain herself.

"Coffee for the boss," Billy mocked as he approached Kerry with a mug in each hand. "Are we doing this here, or did you want me to grab a meeting room?"

Kerry gratefully took the coffee. It was too hot to drink, and she wanted to enjoy it, so instead, she took a long sniff. It was only instant coffee, but it filled her with comfort. "Let's grab a meeting room. I think number two should be free. No need to put a show on for anyone who passes."

"Is there a show?" Billy asked.

"Not really, unless you enjoy watching crowds of people disembark a ferry. But I'm sure the last thing the bosses want is for a still image of the victim to appear in the local paper."

The pair walked towards the meeting room. Kerry had the memory stick and used her laptop as a tray to carry it, her coffee, the power brick, and her notepad. As expected, meeting room two it was empty. The last users of the room had failed to clear away their coffee cups or clean away the crumbs from their biscuits. Billy immediately gathered up the mess and moved it out of the way as Kerry hooked up the laptop to the mass of cables connected to the large flat screen TV mounted on the wall.

They settled down and watched the footage. Both took notes throughout, noting timestamps, people of interest and details of the girl. All the time the video played, Kerry was waiting to see Ella. She was desperate to identify Ella and prove herself as being an honest copper, hoping to right the wrong she committed when she didn't report it as soon as she saw it.

The video now showed the girl as she waited outside. Kerry sat up in anticipation. As soon as Ella's face showed, she paused the video. "Isn't that Jim's wife?" She excitedly announced.

Billy rose to his feet and approached the screen for a better view. "It looks a bit like her. It can't be, can it?"

Kerry felt the relief at blurting out the words. She pressed play, and the video continued. The view of Ella only became clearer until they departed. "I think it is. No, I'm sure it is."

"Wasn't Jim there when you watched this earlier?" Billy asked, already knowing the answer.

"Yes. I think we need to take this upstairs. He has questions to answer."

***

Jim knew the clock was ticking ever faster. Daz had taken him home, where Jim had thrown on a coat and grabbed the spare set of car keys. The next stop was the airport in the hope his car was there. He needed to see what was in that car, if she'd been stupid enough to leave any evidence of her involvement with the dead girl. It was his car, so he couldn't let the evidence point at him even for a second.

They arrived at Ronaldsway airport in darkness. It was late enough that only a few more flights were due in, but none were scheduled to depart. Daz pulled up in one of the short-term parking spaces and Jim wasted little time in hopping out and striding across to where he and Ella would normally park when going away. The long-term car park was pretty full, that added with the darkness, made the black Mercedes a hard car to spot. The lighting wasn't particularly bright or efficient, but Jim was determined to find the car.

Daz had remained in the car listening to the local radio. An update from the police stated they had identified several witnesses that they were in the process of tracking down. Like most of the island, he'd heard all about the naked dead girl found in Laxey. He had speculated, like many others, that she was from the UK and probably brought her problems with her. Few of the Manx population liked to think their own were capable of murder, the island that was so close that it was impossible to pop out without bumping into half a dozen friends or acquaintances on your travels. He looked at his friend in the distance as he walked through the car park, holding his keys impotently, attempting to unlock his car, and make it give away its position.

Jim had searched the car park twice, even the short-term car park had been searched, but it wasn't there. Jim sat back in the car with Daz, who had his eyes closed and snoring quietly. The slam of the car door woke him up, and he sat up in his seat.

"All well?" Daz asked, pretending he had been paying attention.

"No. I don't know what the bloody cow is playing at. It's not here," Jim exhaled, exasperated.

"Fancy a pint? I'm sure we could get in somewhere." Daz asked, knowing that a few drinks normally helped lift Jim's mood.

"No, I'm not drinking at the moment. Could I kip on your sofa tonight? I'm not feeling great. If I get sick in the night, I might need you to take me back to the hospital."

That wasn't the reason at all. At any moment, the police could begin looking for Ella and him, and he wasn't ready to answer those questions just yet.

"And if you die, I can make sure you're not festering for weeks on end." Daz helpfully added.

"Thanks Daz."

***

The superiors were far from pleased with what Kerry had reported to them. A very public case had become messy and potentially very embarrassing. She had broken the news, and they had opted to give the vaguer details to the press to show some progress and help assure the public that everything was in hand. Billy had been dispatched with a uniformed officer to watch over Jim, and they had sent another detective to Jim's house to pick up Ella. Kerry had volunteered for both duties, but the top brass were keeping her there. With DS Jim Walsh now compromised, they needed another lead for the case, and Kerry had impressed them enough to get her chance.

Kerry tried to find the impossible quiet spot where she could rest her head and close her eyes for a few minutes. It had been a long day. But from here, they were only going to get longer.

CHAPTER 13

J UST A FEW DAYS ago, Jim had been a detective whose best days were behind him, and Ella, an unhappy woman trapped in a marriage that had decayed dramatically in recent years. Today, they were wanted in connection with the murder of a young woman. Both had disappeared and were suspected of being on the run together. At the hospital, the nurse described the man who picked Jim up. Kerry recognised the description as Jim's friend Darren "Daz" Corkill. She had only met him a few times, mostly when fishing Jim out of the pub or when he strolled into CID looking for his drinking buddy. She knew he was a local, lived in Ramsey, a drinker and didn't appear to have a fixed career, instead picking up seasonal work and cash-in-hand jobs. They had already dispatched two officers to his home to get some answers.

An emergency meeting had been called first thing in the morning and they had invited Kerry to take part with the most senior officers on the island. She hadn't made it home, instead she had taken the smallest meeting room at the station and booked it out overnight to ensure she wouldn't be disturbed. Managing a few hours of uncomfortable sleep on the floor. When she woke up, she was stiff and just as tired as when she laid on the harsh carpet tiles. She allowed herself enough time to get a coffee and freshen up, ready to face her superiors, hoping she wouldn't embarrass herself.

They roundly saw the whole situation as a disaster, that one of their officers was now on the run on the suspicion of being involved with a murder, was as bad a scenario as they could have imagined. Their best hope was that swift action might save some face once the press became aware, and that they weren't seen as protecting one of their own.

"We still don't know he's guilty of anything," Kerry dared to speak up amongst a room full of her superiors.

"He ran. Innocent people don't run. He is either guilty of murder, or guilty of covering up his wife's crime." DCI Ingham remarked, laying it out as simply as possible. He didn't like Jim, and whilst he had never believed Jim was capable of this, he could believe it with the known facts presented to him.

"It looks bad. It looks bloody awful, but all we know is Mrs Walsh picked up the girl from the ferry. I'm not sure I see them as suspects, but witnesses." Kerry tried to remain strong and not sound emotional. She knew that if she wound up the bosses, her shot at leading the investigation could be a very short one.

"With all due respect, Hughes, your loyalty to Walsh might cloud your judgement. I agree, the evidence does little more than put the wife in a car with the girl. That on its own would be unfortunate, but not inexplicable. But they ran. He's a bloody senior detective. He would only run if he thought it was hopeless. If there wasn't something terrible going on, he would have come to us, not runaway like a common thief." Ingham's anger grew.

The chief constable had barely said a word through the meeting. He was sitting at the top of the table and had listened keenly to what everyone had to say. His concern was now beyond that of a single detective. He had his eye on protecting the reputation of the constabulary. "We should treat them as witnesses. There isn't enough evidence to the contrary and I don't want to make one of our own a murder suspect just because his wife might have been moonlighting as a minicab driver. We don't release the names. I don't want a formal arrest unless we absolutely have to. If asked why Walsh was no longer leading the investigation, we will say he's recuperating after his accident." He had laid out his orders clearly to leave no room for a misunderstanding. He rose to his feet, signalling the meeting was over. Others followed suit, and with a few murmurings and hushed conversations, everyone left.

Kerry remained in the room, hoping for a few quiet moments to gather her thoughts. Billy had different ideas.

He had waited nervously outside of the meeting, not wanting to interrupt those in the room, but was eager to inform Kerry of an anonymous tip received. When the senior members of the constabulary left the room, he was relieved that he wouldn't have to face them. As soon as they were clear, he rushed into the room.

"Kerry, we've found the car," Billy excitedly announced.

"Which car?"

"Jim's. Black Merc, C class. They found it over in Kirk Michael in the corner of a field."

"Who found it? One of ours?" Jim and Ella had only been of interest for a few hours. This was exceptionally quick work.

"No, anonymous report. Local busybody probably," Billy speculated.

"Anyone been out to it yet?" Kerry rose to her feet.

"Uniform has been despatched, the front desk put it straight through to me so I thought you'd want to get there asap."

Kerry stretched and straightened herself up. "You can drive."

***

Kerry had tried to get a little more sleep on the drive to the abandoned car. It took less than twenty-five minutes to pull up to the field from leaving the station, and despite having her eyes closed, it had proved impossible to get any actual sleep with Billy excitedly sharing his thoughts on the case and on Jim. She politely listened and offered reassuring grunts as she tried to rest until the car came to a stop.

Two uniformed officers stood at the entrance of the field, another two were in the field standing next to the car. The gate was open, a smashed padlock and chain were on the floor beside the gatepost. Billy had parked on a grass verge next to a low slate wall that surrounded part of the field. From their position, they could just about make out the roof of the black car in the field. Someone had clumsily camouflaged it with a few small branches covering the roof. As soon as they exited the car and stood beside the wall, the car became obvious.

"What the hell was he thinking?" Billy asked, shaking his head as he looked at the half-arsed attempt at concealing the vehicle.

Kerry didn't say a word. She nodded to acknowledge the two officers and carried on into the field. It hadn't rained for a few days, but the grass was drenched with the early morning dew. The field might normally have housed sheep, but was currently empty. This didn't stop Kerry and Billy being careful not to tread on any animal faeces that may have remained. As they walked closer, Kerry felt uneasy. She wanted to believe Jim wasn't involved with any of this mess, but it seemed unreasonable to believe he was completely clean.

"Have you looked inside?" Kerry peered through the driver's window.

"No, we've not been here long." PC Jenkins replied.

Kerry walked around the car, looking it over. It was facing towards the gate. She looked at the tracks. They were barely visible, but the soft mud and the crushed grass showed that the car had been driven into the field and turned towards the wall to run parallel with it. Barely twenty metres away, a thick laurel encroached over the slate wall and high above it. It ran for several metres, enough to hide a small van; the Mercedes would have been near impossible to spot had it been parked there. It would probably have remained undiscovered until the farmer next moved his flock back into the field.

Kerry put on a pair of latex gloves and tried the driver's door. It was locked. "Can we get someone down here who can open this up?" The frustration in her voice was easy to pickup on and the nearest police officer made the request on their radio.

Billy had also been examining the car, and with his gloved hand, tried to open up the boot. To his surprise, it popped open. "The boot isn't locked."

Kerry quickly joined him at the rear of the car as he swung the boot door fully open.

"Fucking hell!" Billy screamed without thinking. Both he and Kerry stepped back.

Inside the boot, partially covered in a red stained bedsheet, was Ella. Her arms and head were uncovered.

Ella's eyes were open and staring out of the car. There were two small wounds that were easy to see on her forehead, possibly matched by another under the blood covered sheet. Her face was swollen, with several grazes and cuts showing.

"Jenkins, we're going to need a full team down here now." Kerry ordered, without looking away from Ella.

A rustle behind them caused both Kerry and Billy to turn around. On the other side of the wall were Patrick and Linda, with a photographer for good measure.

"Pat, what are you doing here?" Kerry demanded.

"I received a tip that there was a break in the case. It looks like it was right." Pat tried to look around the two detectives for a further glimpse of the car and the grizzly contents in its boot.

The photographer was snapping away, taking as many pictures as he could before an overenthusiastic uniformed officer tackled him to the ground.

"You can't treat us like this. We're the free press and the people have a right to know what is happening here," Linda argued aggressively.

"What is happening here? This is a crime scene. We need to preserve it and gather evidence. What we don't need is an irresponsible journalist printing incorrect or sensitive information before it has been verified." Kerry didn't have the best impression of this woman from her attack on Jim. She liked her even less for pulling the freedom of the press card.

"You'll need to step back." Billy ordered, putting his hands up and motioning them to move away. "I'm going to need you to move down the road by at least fifty yards. Now!" He shouted in an uncharacteristic display of authority.

Kerry jogged back to the car and pulled the boot door down, careful not to close it fully. "Pat, just piss off. You'll get your statement later."

"Excuse me, we have a right to be here," Linda loudly protested.

"Who are you again?" Kerry looked at her with utter disgust.

"Linda Jones, Mersey Post. The tip I received said there was another woman's body in the boot. Can you confirm there is a second victim?" Linda pressed, not willing to be shooed back with no information that she could use.

"My tip also said there was a body. Whatever is in there, your friend Billy didn't seem happy to see it," Pat pressed, feeding off his competitor from Liverpool.

"Get back!" Billy screamed.

"I'm not making any comments. Step back, this is a crime scene." Kerry was angry. It was easier than feeling anything else after seeing Ella's bloody corpse.

PC Jenkins and one of his uniformed colleagues bundled the three members of the press back and out of view of the car as two more police cars arrived at the scene to assist.

Kerry walked back towards the car and stared at the closed boot. "What have you done, you stupid drunken arsehole?" She whispered, trying to fathom how Jim could have fallen so far.

CHAPTER 14

W HEN THEY HAD DRIVEN back to Ramsey, Daz had stopped at the end of his road. Parked outside of his house was a police car. He had made Jim aware, who made it obvious they couldn't stay at the house. There weren't many options open to them, and after driving for over an hour, Daz parked the car on a dirt track off of the mountain road for them both to get a discrete bit of sleep. It could have been the pain that kept Jim awake, but his mind couldn't wander from the situation he found himself in. At sunrise, Jim was eager to get moving and directed Daz to Snaefell mountain. It was the highest mountain on the island and easily accessible. On a good day, it offered views of the whole of the Isle of Man. Daz again didn't question his friend. By now, he knew something was desperately wrong, but he didn't say a word. He parked the car at the bungalow, where the trams crossed as they made their way up to and down from the summit. There wouldn't be a tram to the top for a while, but it wouldn't take half-an-hour to walk up to the top from this point, even with his injuries.

The two men had silently walked across the soft ground until there were at the top. Once there, Jim led them to the side facing Ramsey and plonked himself down on the damp grass. "It's all gone to shit," he said quietly, shame in his voice.

Daz sat next to him and they both looked across to Ramsey. It was a beautiful day without a cloud in the sky and Ramsey looked tiny from this vantage point. "It'll be alright Jim. She'll be back."

"I don't know what is happening to me. They're setting me up, they're framing me for that girl's murder, and I don't know why. I don't know who Ella sold her soul to, but she's fucked me. They've fucked me." Jim all but sobbed.

Daz trusted Jim above anyone else. He admired him and what he had achieved during his time in Liverpool. The stories he had were incredible to Daz, but he knew his friend wasn't a killer. "What are you saying, Jim?"

"I met the girl. Then the next thing I know I've woken up next to her body in what looked like a rundown hotel, but it was all fake. A room in the middle of a warehouse. Now they're sending me reminders, videos, bullets, even a bloody finger." He stopped and waited for a moment as a thought bounced around his mind. "The finger. Where did it come from?" He rose to his feet and paced around in a circle, racking his brain. "She hadn't lost a finger," he muttered to himself as he walked faster. Then he remembered Ella's necklace. "She's not screwing me over. Someone has her. Jesus, they've got Ella!"

Jim wanted to run down the slope back to the car. He wanted to scream, but he knew it was pointless. Jim had no idea who they were, or how they would use her and the evidence against him. He sat back on the grass and put his head in his hands, sobbing.

"Jim, mate, you need to talk to your people. You need to tell them everything. They can help. Can't they?" Daz wasn't sure himself, but this was all above his pay grade. Jim used to fix his problems for him, the first time Jim comes to him for help and it involves a murder and a kidnapping.

"I've seen the evidence, and I'd arrest me with absolutely no doubt that I was guilty. If I hand myself in, I'm done." Jim wiped away the tears and tried to regain his composure.

"But what is staying out here going to do for you? You've got this mob who are setting you up for murder and your mates looking for you." Daz spoke slowly, with sympathy, but lacked the answers Jim so desperately needed.

"If they have Ella and they want something from me, I've got to give it to them. I've got to do what they want, otherwise they'll kill her."

"They might kill you," Daz told Jim.

"I hope they do."

***

Kerry had been trying to call and text Jim since they had found the car and the body, but it had been no good. Calls went straight through to voicemail and texts were unanswered. She had only just returned to the station from the latest crime scene, having spent several hours directing her colleagues and scouring the site. She didn't believe what he had become, but hoped she could talk some sense into him, get him to hand himself in. With one of their own as the prime suspect, it wasn't about avoiding the scandal but facing it head on and getting through the other side as quickly as possible. Her superiors had no interest in cover-ups or sweeping anything under the carpet. Justice had to be done, and the sooner it was done, the sooner the island could move on.

"Have you seen this, Kerry?" Billy asked as he undocked his laptop and brought it to show her.

She looked at the screen, and horror spread across her face. "That bitch," she said without even thinking.

The website of the Mersey Post carried a picture of the black Mercedes with the open boot. They blurred the contents out, but the headline read, 'FORMER MERSEYSIDE POLICE OFFICER WANTED FOR DOUBLE MURDER". Kerry read through the story. It was poorly written and only a few paragraphs long, but named Jim as the suspect and identified both the victims. It was as disastrous as it could be as far as the police were concerned. Almost all the information in the story had yet to be released. Anger flowed through her veins. Someone had leaked information to this woman. There was no other way she would know the names of the victims. "Billy, who's been talking to the press?"

"No one, as far as I know," Billy said, shrugging his shoulders.

"They've named Jim here, and his wife. We've not even formally identified her yet. How the hell did she find out?"

Billy shrugged his shoulders. He couldn't imagine anyone leaking any information, especially to a journalist they had never heard of from a Merseyside paper. He felt Kerry's eyes staring at him, but opted not to look back. "It will not be long before the locals pick this up. They're going to want to get ahead of it upstairs, aren't they?"

Kerry nodded, dejected. "Next time we see her, we need a word."

***

As the morning had turned to early afternoon, more tourists had made their way to the summit of the mountain to enjoy the views and tolerate the strong winds. Jim had moved little, waiting for the solution to strike him, but nothing came.

"Shall I pop into the cafe and get something to eat? I'm starving," Daz offered, hoping Jim would spring back into life.

"Sure." Jim nodded slowly in approval.

"I'll just get a few sandwiches and something to drink, maybe."

"Okay."

Daz walked towards the cafe, glancing back at Jim as he walked, half expecting the man to spring to his feet and run away. The cafe wasn't full, but was enjoying a steady stream of customers who had got the tram that day and now needed refreshments. He picked up a couple of bottles of water, a ham sandwich, and a tuna and sweetcorn one. There was a small queue to pay, but the queue was moving as their purchases were quickly dealt with. The radio was playing, and when the song ended, it cut to a news update. Daz listened intently as the new body was reported and its identity. Before he knew it, he was at the front of the queue and stood in place, gormlessly staring as the cashier coughed to get his attention. Daz snapped out of his trance and paid for the food and drink before scurrying outside.

He plodded back to Jim. It disappointed him to see that Jim was still in the same spot. If he had run off, it would have spared Daz from being the one to break the news that Ella was already dead.

"I think you need to hand yourself in," he said as he handed a ham sandwich to his friend.

"No thanks," Jim looked at the sandwich and handed it back to Daz. "I told you, if I hand myself in, I'm finished, and Ella will be no good to them. They'll kill her."

"They already have." The words passed his lips easier than he thought they would. He waited for Jim to erupt, scream obscenities, and call him a liar. But he didn't.

"How?" Jim didn't look at Daz; he just stared at Ramsey off in the distance.

"I don't know. They said on the radio they found her in a car. Sounded like it was your car." Daz studied his friend for a reaction.

Jim wiped a tear from his eye and rose to his feet. "I think you're right. Can you give me one last lift?"

CHAPTER 15

A N UNEXPECTED BYPRODUCT OF being placed in charge of the investigation was Kerry had spent much of the day in meetings. Briefing those in charge and helping to prepare for a press conference that would surely become a spectacle. All she wanted to do was go out and do police work. But as she had been informed, it was her operation, her job to make sure the senior officials had all the information they needed, and anything they could use to help deflect tough questions. She had already pressed Jake, the pathologist, to hurry his latest report to get her some preliminary findings. Desperately hoping there would be some evidence that cleared Jim and gave them another suspect. She knew it was a tough ask, and that it was unlikely the evidence would do anything other than confirm the cause of death was the two bullet holes in her head, and if they were lucky, some DNA that could implicate Jim further.

Kerry left the conference room feeling more tired and worn than she had ever done as a bobby on the beat, even at the end of a shift during the TT. How she longed to be breaking up a fight in a pub or arresting some small-time drug dealer selling pills to tourists. She had already promised herself some fresh air, a strong coffee and a burger. Kerry had barely eaten in the last twenty-four hours, and as much as her body yearned for vegetables, her heart desired the comfort of a piece of meat between bread. She ducked her head into the office, thinking it was only polite to offer Billy and the other detectives a chance to join her or request a takeaway.

Billy was on the phone, listening intently and staring downwards. Kerry approached and stood next to him and cleared her throat.

"We can be there in ten minutes. Okay, no press. Just me and Kerry, I promise," Billy said excitedly before hanging up. "It's Jim. He wants to hand himself in!"

Kerry sighed deeply. No more caffeine or food for her today. It was a relief that this might be over, that they could now start working on a confession and finding out what really happened and why. DCI Ingham would be pleased; he would hope that with any luck they could get to work putting this behind them within a week. "Where is he?"

"The Albert tower," Billy answered as he rose to his feet and slid on his jacket.

"You can drive," Kerry responded, handing Billy a set of car keys.

"We're not going alone, are we? Shouldn't we have the tactical firearms unit with us?" There was a genuine tinge of fear in Billy's voice.

"It's Jim, not Al Capone," Kerry reminded him.

"He's shot two people. One of them was his wife. I don't fancy us being victims three and four." Billy stated.

"You can stay in the car if you want. He won't shoot us. Well, he won't shoot me. He likes me," Kerry half-joked.

"But he thinks I'm a dick." The realisation struck Billy that there was every chance Jim was looking for one last victim.

"I'll call them as we go." Kerry didn't think Jim would harm them, but it wasn't worth the risk and Jim didn't deserve special treatment.

***

Jim wanted a location away from the crowds, and not related to him. He didn't know if they had circulated his picture and didn't wish to risk being taken down by a wannabe vigilante who fancied taking a swing or two at a dirty copper. He also didn't want to be in his local and have the press there waiting to photograph his arrest and fall from grace. The Albert tower seemed a good enough place to achieve those goals. He couldn't know if the press would get there too, along with the police, but the tower only ever had hikers and the odd tourist to pay it a visit. Closed off, it offered the chance for a few selfies or artistic shots from the outside, but little more of interest to any visitors.

He had told Daz to go so that he could avoid any trouble with the authorities, but he had refused. The two men sat silently at the base of the tower, listening to every car or motorbike that drove by, waiting for the sound of sirens.

"Bloody hell, Jim, you could have picked somewhere with parking, or at least not a ballache of an uphill walk." Kerry breathed heavily as she walked up the last part of the hill to the men.

"You know I didn't do it, don't you?" Jim asked, looking at Kerry for some show of support.

"Jim, I hope you didn't do it. I want to believe. But you need to talk to us. I'm sure you're aware we found Ella in your car, shot to death. We're waiting for Jake to confirm, but we believe it will be the same calibre handgun that was used on the girl. I don't know what you two were involved with, but you just need to come in and talk." Kerry told him with a sympathetic tone.

"Where's Billy?" Jim asked, looking around.

"He's afraid you would shoot him," Kerry answered sternly.

"The gutless shit. So he put you here in front of a murder suspect on your own?" Jim snarled, disappointed.

"I'm pretty sure you won't hurt me."

"Still, that kid has a lot to learn. That's why you're an excellent detective and he's only ever going to be bang average. Is the firearms unit nearby?" Jim casually looked around to see if they were visible.

"Yes," Kerry answered honestly.

"Good. Don't let sentimentality make you do something foolish. I will not kill you. I've never killed anyone, but you don't know that. It's all fucked up, Kerry. Someone is after me, and I have no idea who or why." Jim spoke softly, as if he didn't want to be overheard by those lurking in the shadows.

"You can tell me all about it at the station. You need legal representation, and we can make sure this is done by the book and place everything on record." Kerry approached slowly.

"You need to get the bastards for me, Kerry. You need to find them and make them pay." This was it. Everything he had ever worked for, professionally and personally, had ended. He wasn't dead, but he might as well have been.

"I'm going to need to put the handcuffs on, sorry," Kerry said as she stood in front of him, cuffs in hand in front of her.

Jim nodded and held out his wrists as Kerry placed the cuffs on them.

"Suspect secure. Please proceed," Kerry shouted behind her.

Within seconds, Billy led several uniformed officers towards the tower. Several more armed officers broke cover and cautiously approached, urging Daz to put his hands into the air.

"What's going to happen to me?" Daz asked as he raised his hands as high above his head as he could.

"I expect an uncomfortable few hours of questioning, and then they'll see if they want to charge you with anything," Kerry confirmed.

Billy dashed forwards, cuffs in hand and secured Daz.

"All okay?" Billy asked Kerry, unable to look Jim in the eye.

"Well, he didn't shoot me, did he?"

***

It was impossible for so many officers to make the urgent dash across the island and not have a few of the waiting journos realise something was happening. Once they had arrived at the Albert tower, the police had done a good job of keeping the press at arms' reach, but they couldn't stop them from getting pictures from a distance. At least on the drive back to the police headquarters, none of the journalists or photographers attempted to do anything silly to get their exclusive.

Kerry and Billy had followed the marked car, driving Jim back. All the way, the two didn't speak to each other. Only the constant vibration of Kerry's phone punctured the silence. Patrick McNeil was keen for an exclusive, hoping his new higher profile might secure him a few extra details his press colleagues wouldn't receive. She could see the number of text messages growing in number and desperation. Voicemails and missed calls filled her screen. She would not give him anything, not yet, at least. If he could help her, she might throw him a bone. But at the moment, he had nothing to offer.

The headquarters weren't equipped to unload a suspect in privacy. The public mingled with the press and took their own photos, each camera phone capable of reaching millions of eyes within moments. Amateur journalists live-streamed the event to their social media platforms, each stumbling over their words in their eagerness to be the definitive source breaking the news. They didn't appreciate that outside of the island and the UK, few people would have cared. But to them, they were about to be a breakout influencer. The traditional press screamed inaudible questions at the police and Jim. Hoping against hope that today would be the day that their question would hit so effectively that police and their suspect would stop in their tracks and begin answering the inane question in explicit detail.

Without a word said, those involved entered the sanctuary of the station, lit up by camera flashes, as Jim tried without success to cover his face. Inside the station, his former colleagues stared at him, seeing him as a monster. He had a lot of work to do if he was to clear his name. And he didn't even believe him.

CHAPTER 16

I N HIS CAREER, JIM had worked in the interview room many times. In Liverpool, he would interrogate drug dealers regularly. Compared to petty thieves, burglars or even those suspected of a violent crime, drug dealers were easy. Often they would sell out their own granny if it meant a lesser sentence or avoiding prison completely. Most of the drug dealers he had dealt with were low-level. To them, the thought of spending any time in prison was a petrifying idea. The older, more experienced dealers weren't so easily swayed but could be leaned on to give up a rival. It all looked good on the stats, even if taking out one rival only kicked the drug problem a little further down the road. It was certainly easier than interviewing a burglary suspect on the island who had no information or names to trade. The only thing they had was their freedom, and they grasped it tightly.

Now he was on the other side of the table, looking sorry for himself and sitting next to his advocate, and his brief meeting with them hadn't been productive. Jim had a story to tell, and his advocate was keen on him not to tell it.

For his representative Desmond McGuinness, this was the kind of case he never thought he'd get near, and he wasn't ready for his client to lose it for him on the first day. His advice had been simple: say nothing unless Desmond directed him to. Every client he had ever represented had protested their innocence. They had been fit up, the police got the wrong man or equal nonsense. In his experience, no one accused of a serious crime had ever been ready to accept their fate. And he could work with that. He knew the same details of the case that had been in the press since they had found the first victim, but the small amount of time he had spent with Jim didn't give him anything he could work with. The story of a man pursued, tormented and framed didn't ring true. Even the evidence Jim claimed they had sent him was worthless. He couldn't prove who had sent it to him, and it was more than plausible that he concocted the whole thing as an amateurish attempt to conceal his crimes.

When Kerry entered with DCI Ingham, it was hard to tell who looked more filled with dread, Jim or Kerry. Ingham just looked angry, betrayed by one of his own.

Kerry looked back at the one-way glass and nodded, signalling an unseen officer to start the official recording. She waited for a moment, then began. "For the video, I am DC Kerry Hughes with DCI Ingham. Interviewing Jim Walsh, represented by Desmond McGuinness." She opened up a folder and produced several photographs of the first victim that she spread out on the table in front of Jim. "Who was Cassie McLean to you?"

Jim looked at his advocate, who lightly shook his head.

"Jim. We have video footage that you have seen of Cassie being picked up by your wife at the ferry terminal. Did you know her?" Kerry asked sternly.

Another glance at the advocate from Jim received the same response.

"You know this will not help you." Kerry told Jim.

"My client doesn't wish to answer your questions at this time," Desmond said dryly.

"You called us. You wanted to hand yourself in, and you told me that somebody was after you. Who?" The less Jim answered, the easier it was for Kerry to treat him like any other suspect.

Jim was desperate to tell her, get it all on record, but the Desmond's glare was a firm no. He looked at Kerry; she looked genuinely sad behind her growing irritation. Ingham looked like he was ready to lunge across the table and strangle Jim. He then thought of Ella. They had been madly in love once, and however things were towards the end, he still loved her. What had happened to her was his fault. He just didn't know why. Those bastards were out there and he needed them caught, punished. Not to save himself, but to condemn them. "I don't know who."

Desmond reached across his client, putting a barrier between Jim and the police, hoping the gesture would stop him. "My client doesn't wish to say anything further at this time." He stated firmly.

"He sounds like he does." Kerry remarked.

"No, Dessie. I told you what I wanted to say. You work for me, and I need to tell them what I know," Jim demanded.

"I must insist..." Desmond started before Jim flung Desmond's outstretched arm back at him.

"I am the victim of a blackmail plot. I've been set up for the murder of Cassie. Yes, I met her the night she died. I now believe I was drugged and staged with her body in a fake room. They led me to believe I had killed her, and since then, I have been receiving pieces of evidence that incriminate me."

Ingham sat up. He wouldn't normally be in the room with a suspect, but this felt completely appropriate. When he told Kerry he would accompany her, he had no intention of doing anything other than remaining silent and staring at this poor excuse of a police officer, but now he couldn't help himself. "What kind of evidence?"

"A video of me discarding a firearm. Cartridge cases. A human finger."

"A finger?" Kerry questioned as she hurriedly searched through her notes.

"Yes. Since Cassie had all her digits, I'm guessing it is Ella's, or there is another victim they have linked to me we have yet to find."

"Anything else?" Ingham asked.

"A bloody silver chain. I'm pretty sure it's Ella's too."

"How did they send these items to you?" Kerry asked, trying to regain control of the interview from her superior.

"I have received hand-delivered brown envelopes. When I've seen the guy delivering them, he's been on a powerful motorbike, helmet down in his blue racing leathers."

Kerry stopped and looked up at Jim. She felt a glimmer of hope that he was telling the truth. His mystery motorcyclist sounded a lot like hers.

"What did they want you to do? What was the point of this blackmail?" Ingham didn't believe a word Jim had said and was insulted that Jim would try to prolong this nightmare with his lies.

"I don't know. They never told me. They just showed me their leverage. I was waiting for something, but maybe they didn't plan on me handing myself in."

"So, let me understand you. You are being blackmailed by a person or persons unknown. They framed you and your wife for the murder of a young girl, then they murdered your wife. And they've not asked for a thing. They've made not one single demand? Really?" Ingham's voice was getting loud. He had to control himself from screaming. Ingham snatched Kerry's folder and removed pictures of the black car and the grisly contents of the boot. He rose to his feet and placed the pictures on top of those of Cassie before sitting back down. "Look at the pictures."

Jim didn't raise his head. He didn't want to see what they had done to her.

"Look at your wife, damn it!" Ingham hit the table with his clenched fist, shocking all in the room.

Still, Jim refused to look up. "I didn't kill anyone. I loved my wife."

"We know things were bad, Jim. We've spoken with her parents. They didn't seem to think much of you, even before you murdered their daughter." Ingham sat back down and glared at Jim.

"I didn't kill anyone!" Jim shouted across to his senior officer. He had wondered whilst waiting at the Albert tower if he had handed himself in so that the burden of investigating the case fell on to someone else, on to Kerry. If he was behind bars, they couldn't do anything to him, their leverage worthless, and he would either rot in prison for the rest of his life, or maybe someone would believe him. Maybe they would clear his name for him. Only now, looking at DCI Ingham, did he realise that there was zero interest from those above in finding him innocent.

"The motorcyclist. Describe him." Kerry gathered up the pictures of the victims and stuffed them back in with her notes.

"I didn't get a number plate. Average height, difficult to tell his build in the leathers, but he wasn't a fat man." Jim tried to recall, but knew he only had a vague description to share.

"How many times did you see him?"

"A couple. I was chasing after him when I had my accident."

Kerry produced a blank piece of paper from her notes and slid it across the table with a pen. "Write down every location and time you saw him. If he exists, he'll be on video somewhere."

"Don't forget the station. His first delivery was here. Get the tapes from that morning and have Billy run through them." Jim caught himself in his former role, the senior detective giving the junior colleague orders. "You know what you're doing, sorry."

"Also, the incriminating evidence. Where is it? We want to see it all," Ingham ordered.

"We will not hand over anything that may endanger my clients' freedom without some assurances first," Desmond asserted.

"Lay off Dessie," Jim ordered his advocate with a more relaxed tone. Jim nodded at Ingham and drew a line across the sheet of paper and began listing the details and locations. After a few moments of silence, with just the light scratching of a ballpoint pen on paper, Jim slid it back to Kerry. "I'm done now. You check this all out. I want some time with my Desmond and a rest."

"This isn't the Grand Island in its pomp, Jim. You can't just rock up for a room and get room service. You're not in charge here." Kerry spoke calmly but had been annoyed by the power grab.

"We can sit here for another six hours, but I'm not saying another word." Jim folded his arms and sat back, letting out a sigh. He was so tired he could just as easily fall asleep in the interview room as in his cell.

"We'll take a break whilst we look into these details, but I'll call you back in when I'm ready, not you. Interview suspended. You can talk to your advocate here, and someone will take you back down when you're finished." Kerry rose and left the room, followed by DCI Ingham.

Billy was already out of the observation area and intercepted his two colleagues, an open laptop in his hands.

"You don't buy any of this nonsense, do you?" Ingham asked Kerry.

"We've got to check it out. I've seen that motorcyclist myself. It could be a coincidence, or he could be telling the truth," Kerry responded, hoping to keep some of her cards close to her chest.

"It could be one of his friends. It doesn't prove any ridiculous conspiracy," Ingham told Kerry.

"Sir, I started checking through the CCTV footage from the front desk. The rider was there. His visor was up, but his face was still obscured. I got a plate from the camera facing outside. The bike isn't right." Billy showed the brief video on the laptop screen.

"That was quick work," Kerry confessed, obviously impressed.

"I already had the access. It's easy enough to search if you know where to look," Billy responded bashfully.

"The bike isn't right? Explain," Ingham demanded.

"The plate is real, but it's registered to an old moped that was reported stolen two weeks ago," Billy reported.

"Keep on it. He is still our prime suspect, and I don't want your loyalty to cause any problems with mounting a successful prosecution. Don't waste too many resources on looking for this imaginary gang of conspirators." With that last order, Ingham headed towards his office.

"So, do you believe him?" Billy asked cautiously.

"I want to. You?" Kerry shot back, keen to see if she was letting any loyalty fog her judgement.

"There are easier ways to slot your wife and get away with it." Billy shrugged his shoulders as the pair returned to their office.

CHAPTER 17

T HE CAFE WAS ONE of many that the side streets of Douglas offered. Linda had made it her second office since she had been on the island. When she couldn't stand the confines of her hotel any longer, she headed to the cafe to indulge in fresh coffee and free Wi-Fi. She could work away on her laptop and upload her reports to her editor back in Liverpool. She was friendly enough with the staff, not wanting to offend her hosts whilst she leeched off their power sockets, drinking mostly black coffee and only occasionally treating herself to a homemade cake or sandwich. A smile thrown their way bought her enough goodwill to continue despite her minimum spend, and that the cafe was never busy ensured they didn't hold it against her that she would hog a table for hours at a time. In the few days she had been using the cafe, this was the first time she had ever been with anyone.

Ian Harrison was in his forties, a slim but muscular build, with a stern, unattractive face. He looked like he was permanently looking for a fight, hoping for offence to give him an excuse to throw a punch at an unwilling victim.

They were familiar with each other, but the relationship was cold and businesslike.

"I can't print that," Linda protested.

"You print what we tell you to. If we say he's a paedo, you print he's a paedo. You know the score, you agreed to it." His thick scouse accent added a touch of venom despite the softness he spoke with.

"I know what I agreed to. But I won't be able to continue doing my job if I'm suspended and sent back to Liverpool. I've tested my luck already. We need to take this slowly with actual evidence. You have plenty of it. There's no need to rush this now." Linda took a sip of her coffee, trying to show she was calm and in control.

"There's every fucking need to rush. He wasn't supposed to be in custody. He's supposed to still be dangling on a string, on the run and shitting himself." Ian stated.

"They found his wife murdered in his car. Did you not think they would look at him as the suspect straight away and try to arrest him?" Linda looked at Ian as if he was a moron.

"We didn't think these lightweight bizzies would catch him quickly, and we didn't think he'd be daft enough to give himself up." Ian became uncharacteristically defensive.

"Well, they have him. Your fun is over. Now it's my turn to play and you can step back in when I tell you."

Ian turned away, trying hard to conceal his anger. "We have some exclusives coming your way, with the evidence you want."

"The evidence I need, you've got enough of it. If you're in such a rush, give me something today, or you're just wasting my time." Linda was enjoying the shift in their relationship.

He stared at her hard. Ian knew who she was. He knew he couldn't touch her, but he was a brute by nature. He wanted to reach out and slap her, to put her back in her place. But it wasn't worth it. He slipped his hand into his jacket pocket and produced a small envelope with Jim's name written in red marker. "Your editor should approve of that. I meant it for him, but that will not happen now, will it?"

Linda opened the envelope and slid out a blue USB memory stick. She keenly inserted it into her laptop and explored the contents. There were two folders, one marked 'Videos' and the other 'Photos'. She went straight for the videos. There were two files. She opened the first. It showed the drone footage of Jim burying something amongst the trees. "Is that the gun?" she asked in a whisper.

Ian nodded, knowing precisely what she was referring to.

Good and usable, Linda thought. The second was blurrier, taken at night. It was ten seconds of walking down the street in near-total darkness, then a few brief frames showing Jim and Cassie walking together, illuminated by a streetlight. It put them together, but it was nearly too blurry to be definitive. She knew they had more juicy videos than this one. The fact they had given it to her was disappointing, considering their apparent impatience. The next folder had a single image. It was a hotel room, with Cassie completely naked on top of Jim, his trousers down by his ankles, and a collection of bottles of alcohol and lines of powder in view. Linda smiled. "I can use this. Just two questions. Who was supposed to have taken the picture, and why are his eyes shut?"

"Does it matter? You have the prime suspect shagging the victim. Who cares who took the picture?" Ian snarled.

"Can I use this all now?"

"That's all you're getting for a few days. If you want to blow your wad all at once, I don't give a shit." Ian got to his feet and walked out of the cafe.

Linda didn't like Ian. She didn't even know his full name, but her father had told her to listen to him. Linda had only met him once before and he had been as friendly that time as he was today, but at least today, he came bearing gifts. She would run the photo first, with the necessary details obscured so as not to offend readers over their breakfast. It would nail Jim well and truly to the wall. She would then use the video of Jim burying the pistol to be the basis of the following day's story. The brief few frames of Jim walking down the street with Cassie weren't much use on their own. But she didn't have to use them herself. She had met a few of the local journalists and they didn't seem keen on someone from the UK muscling in on their territory, even less so when they knew the paper she worked for. A local Merseyside paper wasn't any good to them and their careers. At least if she worked for one of the national papers, she might have been a useful contact for them in the future, but working for the Mersey Post, she was on the same rung of the ladder as they were. Maybe she could use the video to buy some favour.

It hadn't taken her long to work out that Patrick McNeil was the top journalist. His work for a broadsheet in London made him even more valuable. She had made sure he had received the same tip that she had so that they would be there together when the car was discovered. She had tried to strike up a friendship then, but he hadn't been receptive. Like the others, he couldn't see a use for her. She would return to her small newspaper and wouldn't be seen or heard from again. Helping her would have been a waste of his time, and he was a man going places. He could ill afford people holding him back. Linda knew she needed a local friend but received the message loud and clear. Unless she could help him, he wouldn't even give her the time of day.

Linda didn't want to wait until the likely briefing from the senior officers that evening. She wanted to get to work now. She looked up the Manx Times website and pulled up the number, then entered it into her mobile phone, hit the call button, and placed the phone to her ear. "Hello, I'm Linda Jones of the Mersey Post. Can I speak to Patrick McNeil, please?" she waited a moment as they tried to transfer her call across unsuccessfully before returning. "No, that's okay. I'll drop by your offices in about ten minutes. I'll see him then." She hung up the phone, started copying files off of the USB drive, leaving only the video she wouldn't use still on it.

She was about to make Patrick's day.

CHAPTER 18

K ERRY HAD BEEN FURIOUS that Ella's identity had been leaked so soon after her body had been discovered, nearly as furious as her superiors. She trusted Pat as far as she could throw him, but didn't believe he'd leak the identity to another news source and not use it himself first. The other journalist seemed much more likely to burn bridges. It didn't matter. As soon as the news was out there, all the papers and radio stations saw it as fair game to report. Since they initially brought her name to the public, much dirt had been raked up about Jim. Unbelievable detail that was embarrassing for anyone associated with him. Kerry looked no better than her bosses or colleagues, less so than many since she had worked so closely with him. Billy had wisely kept his head down and was happy for the chance to get away from his desk and accompany Kerry to visit the pathologist.

It was the middle of the day at Noble's hospital, and it was as busy as any hospital would expect to be. Visitors filled the small shop and cafe close to the entrance as staff went about their business. The two police officers didn't need to stop and ask directions, and they could walk through the hospital with no fanfare.

"Billy, pick up three coffees. Make two of them black and one however you want yours. Grab a fistful of sugar too," Kerry ordered without breaking her stride.

Billy didn't answer. He just set about his task, joining the small queue by the coffee counter.

Jake was expecting Kerry. Just like with the first victim, the police were eager to get at least a few notes from the report and he had worked nonstop to facilitate them. A knock at the door prompted Jake to straighten himself up.

"Come in," Jake answered.

Kerry entered with a smile. "What have you got for me?"

"A seventeen page preliminary report," Jake replied, holding a printout in the air.

"Excellent. What does it say?"

"Headlines are no sexual activity. She was beaten, viciously. One of her fingers was missing. It hadn't been removed with any care. Broken ribs, jaw, her remaining fingers were either broken or subject to trauma, and she was missing several teeth. Of course, that didn't kill her. Two gunshot wounds to the head and one to the chest. I recovered three bullets. All had mushroomed, but the one I got from the chest was in slightly better condition. It was a jacketed hollow point. Again, like the first victim it was a .25."

"Same gun?" Kerry asked.

"Strictly speaking, not my area. It's only a personal interest that I know it's a .25 ACP round to begin with. I couldn't tell you it was the same gun, but it's not a common cartridge these days, so too much of a coincidence, in my opinion," Jake replied.

"No DNA on her. Anything useful like that?"

"I'm still running some samples, but everything so far has been all her."

Billy entered, carrying a cardboard tray with the three coffees.

"DC Mulligan, you come bearing gifts." Jake smiled, always pleased to receive a free hit of caffeine.

Billy offered the hot drinks to the others. Kerry instantly dumped in four packets of sugar and Jake happily took his as it was.

"What do we have?" Billy asked eagerly, expecting them to have waited for his arrival to start.

"A seventeen page preliminary report you can take away and read. I didn't type that blasted thing up so that I can sit here and read it to you like an adult version of Jackanory," Jake scolded. He seemed serious, but a sly smile at Kerry confirmed he was just giving the most junior detective in the room a hard time.

"Probably the same gun as before. She was badly beaten beforehand. As yet, no DNA to point the finger at Jim or anyone else," Kerry summarised.

"Did you want to take a look at the body?" Jake offered.

Kerry and Billy looked at each other, waiting for the other to respond.

"Maybe once you have completed all your work. This will be enough for now. Thanks," Kerry replied.

Billy and Kerry smiled and left Jake enjoying his coffee.

"That was a bit of a waste of time. That could all have been done on the phone and through email." Billy sulked, again missing out on the interesting stuff to be treated as the lacky.

"Jake likes you to show your face. He gives Doolan early access because he's terrified of him. He gives us early access because we're nice to him and bring him coffee. If you want to stay in the office, you may as well go work in the bank."

"I don't want to stay in the office. It's just, it feels like all we do is the boring shit. I spend half my time on the phone talking to officials in other departments in their meek offices, and the other half fetching hot drinks. And that's when I'm not acting as your chauffeur. Just once, I want to feel like a proper copper, not some village bobby." He wasn't angry, he just sounded sad. Depressed at the realisation that even when violent murder came to the Isle of Man, he would not be kicking doors down and heroically duking it out with a crazed killer.

"It's the job, Billy. You've not been doing this for much less time than me. It's just you treat it like a game, like you're a big kid playing cops and robbers. That's fine up to a point, but if you want to be taken seriously, you've got to be more serious and less like an excited puppy." Kerry tried to keep her tone kind, but knew that basically calling him a manchild would probably go down poorly.

They both walked back to the car in silence. Billy sulked, but Kerry was trying to put together in her own mind the level of violence that had taken place. It didn't seem like Jim. He was a big man, an alcoholic, but he didn't seem like a mean drunk. The marriage obviously had been in trouble, but a horrific and prolonged assault followed by two bullets in the head and one in the chest was the most extreme result imaginable. Jim was many things, but he wasn't a fool. The half-arsed dumping of the body and car was amateurish at best, but for an experienced detective, it was impossible to believe he would have been stupid enough to leave in such an easily discoverable location. The more the evidence pointed towards Jim, and the more she thought about it, the more certain she became he was being framed. She wasn't brave or foolish enough to defend Jim yet to her colleagues or superiors, but she knew the time would come. And she was dreading it.

CHAPTER 19

D AZ EXITED THE POLICE headquarters, with few paying him much attention. His name was known to the waiting press, but not his face, allowing him to walk through the few assembled journalists and photographers towards the centre of town. It had all been a shock to him. He believed Jim, but even he knew there was a mountain to climb if his friend was to ever be free again. He had cooperated with the police. It was easy to do when he knew absolutely nothing. Jim had been clear whilst they were waiting for the police to arrive at the tower; tell the truth, don't protect him and don't worry. The first two he accomplished with ease, but not worrying was an impossibility. Despite his cooperation, they made him absolutely certain that they could still charge him for his involvement, and he could easily do a few years in prison. His advocate had done little to calm those fears, but despite the threats, they had released him. He had been told to stay on the island and that he was still a person of interest but would not be charged at this time.

The police had confiscated his car, leaving Daz to catch a bus to get back home to Ramsey. There had been enough adventure in the last day, and he was looking forward to a piece of toast, a cup of tea and a few hours' sleep in his own bed.

The motorcycle rider and his three accomplices had seen Daz leave the station, even if the press didn't know what he looked like. They did. The rider held back, parked against the side of the road. Using his mobile phone, he texted instructions to his three men inside a small blue transit van. He waited patiently for Daz to pass on the other side of the road, then quietly as possible, started his bike. There wasn't a great deal of traffic and the rider was able to slowly follow Daz, keeping a healthy distance between them. As Daz cut into a side street, the rider followed, careful not to ref the engine or force the bike to make a noise that may cause his prey to turn.

It was difficult following Daz. He walked erratically and seemingly wasn't sure where he was going. The rider stopped thirty feet back from Daz and messaged the other three men. Within a few seconds, they joined the road and overtook the rider. They slowed as they approached Daz, and without warning, two men leapt from the sliding door on the side before the van had stopped. They caught their target completely by surprise. A swift punch to the face and a crack across the back of the legs with a bat were enough to remove any fight from him. They bundled Daz into the back of the van and it was slowly driven off, with the rider following.

Inside the van, Daz tried to regain his senses, but repeated blows to his face and chest were too much. He slumped back, and they forced him onto his stomach, his hands pinned behind him and bound with cable ties. An old rag was stuffed into his mouth and held in place with electrical tape with a black cotton bag pulled down firmly over his head. Even if he was conscious, he could no longer pose a threat or attempt to defend himself. The three men didn't say a word as the van carried on.

***

The small farm no longer tended to cattle or grew crops; it was now mostly used as a holiday let. During the TT, the retired owner made a fortune renting it out to wealthy families, and such was the success; he had even converted the barn to maximise the income. Out of season, it ticked over with a few visitors looking for a quiet base with no neighbours and plenty of space. The parish of Cronk-Y-Voddy was small and far enough out of the way that it was an ideal location to relax and an even better one to base a criminal enterprise out of for short periods of time. Between the cottage and the large converted barn, the eight men had ample room to conduct their business and torture poor, unsuspecting friends of detectives. The booking had been placed through a shell company, unrelated to any of the men or their boss back in Liverpool. They had already used this property once, and many others like it before. After they left, they would ship an experienced cleaning crew from England over to make sure that not a fingerprint, hair or speck of blood would remain. Normally, there was less blood to deal with than would be the case after this booking.

It was nearly a quarter of an hour since they had thrown Daz onto the converted barn's wooden floor, still bound and hooded, and he had yet to move. A small pool of blood had gathered under the hood. Two large men stood over him, concerned. Both were white and in their late thirties.

One was covered with tattoos up to his chin and sported a small ponytail, the other had a shaved head and part of his ear was missing. Neither looked like the kind of person who you could accidentally spill their drink in a pub and expect a polite smile in return.

"How hard did you hit him?" The man with the shaved head asked.

"Not that hard. The prick has a glass jaw." The man with the ponytail gave the still figure on the floor a tap with his foot, with no reaction.

"Is he breathing?"

"I think so. Take his hood off."

The shaven-headed man bent over and yanked off the hood. Daz had a large cut across his forehead. It was responsible for most of the blood. His left eye was badly swollen and the rag in his mouth was stained red.

"He's going to be pissed if you broke his jaw," the shaven-headed thug announced.

"I didn't fucking break anything." The man with the ponytail pulled off the tape and removed the bloody rag from the mouth. He grabbed the jaw with his hand and gave it a squeeze, trying to feel for an obvious sign of it being broken. To his surprise, Daz opened his eyes and threw his face forward, clamping down on the man's hand and biting with all of his might.

The man staggered back, but Daz didn't let go, rising to his knees as he was dragged across the floor until a swift left hook to his face sent him back to the ground, with his mouth covered in blood.

"I guess the jaw isn't broken," the shaven-headed man stated with an amused smile.

"Fucking bastard!" the man with the ponytail shouted before stamping on Daz's knee.

Daz rolled over and screamed with pain. If his hands weren't still bound, he would have been clutching the knee to soothe it.

"Boys, lighten up on the man. He's here to help, aren't you, Darren?" A man clad in blue leather entered and removed his motorcycle helmet. It was Ian Harrison. He smiled, but it was awkward and more frightening than reassuring.

Daz turned and faced Ian. "What do you want?"

"Good man, straight to business. I like that; it's efficient. My boss likes that too. He likes quick; he likes efficient. Things here have been pretty quick. Your friend Jim, he's been a bit too quick. He wasn't supposed to be in custody yet. He was supposed to do a few tasks for us. But the prick went and fucked that up, didn't he?" Ian paused, waiting for a response. When one wasn't forthcoming, he continued, "I don't need much from you, barely anything at all, really. Just speak a few words into a phone for me. Now, I won't lie. We're going to hurt you a bit first. It's not personal." Ian looked at his man with the wounded hand. "Well, maybe a bit personal from him, but we need you to know that we're serious, okay?"

Daz looked around, hoping for help, a route to escape, but it was useless. He was bound and bloody, three violent men standing over him, ready to do him harm.

"No more in the face, lads, no blades, no bullets. Feel free to break a leg or two."

The two goons moved closer to the terrified Daz on the floor as Ian left the room and immediately pulled up a number on his mobile phone and lifted it to his ear. "Yeah, we're on it." Ian looked at his watch, unimpressed. "I know, boss, we're heading in the right direction. You'll get what you want. Fuck, his life is bollocksed already." He held the phone away from his ear as the voice on the other end of the line screamed at him. "I know. We'll get it done." The other voice calmed and carried on speaking at a normal volume. "Nothing from the paddy's or the jocks. We're keeping them in the dark. I've only used our people and done it all off our books, not the Kings." He listened for a moment, then disconnected the call and slid the phone back in his pocket.

Ian didn't agree with his boss; bringing personal problems into a profitable business would only end in trouble. He had worked his way up from the streets in Liverpool and always kept himself out of the way of the police, but now, on this rock, he was being put in a risky situation for another man's lust for vengeance. He didn't like his boss or his daughter.

CHAPTER 20

For Kerry, the days had all blurred into one another. Looking at the clock on the wall in the office, she couldn't be sure if it was 8am or 8pm. Looking out of the window, she decided it was probably the morning. Daz had proved useless, and Jim was sticking to his story. All of her superiors were calling on her to charge Jim, but she wasn't ready despite the clock ticking. The evidence was overwhelming, but she knew something wasn't right. She didn't dare tell them that, instead insisting she wanted to bring the strongest case possible against her former senior officer. But that would only buy her a little more time before the pressure increased again.

"Kerry, I think I owe you a coffee," a voice bellowed from the entrance to the CID office.

Kerry jumped in her seat and turned to see Patrick standing in the doorway, straight-faced. "Jesus Pat, you've got to stop doing that. I'm bloody shattered. Who let you in any way?"

"Sorry. Just been speaking to one of your superiors. He wasn't very open. I owe you a coffee if you can spare a few minutes." Patrick looked worried.

"I'm in the middle of a murder case, and I'm not telling you anything, either on or off the record," she replied, anticipating his motive.

"Kerry, please." Patrick pleaded.

Kerry picked up her jacket and threw it on. "You can get me a bacon and egg bap, too."

***

Pat and Kerry stood on the promenade, looking out over the sea. It was nearly high tide, and the water was a dark blue but calm. Pat sipped at a disposable coffee cup. Kerry had rested hers on the wall as she launched herself at her breakfast.

"I thought you should know. We're going to print with a picture of Jim with the first victim," Patrick confessed.

Kerry nearly spat out her mouthful of food, but instead chewed more quickly before speaking with anything in her mouth. "What picture? We haven't released any."

"I know. A source gave it to me. It's not a horrific picture, just one of him and the girl together at night walking down the street. It's taken from a brief video clip. Quality is terrible, but it's him."

Kerry felt relieved. That wasn't so bad. Jim had explained how he met the girl; what happened afterwards had been up for debate, but placing them together in public was far from the end of the world. All the papers carried his picture already. This was just another for the collection. "We'll need that, and your source."

"You know I can't give you my source just like that," Patrick protested.

"Well, you're obstructing a police investigation."

"That won't work on me. Look, I'll get you the memory stick. It's no good to me now, but I don't have to tell you my sources. But I may be tempted if you could help me."

Kerry wrapped the rest of the bap up in its packaging and stuffed it into her pocket. It wasn't looking likely that she would have a chance to enjoy the rest of it until she was alone. "How good is your source?"

"Remarkably so." Pat smiled. He felt he had her on the hook and now just needed to be patient reeling her in.

"What do you need?" Kerry asked.

"The source is a reporter. I don't know who their source is, but I know the picture they gave me is nothing compared to what they have. They didn't give me any details, but if it's not a picture of him murdering the girl, it's something nearly as sensational." Pat genuinely did not know what Linda had, but she was extremely pleased with herself, so he knew it must be good.

"So, what do you want from me? I'm not giving you any inside tracks."

"I want what they have, so I can print it first. This could elevate me to the next level, and maybe I get the chance to head to fleet street permanently." Pat looked excited.

"Piss off. I can't do that. I'd be back in uniform before the week was out, if I was lucky." Kerry took a long sip of her coffee and savoured the caffeine hit. "You want me to steal from your rival? No chance."

"You know me. You know you can trust me to treat it with respect. If they release it, who knows what they'll show the world," Pat argued, hoping the devil Kerry knew would be better than the alternative.

"Whatever they do with it isn't my fault, and I can't stop them. If you want to tell me who they are, great. If not, I'll log this conversation and we'll see what happens when this sensational story hits the presses," Kerry replied angrily.

"She will do it, and you would have blown your chance to remain in control." Patrick tried a final time.

"She? Is it that scouse bitch again?" Kerry asked, already sure it was.

"Please. If you help me, I can help you. A friend in the press is a valuable asset to an up-and-coming detective."

"But you're looking to piss off to the mainland to work for a proper newspaper, remember? What good is it to me trying to locate stolen farming equipment or investigating an assault if you're not working for the Manx Times but The Telegraph or the Independent? How's my friend in the press going to do anything useful for me then when he's getting pissed in London?"

"Kerry, please. Throw me a bloody bone here. London is losing interest in the story and me. I thought for sure a bent police officer would have been enough, but it isn't. I need more."

Kerry almost felt sorry for him. She could see he genuinely believed this was his one chance to get off the island and make his name. But she wouldn't risk her own career to help build his. "I will not promise you anything. I appreciate the heads-up, but I won't risk my job for yours."

"I don't know how she ties in to all of this. Her paper isn't much bigger than any of the Manx ones. It's not as if it was known that the girl was from Liverpool when she was found. It's not like they're running out of crime in Liverpool to fill their papers with. I don't know why she's here." The question had popped into Pat's head a few times, but he still couldn't tie it together. Papers on the mainland had a minor interest that had benefited him, but they didn't even want to send their own people to the island. The few lines of his they printed were safely nestled deep within the paper, where most readers would happily skip past without caring. The Mersey Post was all over the story, giving it as much prominence as his own Manx paper.

"Why do any of you do this? Afraid she might scoop you and take your national paper gig, and you'll be stuck here forever?"

"I'm not worried about me. If you don't want to help me over an outsider, I can't help you again." Pat turned, as if he was withholding a valuable resource, but he knew he had nothing.

"I will not help her. If she has information, I'll talk to her. I've got to go. Thanks for the coffee and grub." Kerry headed back to the station, hoping Billy would be ready to call around hotels to find their journalist.

CHAPTER 21

I T HAD SURPRISED JIM by just how easily he had fallen asleep since his arrest. He'd never been one to drift off easily, even when exhausted. Normally, alcohol would aid him in finding sleep, even if the overall quality was poor. His cell was as basic as it could be. A simple solid bed, topped with a thin mattress covered in a thick plastic cover and a wool blanket, provided the sleeping arrangements. A small basin, toilet and a single towel provided the washing facilities. They did not design the cell to house anyone for more than a night or two. That honour would go to the only prison on the island in Jurby. In his polyester overalls, it would have been easy to imagine getting no sleep on that wafer-thin mattress, but he had slept like a baby. When he surrendered himself, a tremendous weight had been lifted. Jim was facing a lifetime in prison, his wife had been brutally slain, but for the first time in a long time, he felt he had taken control. He had allowed himself many tears to be shed for Ella, but he knew they wouldn't bring her back. He felt guilt for not avenging her and bringing her murderers to justice, but he knew he wasn't the best person for that job. Stepping aside, he'd unleashed a more honest, determined and intelligent copper than he would ever be. Kerry's instincts were top-notch, and despite the hard time he had given her since they had been working together, he knew she would give everything in the name of justice. And unlike Jim, she could maintain her rationality in the face of what was still to come.

They had delivered a tray of food that morning, little more than a tuna and sweetcorn sandwich, a coffee, a cup of water, and a banana. Not the breakfast of champions, but it was enough to ensure the guest wouldn't starve. Jim had ignored the sandwich, knocked back the coffee and water, and eaten half of the banana. He had little appetite, so discarding the sweetcorn-tainted sandwich was easy to do. Jim was sure the officer who delivered him his meal was aware he hated sweetcorn. He had probably sent the lad out more than once on a lunch run when CID was too busy, so the young constable could easily have been aware. A small dig at a disgraced detective, hardly the worst thing to have happened to him in the last week.

A knock on the door signalled the slot on the heavy steel door was about to be opened. Jim slowly sat up on his bed and looked at the door.

"Your brief is here, Jim," the young officer remarked.

The door was unbolted, and three officers waited for Jim to rise to his feet. He stretched and winced with pain. His wounds were far from healed, and now living out of a cell, his prescribed pain medication was unavailable. It would be a job for his advocate to sort out. Until then, he would just have to live with the dull aches and sudden spikes of agony that would take him by surprise. He followed the two officers out, leaving the youngest holding the door for him. "What's the time?"

"If you're going to start clock watching, this is all going to go really slowly. How was the sandwich?" The young officer grinned.

The bastard, Jim thought to himself. *He always was a twat.*

The custody suite was mainly in the process of discharging the previous night's punters. Today, just a single hungover and sorrowful face stood in front of the custody sergeant as they were being released, their previous night's drunkenness resulting in a warning and a stern telling off. As they passed through, Jim remained uncuffed, and it almost felt like he was doing his job again. Had he been in a cheap suit rather than the cheap overalls, he could have believed it himself. Coming from the other direction, a man in his late twenties and a shaved head was being led through to be checked in for his own brief stay.

They took him to an interview room where his advocate Desmond was already standing in the room's corner. Jim looked at Desmond, expecting to see masses of documents to sign, a recording device, and anything else his representative might deem important enough to clear his client. But he had nothing. He hadn't even brought his briefcase with him. They waited for the door to close and to be alone before either spoke.

"I'm really sorry, Dessie, for how I was the other day. I promise, I'll do as you say now. I was tired, under stress and had to tell them what they needed to know so they could find the bastards responsible." Jim was contrite, but calm. Desmond McGuinness was a friend doing him a favour, one Jim had thrown back in his face when he had ignored him.

"Jim, I can't carry on representing you." Desmond couldn't look at Jim as he spoke.

"What? I said I was sorry. I know this is a crap situation, but I need you to help me." Jim felt a surge of adrenaline as he saw his situation take another nosedive.

"Cathy said I was wrong to take this case. I told her everyone deserves to be represented and that you deserve the best defence that could be offered." Desmond spoke quietly, with shame in his voice.

"So, why are you doing this?" Jim asked.

"Jim, Ella was as much our friend as you were. Jesus, Cathy, and Ella were far closer than we were. When I saw the picture of you having intercourse that girl, saw what you had done to Ella. Cathy would divorce me if I kept you on, and I couldn't look at myself in the mirror."

"Dessie, I'm innocent. I don't know what you've seen, but it's not me. Someone is setting me up. I told you this," Jim pleaded.

"Find yourself another advocate. I can make a few recommendations. Someone who doesn't know you and didn't know Ella. They will give you a far better defence than I could." Desmond walked to the door and banged on it. The door opened, and he walked out.

Jim sat in silence, trying to work out what to do next. Dessie was highly skilled, better than anyone else he could normally afford. He had sat opposite him several times in the interview room and always been impressed by his friend's professionalism and brutality. Now, he was back to square one.

***

Desmond didn't wait around at the police headquarters. He felt bad about what he had done, lying to a friend even if there were more than a few ounces of truth to what he had said. He had seen evidence against Jim. Desmond had argued with his wife, but he was a professional and would defend the devil himself if he was a client. But he hadn't walked away because of a photo, pictures of a dead woman, or any of the other evidence. The reporter had been hard, vicious in her attack on Jim when she had confronted him. But it was the man who had genuinely scared him. He had followed Desmond after he had met with the reporter. It had taken little more than a threat to his family to give Desmond second thoughts. He was only a few years away from retiring and both of his sons studying in Liverpool, away from any protection he could offer. The picture of the pair of them from that morning, unconscious and naked, gave him little doubt that if he didn't walk away, his boys would never be seen again.

He walked down the promenade until he reached a bench with a man sitting on it facing the sea. He sat next to him but made sure not to get too close.

"We done?" Ian asked.

"Yes, now what about my boys?" Desmond couldn't hide the fear in his voice.

"They're fine. They'll wake up and think they've had the best night of their lives. Don't do anything stupid. You can't protect them, yourself or your wife." Ian stood up and moved directly in front of Desmond and handed him his mobile phone. "Stay away from Jim Walsh and this is all over. Let that fucker rot." Ian walked away to a waiting car. He entered the passenger seat, and it drove away.

Desmond unlocked the phone and scrambled for a contact for *Jason McGuinness*; he hit call and pressed the phone to his ear. "Jason, are you okay? Is your brother with you? Oh, thank God!" He burst into tears as he allowed the trauma to hit him. He hadn't been a good friend, but he had been a good father.

CHAPTER 22

L INDA WAS DEEP IN concentration at her laptop as she
hammered on the keyboard, pressing each key harder
than the previous one, hoping her words would be
captured more efficiently. She had nursed a single cup
of tea for nearly two hours, but the staff was too fearful
of upsetting their squatter to dare to confront her. It
wasn't worth the aggravation when she was one of only
three customers. She had been pleased with her work. Her
editor was nervous but enjoying a surprising spike in visits
to their website, even if the physical circulation remained
unmoved. Advertisers on the Mersey Post's website were
growing in importance to the paper and its financial
position. A successful and intriguing story, even with the
remotest of links to their little part of Merseyside, helped
bring traffic to them. But it wasn't just her editor she was
eager to please, but her father. The little feedback he had
sent her way was full of praise. Whatever was happening
with DS Walsh, she was doing her part, and she couldn't
worry about what Ian was fucking up. She wanted Jim to
suffer, to feel pain, both physical and mental. She had little

doubt the bastard was psychologically broken. Everything he had was being ripped away from him. She had wanted him to suffer, and he had. It had been her idea to stage his public fall from grace and play his own mind against him before making those close to Jim his enemy. The only thing he had left was his life.

It would be hard for them to take that from him now.

Kerry entered the small cafe calmly. She was fed up. Any anger she had experienced had already faded away. Billy had done the legwork but could not find her booked into any hotel on the island. Pat had been all too happy to rack up a favour owed by sharing that Miss Jones spent a lot of time at a small cafe not too far away. When Kerry arrived, she told Billy to head back to the station or take a few hours at home if he needed a break. He had been hesitant to leave her, but she was walking into a greasy spoon to meet a journalist, not raiding a drugs den with just a baton and a stab vest. He was happy to return to headquarters and try to steal an hour of sleep if he could. Kerry spotted the small makeshift office immediately.

Linda didn't look up, concentrating on her work. Kerry walked to the counter and ordered herself a coffee, before joining Linda unnoticed. She sat opposite the reporter and watched her work for a good minute before Linda looked up, agitated. "What do you want?" she snapped.

Kerry stared at her for a moment. "I guess I should say world peace. Maybe an end to hunger and starvation. But I'll be honest, I just want some sleep and for things to return to normal."

"Normal? You've been working with a murderer. Who knows what else that bent prick has been getting up to?" Linda closed her laptop screen and sat up, ready for an argument.

"Look, I'm not here to fight. You have a job to do, I understand that. But you can't just publish pictures of the victim, of Jim or anything else. Naming the victims, that's just not right. You need to work with us." Kerry didn't like Linda, but she didn't think shouting and screaming would get her anywhere.

"Work with you? So you can cover up everything he has done and fit up some poor kid?" Linda accused.

"Nobody is covering anything up or looking at framing anyone. We all want justice, even if it's uncomfortable. You can't do what you're doing. You're harming our investigation. I'm asking you to please stop, work with us, and I promise justice will be done."

"Of course I can do what I'm doing. The truth needs to be told. If you have a problem, talk to the Press Complaints Commission." Linda retorted.

"Why are you here, and what is your problem with Jim? You don't even know him." Kerry asked.

A waitress approached nervously, having heard the conversation and not wishing to intrude, but she had a cup of coffee to deliver. Kerry gladly took it from her and quietly nodded her thanks.

"He's bent, and he's dangerous. My brother is dead because of a police officer who didn't care about doing what was right. Walsh deserves everything that's coming to him and more." Linda's anger couldn't be concealed.

"Let us do our jobs. If he's guilty, he'll be punished. Please, just don't publish anything that might hurt our investigation. If it's evidence that will help us, give it to us to strengthen our case."

"So that it can conveniently go missing? It's too late, anyway. It's all live on the website, and it's already being picked up by the nationals. Any doubt in anyone's mind that he might be innocent will have gone now." She opened her laptop back up and launched a web browser, loading the Mersey Post website, and turned the screen to face Kerry.

A still image of Jim in a wooded area, taken from above. She clicked the picture, and it loaded up the story. On the page, a video automatically played of Jim burying what looked like a pistol in a small hole.

"Where did you get this from?" Kerry's face had dropped in shock, but she couldn't keep her eyes off of the screen.

"I don't need to divulge my sources," Linda replied with a vindictive smile.

"How do you even have sources? You're from a little paper from Liverpool. It's probably read by fewer people than the wanted section of one of our own locals. Why would anyone give you the inside track?" Kerry tried to hold herself back, desperate not to lose her temper and scream at this woman.

"Maybe it's because I'm not from this cesspit of a rock!" Linda screamed, gaining the attention of everyone in the cafe.

Kerry took a large gulp of the coffee. It was too hot to drink, but she didn't bat an eyelid. She would not show any weakness. "I guess we're no Liverpool here. We don't enjoy your higher levels of crime or drug use. The poverty that parts of your city experience is not something that we can claim to match. We're just a nice little island of friendly people." She took a more leisurely sip of coffee and placed the cup back on the table with a smile.

"If you're finished, I have a deadline." Linda stated coldly.

"Who is using you, Linda? Someone is playing a game here, and they don't care who gets hurt. When this blows up, you'd be better off away from this place. You don't have any friends here." Kerry took another uncomfortable swig of her coffee and roughly placed it back on the table, a few drops splashing onto Linda's paperwork and laptop. She produced her contact card and held it out to Linda, who looked at it but ignored it. Taking the hint, Kerry placed it on the table. "Please, just call me. I promise we're not looking to hide anything."

Both women stared at each other for an uncomfortable moment before they simultaneously broke eye contact. Linda turned her attention back to her laptop and began working once again as Kerry walked towards the exit of the cafe, nodding in appreciation to the staff on her way out.

CHAPTER 23

T HE NORMALLY TRANQUIL HOLIDAY let had never before seen this level of violence. The large, brutish men had taken an unnatural pleasure in their task of beating Daz until he was ready. They had obeyed their orders and didn't touch the face or use any weapons to accomplish their task. Their large mitts encased in thin leather gloves were more than capable of inflicting sufficient harm to make their victim do nearly anything they wanted. Ribs were broken, fingers shattered, arms dislocated and privates smashed to a painful pulp. They had succeeded in their mission in less than twenty minutes. It took three attempts for Daz to record the message. The first two tries, he couldn't hide the pain or fear in his voice. It hurt to breathe. Even sitting still, he could feel his injuries swelling, the throbbing pain all over. Threats of further violence focused his mind. After he had eventually recorded his message, admitting his part in the murders, his guilt at what he had done with Jim and how sorry he was, his tormentors no longer needed him.

The next few minutes would be just as devastating. With the message recorded, any rules were relaxed. The pony-tailed thug with the injured hand had already dealt out the most damage, but he was eager to inflict more pain. He acted kindly, helping Daz to a wooden chair and carefully placing him on the seat. "It's all over now. Can I get you something?"

"Water, please," Daz answered weakly.

The man nodded gently and turned away, ready to walk to the kitchen before turning back sharply and swinging his fist into Daz's face, sending his victim straight to the floor. "There, now I think his jaw is broken!" The man laughed loudly. "Do we have a hammer?" Those in the room shrugged their shoulders. He grew frustrated and looked around the room. The wooden chair presented too tempting an option, and the attacker knocked it to the floor and smashed one leg off with his boot. He bent down slowly as Daz stared at him in horror. With the chair leg in hand, he started wailing on Daz with all his might. Bones cracked and blood splattered in most directions. No one else needed to join in with the attack, and it wasn't long before Daz lay motionless and his attacker slowed and then came to a stop. The chair leg dripped with blood and the pony-tailed man mopped the sweat from his brow.

After the gruesome job was complete. Daz was barely alive. Two men gingerly rolled him up in a large bedsheet and moved him to the corner of the room. The sheet was stained with blood and it barely moved with each of Daz's weak breaths.

"Clear this shit up, and when you're done, you can wait until the early hours, then dump him." Ian had watched much of the torture from a distance. There hadn't been a need for him to get his own hands dirty. He was happy to quietly supervise, but found his men needed no instruction. With a glass of whiskey and a comfy seat in the room's corner, away from any likely blood splatter, Ian could enjoy the violent show. "Head up to the mountains, throw him off the steepest bit of hill you can find near the road and don't be seen."

The men looked up, contemplating if they'd rather be scrubbing floors or dumping a soon-to-be corpse.

"Well, go on then!" Ian barked, causing two of the men to do as ordered.

Several men got about scrubbing the floors, mopping up the puddles of bodily fluids.

"Wait, bring me his phone." Ian picked up a small digital dictaphone and replayed the message they had forced Daz to record. He went back to the beginning of the message and dialled a number on the old phone. An answering machine for the Mersey Post played its out-of-hours message, and as soon as the tone beeped, Ian played the message once again. When he was happy with his work, he hung up the call, necked his drink, and stood up, tossing the phone to the floor before stamping on it several times until the screen was shattered. "Put that in his pocket before you dump him."

***

It was nearly 2am. The mountain roads were quiet, but visibility was good. The two goons didn't know the roads well, but well enough, they knew where to dump Daz so that he shouldn't be found for a few days. Their blue van moved cautiously over the mountains, trying to find the spot that both men vaguely remembered.

"I think he's still alive," the pony-tailed goon stated, looking back at the bedsheet-wrapped mass.

"Well, go back there and finish him off then," the shaven-headed driver suggested.

"Piss off. That takes me from manslaughter to murder. I'm no mug. Right now, we're all a little guilty. I go back there and put my size twelve on his throat, and suddenly, you're looking at GBH, maybe GBH with intent and I'm the fucking murderer," the pony-tailed thug answered.

"GBH ain't a slap on the wrists. Dougie got fifteen years for GBH with intent; he's six years into that already. He's looking at least at another two years before he gets a sniff of freedom."

"Dougie was a prat, and as I said, I ain't no mug. We'll toss him, and hopefully, these local bizzies will believe it was a hit and run." The man with the ponytail had wished he hadn't brought it up. "I think it's round here." He tapped his shaven-headed colleague on the shoulder and pointed to the spot.

The van's headlights were turned off as they came to a stop. It was a clear stretch of mountain and they could see far off into the distance, both ahead and behind them. They would spot any car coming their way in enough time that they could get clear. Both men jumped out and quickly got to work. They dragged Daz out of the van and onto the hard, tarmacked road. They unwrapped him and rolled him down the steep side of the mountain. Daz travelled a couple of metres, then became lodged on the rough terrain.

"Bloody hell, give him a shove." The shaven-headed man looked at the awkwardly placed body. It was just out of view, but was supposed to tumble to the bottom of the steep embankment, not sit near the top.

"I'm not crawling down there," the pony-tailed man declared.

In the distance, two sets of motorcycle headlights came around the corner at speed. It wouldn't take long for them to reach the van. Both men thought better of trying to move the body and jumped back in the van. They started off down the road immediately as the first motorbike whizzed by at an incredible speed. The second followed closely behind it as the van began putting distance between itself and the body.

"He's going to be pissed when he finds out." The man with the pony tail thought aloud.

"I'm not going to tell him, are you?"

"Of course not."

"Well, it's fine. They'll still take days to find him, and by then, we'll be back in civilisation."

Daz could only just open his eyes. He felt cold, but the pain had started to fade. Daz let himself believe that maybe he was getting better. He just needed to rest a bit longer. He tried to move his arms and legs, but struggled. With all the strength he could muster, he reached his arm out and felt the cold, damp grass on his fingertips. His mind couldn't focus, and his strength was now all but gone, and he could only lie still. He turned his head a few degrees, but in the darkness, couldn't see anything. He closed his eyes, ready to fade back to sleep, hoping someone would help him.

CHAPTER 24

K ERRY DIDN'T WANT TO go home, but they had ordered
her to. Her superiors would have loved nothing
more than for her to clear her colleague, one of their
own detectives, but it was looking increasingly like a
fool's errand, and one which looked bad to the public.
Kerry burning out would only put them another detective
down. Any hope that DS Walsh was innocent had become
drowned in a tidal wave of evidence against him. They
had more than enough to keep him in custody as they
continued to build their case. Whilst Kerry was eager to
stay working, those higher up didn't want their young
detective to frazzle trying to save an obviously guilty,
washed-up waste of a human being. It was 3am when she
had taken the irate phone call from DCI Ingham. He had
made it perfectly clear. If she was at work before 3pm the
next day, she should report in her uniform and avoid the
CID office.

Her small apartment block was buried amongst many
others on the outskirts of Douglas. It offered little in the
way of luxuries, but proved popular with the young and

those on low incomes. The shared communal entrance was as tired as the rest of the building. Paint peeled back, revealing the rotten wood of the doorframe. A small crack in a glass panel had been patched up with a thick adhesive tape, and even the concrete step in front of the door had a large split with a few weeds poking through. Kerry shoved the door hard and it popped open. There was no lock or keypad to enter. The door served little purpose other than keeping the harsh winds and driving rain out of the building and from degrading the already heavily worn carpet tiles. A sickly fluorescent light tube illuminated everything inside with a yellow hue whilst emanating an irritating low hum that couldn't be unheard.

Kerry warily carried on up the narrow stairs, purely on autopilot, dragging her feet as her body realised it was close to sleep. The occupants of the other apartments were fast asleep, and the building was eerily quiet. Kerry was used to coming and going at all hours, a good excuse to not have to mix with her neighbours, several of whom she would likely have had contact with as part of her job. She didn't broadcast she was a detective, and being recognised by a disgruntled drunk or petty thief wouldn't be an enjoyable experience. She reached the first floor and exited through the propped open fire door and walked down the narrow hallway towards her apartment. As her key entered the lock, she could feel her eyes closing. Her mind and body instinctively knew that they were about to get the rest that they had craved.

As soon as she stepped into the apartment hallway, Kerry felt uneasy. In her fatigued state, it was all too easy to dismiss the feeling and write it off as tiredness. Her intention was to pour herself a large glass of water and take it with her to bed, sipping it as she went. Her heart skipped a beat as she flicked the switch in the small living room on. Sitting on her small two-seater sofa, a masked man, clad in racing leathers.

"Do you know how long I've been waiting? I should have been tucked up nice and cosy in bed. Instead, I'm in this little shithole. Honestly, how much are they paying you? I know junkies who wouldn't live like this," Ian remarked, looking around the small and sparsely decorated room.

Kerry edged back and bumped into a large man who had been hiding in the bedroom. She turned to see the tall masked figure looming over her. She turned, placing her back against the wall so that neither man could easily move without her seeing. "What do you want?" Adrenaline was coursing through her veins, and any hint of tiredness had left her. She didn't want these bastards to think they could intimidate her. Despite the seriousness of her predicament, she remained calm, and her voice was strong.

"Just a talk, for now," Ian replied as he slid back in the chair to make himself more comfortable. "You have to ask yourself, DC Kerry Hughes, do you really need to look after that fuck, or can you just let him rot in a cell for the rest of his miserable life?"

"If he's guilty, he'll answer for his crimes," Kerry answered confidently.

"If? How much more evidence do you need that the prick slotted two innocent women?" Anger crept into Ian's voice. "That bastard needs to be put away. You've done your job finding your murderer. Now follow it through. Two women are dead. You don't want to be the third."

"Don't you threaten me!" Kerry screamed. She knew how dangerous the situation was. Kerry knew these men could overpower her, but she was tired and angry. She wouldn't go down without a fight.

Without warning, Ian's accomplice grabbed Kerry firmly by each arm and slammed her body into the wall three times until she went limp. She could feel the pain. They had knocked out the wind of her. Kerry tried to remain on her feet and not collapse to the ground. She swayed as she struggled for breath before she dropped to her knees and steadied herself; her attacker stood over her. Kerry looked up at Ian and back at his goon. Like a viper, she struck the man in his groin with a fast and well-placed fist. He groaned as he dropped to his knees beside her and replied with a weak headbutt that only partially met its target, glancing off Kerry's temple.

Ian looked at his own man, now holding his privates and his own head in discomfort from the physical altercation. He looked at Kerry, barely 5ft 8in tall and half the weight of his thug, but she hadn't given up. Ian admired her and cursed her. He was sick to death of this petty job he had been given; his boss was willing to risk it all to destroy one man. "Just don't be a silly girl, and no one else will get hurt. Not you, your mother, your dad or your little sister." Ian gathered himself, ready to leave. Kerry lunged at him but missed by a country mile. Ian's eyes had a wicked glint, and he couldn't help himself as he punched Kerry hard in the back of her head. She was unconscious before she landed on the floor. "Bollocks. Come on, let's get out of here. Tell that silly journo cow it's done. She'll have to handle it from here."

Chapter 25

T HE MORNING WAS BRISK, but the sun had won out over the clouds as it rose over the island. The green slopes of the mountains basked in the light as a gentle breeze whistled through the tops of the peaks and the valleys far below. Daz had barely moved all night and hadn't been conscious for more than a few minutes at a time, not nearly long enough to prepare himself physically to try to move. He had been roused from the blackness several times by motorcycles screaming past at tremendous speeds. By the time he composed himself to raise a hand for help, they were already far off in the distance. Daz had accepted his fate and just wanted it over. The chilly night had helped dull the pain, but it was still there. His whole body let him know it was damaged. The numbing powers of the low temperatures masked the pain but helped ease him closer to death. He knew that every time his eyes shut, they may not open again, and whilst that thought was initially frightening, now it was comforting.

From the road half a mile away, Daz was just a dark spot near the edge of the next mountain slope. Easily mistakable for a deposit of slate, a dried-out shrub or shredded tyre, it wasn't until someone was within 100 metres that they might realise it was a human body. With only an outstretched arm and mop of bloody, matted hair potentially visible up close, many had passed him in the night's darkness. Now the sun had illuminated his pale hand. It was just enough to catch the eye of an observant motorist. As soon as they saw the hand in the light inches from the edge of the mountainside, they pulled over and investigated. Daz was secure enough that the man didn't dare touch him, but he instantly pulled out his phone and called for an ambulance. He flagged down another motorist, who pulled their car up behind his and recovered a blanket from their car boot to cover the poor soul who they determined was still alive. Within 10 minutes, a small crowd of motorists had stopped to gawk at the scene. Many more slowly pushed through the artificially narrowed road to carry on their journey. They had no interest in this drama and found the slight delay aggravating.

By the time the ambulance had arrived, two men had dragged Daz onto the road, and they had found more blankets to cover his bloodied, near pale white skin. Many who had stopped to get an eyeful of this bloody scene couldn't bring themselves to look at the badly injured man before they turned away and made their excuses to leave and carry on their journeys.

***

As the ambulance had raced towards the hospital, the paramedic tending to Daz had fought every inch of the way to keep the battered man alive. His injuries appalled her, and she questioned if it could only have been a single car that had struck him. The bruising was coming through strong and stood out against the pale ice-cold skin splattered with dried blood. "He's fading. Make sure they're ready for him!" the paramedic called out to her colleague, panic in her voice. She had little belief he would survive the journey.

They had cruelly given Daz hope, and now, once again, death frightened him.

A team was waiting outside of the accident and emergency department at Nobles hospital. They were well versed in attending to horrifying accidents involving motor vehicles. The TT races didn't just bring badly injured riders to their door, but unfortunate spectators who had chosen their position for better views rather than any protection. A rider losing control of their bike going over 130mph creates an often devastating missile that all too easily maims or kills anyone unable to evade its path. As they removed Daz from the ambulance, the experienced team began to work, collecting details from the paramedic whilst other colleagues began performing their own checks. They burst through the doors, wheeling the patient through the waiting area and directly to a space in the ward where they could begin to try to save Daz's life.

Kerry had heard the commotion as she waited patiently with the handful of other early morning A&E visitors. She had been hesitant to visit the hospital, eager not to have anything put on record. She didn't want to face up to what had happened the previous night, much less be made to feel vulnerable by her colleagues. There had been a small patch of dried blood matted in her hair, and she had been unconscious. After regaining consciousness, she had an incredible headache that paracetamol did little to help with. She was feeling sorry for herself, physically and mentally. Ready to give up, ready to throw in the towel and go with the flow, even if it resulted in Jim going to prison for the rest of his life. With Daz rushing past her, she had to do a double-take. The man was in terrible shape, but she recognised him instantly. She could only wonder if Daz had been paid a visit too, and that he had failed to come off as lightly at her.

"Miss Hughes?" A nurse called out. She stood with a clipboard in front of the waiting area, looking for her patient amongst the small gathering of sorry looking visitors.

Kerry was too distracted by Daz and failed to respond, as she was deep in thought.

"Miss Hughes?" the nurse repeated, looking directly at Kerry, having ruled out the others in the waiting room.

Kerry looked up, confused. "Sorry," she offered as she looked back in the direction where Daz had been wheeled away to. "Who was that man?"

"Which man?" the nurse responded.

"There was a man just wheeled through on a trolley. He looked really badly hurt," Kerry answered, pointing to where he had been taken.

"I'm sorry, I can't discuss other patients," the nurse replied sternly.

Kerry fumbled in her coat pocket and produced her warrant card. "I'm DC Kerry Hughes. I believe that man is involved with an ongoing case. Can you tell me who he is and what happened to him?"

"I'm sorry, I don't know his name, but they found him on the mountain road. It looks like he had been hit by a vehicle and left for dead," the nurse answered excitedly, now feeling part of the drama.

"I'm going to need to see him."

"That won't be possible yet, but once we have looked at you, I can see if someone can talk to you and answer a few questions."

"I'll be fine," Kerry stated as she followed the direction that Daz had been taken.

"You can't go through there!" the nurse shouted after her.

Kerry just raised her warrant card back into the air, facing behind her as she passed a man in scrubs coming out of the treatment area before the door closed behind her. There were several curtained off areas used to treat patients with a degree of privacy. A few medical staff moved around, going about their duties; one or two paused to look at Kerry, knowing she shouldn't be there but not sure whether to confront her.

Finally, an especially tired looking woman in her fifties approached her. "Can I help you?"

"Excuse me, nurse, where is the man that was just brought in?" Kerry asked.

"It's doctor, and I'm sorry, friends and family have to wait outside," she responded curtly.

Kerry flashed her warrant card. "He's not my friend or my family. Where is he?"

The doctor looked at the identification, seemingly unimpressed with it or Kerry. "He's not conscious, and there's a good chance he's going to die. You will have to wait." She walked back towards the door and pressed the button to release it before swinging it open and holding it in place, inviting Kerry to return to the waiting area.

Kerry stopped for a moment, ready to argue, but then thought better of it. She begrudgingly walked through and could hear the door closing behind her with a noticeable click as the mechanism secured it once again. She reached into her pocket for her phone, pulled up a contact, hit the call button, and held the phone to her ear. After a moment, the other end answered. "I don't care what time it is, Billy. I'm at the hospital. Darren Corkill was just wheeled in. He's messed up. They're saying a hit and run, but he's unconscious, and I can't get near him. Head straight over, but don't tell anyone I'm here. I'm supposed to be resting."

CHAPTER 26

THE NURSE THAT KERRY had dismissed had been kind enough to make time for her as she waited for Billy's arrival. She used two stitches to close the minor wound on the back of her head and gave her a quick once over to make sure nothing serious had obviously occurred. The bruise to her temple had swelled and discoloured and was sore to the touch. Paracetamol, a bag of frozen peas and rest was the advice given with instructions to come back to the hospital if anything changed. Waiting for Billy, Kerry again had time to feel sorry for herself. This time though, rather than thoughts of giving up, she was angry that she had even considered it. Whoever these men were, they couldn't get away with this.

Billy arrived looking tired and dishevelled. His suit creased, and yesterday's shirt was complete with a trace of the baked beans from his lunchtime baked potato. He spotted Kerry straight away and headed over. She hadn't seen him arrive. He quietly approached from behind and moved closer to her ear. "What happened to you?"

Kerry nearly jumped out of her seat and was ready to punch Billy in the jaw. "Jesus, Billy, what the hell is wrong with everyone? Do I just give off a sneak up on me vibe?" She shouted, getting the attention of everyone in the waiting room.

"Sorry, I thought it would be funny," Billy sheepishly answered.

"Well piss off. It's too early for that shit."

"You woke me up. I've been working silly hours too, you know. What happened to you?" Billy looked at the swollen bruise on her temple.

"Sorry, I'm a bit on edge. I just slipped in the shower. I guess I'm just tired." Kerry lied, still unsure if she wanted to admit they had attacked her in her own home.

"With your hard head, I bet the shower came off worse," Billy responded with a smile. "Are you okay?"

"Yes, just a bruise and a few stitches on the back of my head."

"Bloody hell, you weren't messing about." Billy adjusted his position to get a look at the wound, but her hair hid it from view well. Just a few drops of blood on the collar of her t-shirt and some dried blood matted in her hair. "Why do you need me?"

"I'm not supposed to be working until 3pm, and I'll get a bollocking from Ingham if he thinks I ignored him. We're going to find out what is happening with Corkill, and you can get all that credit."

Billy liked the sound of the credit part, but still wasn't convinced by the need for the deception. He trusted Kerry, so he followed her wishes. The pair approached the front desk and both showed their warrant cards. "We're going to need to see someone who can assist us with your patient, Darren Corkill."

***

Kerry had found her way back into the treatment area, this time invited. Billy stood beside her as they waited for the doctor to get off of the phone to speak with them. He was young compared to his colleagues, but spoke fast on the phone with a high level of confidence. He hung the corded phone up and turned to Billy and Kerry.

"You're the detective keen to talk to my dead man?" the doctor said cockily.

"He's dead?" Kerry responded, shocked. He looked badly hurt, but if he was dead, why had they wasted her time?

"He was, but I dragged him back to this plane of existence. He won't able to talk to you for quite some time, if at all. There was massive trauma to multiple parts of his body. A collapsed lung, a bleed on the brain, his jaw is broken, multiple broken ribs, a ruptured testicle, shattered kneecap, multiple breaks on all of his limbs, luxation of his right eyeball. And that's before we get to the blood loss, hypothermia, and all the small niggly wounds he has suffered." The doctor smiled, impressed with his own recall of the injuries.

"I heard them say it was a hit and run?" said Kerry.

"I'm not sure about that. It's possible. Maybe two vehicles caught him. A few more injuries by being tossed a few feet down on to a rocky patch of the mountain. I don't know, maybe. But I've seen people hit by vehicles at high speed. Don't get me wrong, he's severely injured, but someone in a car on the mountain roads going as fast as they dare could have liquified him and shattered every bone. He looks to me like he's had been on the wrong end of a sustained attack. Torture even." The doctor mused.

Kerry glanced at Billy, then back at the doctor. "We'll need his clothes and belongings."

"He'll be in the theatre in the next few minutes. They will start trying to repair some of the damage, but I wouldn't hold out for any evidence on his body. His clothes, wallet, phone and watch have been safely stored for him. I'm not sure if you need any court orders or such like to get them, but I'm sure we'll happily follow your lead after we get some confirmation." The doctor led the pair towards the nurses' station and started rooting around the large drawers and storage cupboards until he found a sealed, clear plastic bag containing blood-smeared clothes and a small parcel with the valuables in. Kerry reached out to take it from the doctor, but he pulled it away.

"We're going to need those," Kerry stated calmly.

"Feel free to take a look, but you'll need to talk to the nurse in charge before anything is taken off-site. Just grab someone if you need anything," the doctor instructed, holding the bag away until Kerry nodded. He handed it over and she eagerly grabbed the bag and opened the seal. The doctor had done his part and left the two detectives, caring little if they did what he asked.

"What are you looking for?" Billy queried, unsure of what they could possibly find.

"Something, anything," Kerry replied as she carefully searched through the contents of the bag.

"What about DNA?" Billy asked.

"Good samaritans, paramedics, doctors, nurses, the person he sat next to on the bus. It's tainted with everyone he's been in contact with. Maybe he scratched one of them, but who knows? What is in this bag might help us now. There has to be something else we can use."

"It could just be an accident. It happens," Billy pointed out. "You've still got an open hit and run on your pile."

"You're probably right. He went for a late night stroll across the mountains and was hit by a car half a dozen times. It happens to the best of us." Kerry rolled her eyes as she plucked a mobile phone from the inside of a jacket pocket.

"Well, what then?" Billy asked.

"You heard that obnoxious doctor. Daz was beaten. There are people here who have an interest in Jim going away for a long time. They wanted something from Daz. They wanted it bad enough to kill him." She examined the handset. The phone was a cheap, old dumb phone. It was in nearly as bad a condition as its owner. The plastic casing was chipped and cracked, and the screen was shattered, but still just about operable. Kerry powered it on and waited for it to light up. The menu was basic: no apps, just the basic functions of a mobile phone; calls, contacts, messages and a built-in puzzle game. She selected messages, and it was empty. Likewise, there were no contacts, and the puzzle game even lacked any recorded scores. Just one call had been placed in the last week, the day before, to a non-Manx number. She showed it to Billy.

He focused on the screen, and a flicker of recognition showed in his eyes. "That's a Liverpool number."

"And you're going to find it for me."

CHAPTER 27

T HE CELLS IN THE police station were reasonably modern but designed strictly for short-term guests. Jim was already approaching the record for the longest visitor, and with the evidence overwhelmingly pointing to his guilt and his presence having a damaging effect on morale, they decided to move him to Jurby prison. His transfer would be a low-key event, originally planned for an unsocial hour to avoid prying eyes. They had brought it forward for reasons only the head of the prison service understood. An ill-fitting pair of trousers, shirt and jumper had been provided to avoid the spectacle of him appearing in his issued white boiler suit. The unflattering short legs of the trousers looked especially amusing on Jim, whose taller frame made the entire outfit look ridiculous. From the moment he had tried it on, he wished he could have remained in the forensic overalls they had given him when his clothes had been confiscated.

He waited patiently in his cell, ready for the door to open and to be led away for the next installment of his nightmare. It was the Isle of Man. The prison was hardly full of murderers and killer gang members. Even so, for a police officer, it would not be a pleasant experience. He would constantly be on the alert for an attack by someone wanting to improve their standing, or maybe anyone who just wanted the chance to kick the shit out of a copper. Promises of segregation sounded okay, but in practice, it couldn't last forever. He had already resigned himself to the fact he was going to have to inflict and receive an uncomfortable amount of physical pain in the coming weeks and months. The door opened, and Jim rose to his feet and held out his touching wrists, expecting the cuffs to be placed on him, ready to go.

"Put them down Jim," Kerry ordered. "I see they dug the good clothes out for you," she smirked.

"Kerry, are you my taxi?"

"God no. We don't have long. I had a visit from some of your scouse friends last night." She flashed her bruised head in his direction.

"Are you okay?" A genuine look of concern spread across his face.

"My pride hurts the most, but I'm fine. Jim, whatever is happening here, you're the victim. They're working too hard to get you sent down. Everything is tying back to Liverpool. What the hell happened there?"

"I was a good detective. Maybe I sent somebody down who took offence, but this is a bit bloody much. They're criminals. Getting pinched is a cost of doing business. They're not stupid enough to make it personal. The only one who ever went that extra mile was the twat who stabbed me. But he's currently back in prison and won't be out for many years yet."

"Well, this looks pretty damn personal. Jim, be honest with me. Tell me something you haven't already. There must be something, isn't there?" Kerry was becoming desperate as the time ticked away. She had to have something to work off if she was to save Jim.

"The warehouse. It's where this nightmare began. I woke up in that shithole of a room, but it wasn't. It was a bloody fake created in the middle of a warehouse out near Laxey. The girl was there, dead, and I just panicked. I didn't know what had happened, what I had done. Of course, I was shitfaced that night, so I remembered nothing. But I know I didn't kill her, but they were watching and following me every step of the way. I've never seen the place before. It's in one of the valleys, and it's brand new."

"I can take a drive over there. I don't suppose you have an exact address?"

Jim shook his head. "I found it again, so I'm sure you should be able to track it down. Take Billy, don't go alone. You know they're dangerous."

Kerry again flashed her bruised head. "I know. They threatened me, my family. And then there's Daz."

"What about him?" Jim asked, concerned.

"Billy said he was going to come and see you?" Kerry looked at Jim, expecting an acknowledgement, but he just shrugged his shoulders. "He's in Nobles. They're not sure if it's a hit and run, or if he was attacked. But it looks like a beating to me, I'm sure of it."

"Damn it, what have I got him involved with? Is he okay?" Jim asked, upset and angry.

"He's been pretty badly hurt. He was in surgery. The last I heard, he was out and stable, but he's not in a good way. They tried to kill him, Jim. It's just dumb luck he was found alive."

Jim looked angry. He was utterly helpless, and he doubted his decision to give himself up. Should he have stayed outside on the run and gone after these callous bastards himself? They had taken everything from him, hurt those close to him, and he couldn't do a thing about it now.

"I need to get out of here," Jim stated coldly.

"That's not happening, you know that. Trust me to do my job." Kerry quickly shut Jim down.

"I do trust you. I don't trust them to not destroy more lives."

"I will do everything possible to clear your name. This is all Liverpool. I know just the scouser to talk to." Kerry heard a sound behind her and turned to see two uniformed officers entering the cell, a set of handcuffs on display. They stood by the door, waiting respectfully for Kerry to finish. She rested her hand on Jim's shoulder and he held his hands out, with them cuffed instantly.

The officers led Jim out of the custody block, past his former colleagues. Some couldn't bring themselves to look at their disgraced colleague; others couldn't help but stare. Jim hung his head low and willed his escorts to pick up the pace and get him out to the transport van as soon as possible. His mind was a mess as he walked through the corridors. Thinking about what had already happened and again thinking of what his future in prison would look like. As they exited out of the back of the station, the expected van was noticeably absent. An unmarked police car pulled up. Two plainclothes officers sat in the front, and another exited the car from the back. He wasted no time in opening the other passenger door and assisting Jim into the seat, hustling the shamed detective's head into place.

Jim tried to reach for his seatbelt, but his cuffed hands and broad frame made it difficult. "Could you?" he asked of the plainclothes officer, who considered the request for a moment before obliging and fumbling with the seatbelt until it clicked into place.

With all three officers and their prisoner in the car, it slowly pulled away and out of the rear car park. They were in no hurry as the car edged out onto the road in front of the station. Ian watched from the other side of the street, clad in his blue racing leathers, his helmet resting on the seat of his motorbike as he stood on the path beside it. He lifted his phone to his ear. "We're coming. You'd better be ready."

***

The CID office was subdued. Murders on the island were one thing, but one of their own being responsible hurt every member of the service. The usually proud detectives held their heads a little lower. Any banter was replaced with hushed pleasantries and silence. Jim's guilt tainted Billy and Kerry. The fact they had worked closely with him condemned them to odd looks and a pariah status amongst their colleagues. Having worked on the investigation that produced so much evidence against Jim did little to restore their good names.

Billy was sitting at his desk, slowly typing up notes. He hadn't spoken to anyone since he had arrived back at the station, and he was happy to keep his head down. He knew this would all blow over eventually. It might take a year or two, but if he kept his head down, it would work itself out. Kerry entered and headed straight over to her desk near Billy.

"That number from Daz's phone. It was unlisted but when I called, it went straight through to an answerphone for a paper," Billy whispered.

"Let me guess, the Mersey Post?" Kerry stated knowingly.

"She shoots, she scores." Billy smiled.

Kerry picked up her desk phone and fumbled through her notebook, searching. She stopped at a page, placed her finger on it, and rested the phone between her shoulder and ear as she dialled a number. She waited a moment before sighing. Kerry waited a few more moments before she spoke. "This is DC Kerry Hughes. I need some assistance with our enquiries. You have our number. Please call me as soon as you get this." She put the phone down and allowed herself a moment to think.

"Who was that?" Billy asked.

"It doesn't matter. We need to go to Laxey."

CHAPTER 28

T HE CAR WAS ALREADY outside of Douglas on its journey to Jurby Prison. The three men accompanying Jim remained silent, keen that the thirty-minute journey be over as soon as possible. They all knew him, not necessarily well, but before all of this, he was one of their own. This was the Isle of Man. It wasn't London or Liverpool. There, the thought of a police officer going rogue was extremely unlikely, but on the island, it was impossible. They all could barely believe it, but his reputation proceeded him, and his time with the Merseyside police force made it easier to think of him less a Manx policeman; and more just another outsider. As they began their way up the mountain road towards Snaefell, Jim looked out of his window across the beautiful countryside, trying to drink in every sight, knowing he was unlikely to see it many more times in what remained of his life.

"Any chance we could go a little slower?" Jim asked, hopeful that a former colleague might feel sorry for him.

The sound of the engine being put to harder work soon made it clear he would receive no benefits for his past service. The countryside whizzed past at a greater speed and he had to fix his focus at a greater distance to avoid feeling sick.

The motorcycle followed with a respectful gap. Ian didn't want to get too close just yet but was pleased as the car picked up speed as it began the ascent on the mountain. There wasn't much he enjoyed about the island; he much preferred the big city life. But whenever he was forced to visit to ensure operations were running smoothly and their interests were being looked after, he would spend hours riding across the mountains and the surrounding areas. Ian could easily have sent his men to do this piece of dirty work, but he led from the front. He had exposed himself to risk several times, but he knew getting everything right was important to his boss, and another excuse to get on the bike always helped. He sped up closer to the car until he was close enough to see the backs of the occupants' heads. It was nearly time.

The car barely slowed as it took the wide turn left just before it reached the Bungalow tramway crossing. Several tourists turned as the sound of the shrieking tyres momentarily caught their attention before they continued their ascent to the top of Snaefell by foot. Jim struggled for a better view of the mountain peak before the terrain prevented it.

Ian continued to follow, dropping back slightly to avoid being noticed. He was just another motorbike on the mountain, and that's what he needed them to believe. The pace didn't slow too much, even though the road now felt a little closer, with more frequent bends and often a little less visibility. Ian knew he had to move. He sped up and whooshed past the car, earning a tut from the driver and piquing Jim's interest. Jim knew that bike, and he knew that rider.

Before he had the chance to speak, the car's side was struck, sending it into a spin. The skilled police driver struggled to gain control of the car as it bounced off the stone wall and grass bank that lined the tarmac. It slowed before coming to a sudden stop and smashed into the wall, sending the passengers forward in their seats. The two in the front struck the deployed airbags and were dazed, suffering a probable broken nose each. Jim and the officer who sat next to him were confused but mostly uninjured, a few minor cuts from the broken glass were their only concern. The car had been totalled, its windows were either missing or smashed, and the engine was exposed, with the bonnet having been peeled off somewhere further back along the road. The tyres each faced a different direction, and oil dripped onto the road surface amongst the broken glass.

Jim looked back behind the car. A large tractor partially blocked the road behind them, the damage to its front matching that of the side of the car. A masked man approached on foot, a small machine pistol in his hand. He struggled to jog in a straight line, his own balance affected by the crash, forcing him to slow to not fall over.

"You have to uncuff me!" Jim shouted, unsure of what was about to happen, but knowing having his hands free would be infinitely better than not.

The surrounding officers did not know what was happening. The two in the front were still struggling, whilst the other in the back turned behind to see the man approaching. "Shit!" he screamed.

The Skorpion machine pistol was small, fired a lethal but not overpowered round and was wildly inaccurate in anything other than skilled hands. The out-of-breath man, struggling not to stumble to the ground, would not win any marksmanship contests until he regained his senses from the crash. He let out a burst of gunfire. One round struck the car; the other two flew over the top. It was enough to get the attention of the two rear passengers of the car and his masked partner running towards them from the opposite side with a semi-automatic pistol in his hand. All of them instinctively ducked despite the bullets having already passed.

Ian had stopped further ahead and looked back, admiring his men's handiwork. Satisfied the hardest part of the job was done, he sped off, eager to return to the farm and make sure the rest of his thugs were ready for their job in the converted barn.

Jim was the first to brave raising his head to look back at the man. He was much closer now, only a few feet from the crippled car. His weapon was still raised, but he didn't fire at the target Jim presented him with. With his attention on this large man, he hadn't noticed the other as he forced the passenger door open and shoved his pistol in Jim's face.

"Get the fuck out of the car!" the man screamed, making sure every occupant knew who was in charge and that he would punch a 9mm hole into anyone who disagreed.

Jim struggled, but with his seatbelt still plugged in and his hands still cuffed, he couldn't free himself. The other man swung open the other rear door. "Everybody out! You do his belt!"

Jim's seatbelt was unclipped, and the four men exited out of the car. Each struggled to varying degrees to get out of the vehicle, the two front occupants seeming the worst affected, unable to find their legs as if they had spent a month at sea.

"Get on the floor, onto your stomachs, and put your hands on the backs of those heads!" they bellowed the next order.

Jim tried to follow the command but was pulled back by one of the men. "You stay here."

The three officers awkwardly laid down onto the broken glass on the road and placed their hands behind their heads as requested. One of the masked men rooted around the car, producing two radios which he placed on the floor.

"Phones!" he screamed as he kicked the nearest man on the floor. "Get them to me now!"

Hands desperately scrambled around in pockets, and the devices were gathered up and added to the radios.

A full burst of gunfire made everyone flinch as the pile of phones and radios were smashed to pieces by the rest of the Skorpion's magazine being emptied into them. The man reloaded as he talked. "Yous is going to stay here. You ain't gonna move, and if ya do, we'll find you and kill you."

The other man was leading Jim away by his collar to a waiting old blue estate car. The machine pistol wielding man began to follow, walking backwards, facing the men lying on the ground, ready to send a spray of bullets in their direction if they so much as thought about disobeying his orders.

They bundled Jim into the back of the car with a gun shoved into his face. He stared at the dark metal weapon. Compared to the pocket pistol they had framed him with, this was a cannon. It wasn't the first time a pistol had been pointed at him, but it was something he would never be comfortable with. A nervous young dealer in above their head in Liverpool might accidentally discharge the weapon, but these thugs were killers. They had already brought bloodshed to the island, to him. Maybe he was too important to kill. They could have killed him dozens of times, but that wasn't what they had done. They wanted to hurt him. And they had.

As the second man reached the passenger door, he fired two aimed rounds into the wrecked unmarked car. The plainclothes officers on the floor pushed their heads into the tarmac, desperate for cover. The man with the pistol entered the driver's seat, and the other man got into the back with Jim, digging the barrel of his weapon into Jim's ribs.

"Who are you?" Jim asked the men. Maybe now he might get some answers.

"You can just shut the fuck up," the driver ordered.

"Yeah, you shut your fucking trap," the other man chimed in unnecessarily, digging the machine pistol further into Jim's ribs.

The car drove at speed for a few minutes before driving through a gate and into a field and coming to an abrupt stop twenty yards away from a parked blue van. First out of the car was the driver who jumped out and ran to the car's boot, where he produced a small petrol can. The other man got out of the back and dragged Jim by his cuffed hands out of the car and into the field a few metres away. The driver began pouring the petrol over the outside of the car and emptied the rest of the can inside of it until it was drenched.

"Where are the matches?" the driver asked his colleague.

"Dunno, the van?"

"For fuck's sake." The driver stormed off to the van and began searching the cab.

Jim remained on the ground, his guard staring away from him and towards the van and paying Jim no attention. Jim knew he was dead. Whatever this jailbreak was in aid of, it wasn't about freeing an innocent man and making sure justice was done. He clasped his cuffed hands together and sent them up between the man's legs and into his genitals. The air left his victims' lungs, and he could only fall to the floor retching. Jim wasted no time in smashing the bastard several times in the back of the head with his fists until the man barely moved and blood dripped through his hair to the mud below. The commotion hadn't gone unnoticed, and the driver turned from the van's cab and began firing his pistol. Jim put himself flat on the ground, seeking cover behind the other man. The Skorpion pistol was near, but just out of reach. Jim didn't take any time to think and scrambled forward to pick it up and, in one motion, scooped up the gun and fired towards the driver. Three rounds left the barrel; the first struck the driver's thigh, the second the front wheel of the van, and the third whistled off into an earth bank fifty yards away. The driver collapsed to the ground; his pistol slipped from his grasp as he clutched his wound.

Jim paused for a moment. He could stay here and wait for the police. *Surely this was proof something was going on, that he could be an innocent man.* No. He knew the evidence against him was too strong. Whatever this was wouldn't clear him on his own; it would only ask more questions of him. He rose to his feet and checked the man closest to him. The man stirred but was no longer in the fight. Jim raised his gun towards the other injured man and hurried to the driver's seat of the car. The keys were still in the ignition, but the stench of petrol hit him straight away. He was already covered in petrol and felt that he had no choice. With his cuffed hands, he struggled to operate the car, but could turn the key and get the engine running. He put the car into gear, lifted the handbrake and awkwardly grabbed the wheel as the car slowly moved off.

The downed driver had regained some composure. With his blood-covered hands, he had picked up his pistol and fired several unaimed shots at Jim, all failing to hit their target. The car juddered as it pulled out of the field and down the road. The bloodied driver pulled himself up to his feet and winced with pain as he looked down at the wound and the growing patch of red emanating from it. His partner staggered towards him, clutching his own bloody head wound, using his scrunched-up mask to help stem the bleeding.

"What the fuck is wrong with you? We're dead men." The driver shouted angrily.

"Piss off. You were supposed to light up that motor." He looked at the tyre, that was already deflated. "We can't drive that."

"Well, we can't stay here, and my dancing days are over. Get the boss on the phone. We'll take this piece of shit as far away from here as we can and he can get us picked up. You can fucking drive." He limped to the passenger door and climbed in. "We're in so much shit."

CHAPTER 29

J IM'S DIRECTIONS HAD BEEN vague. Kerry could only assume that he had been so out of it he couldn't keep any useful information, but knew if she had more time, she could have teased a few extra details from his tarnished memories. She didn't know of any warehouses near Laxey. The land was mostly farmland or more green hilly fields left to the elements and wildlife. With a lack of mobile phone reception, she couldn't check in with the station and it had become increasingly obvious Billy was getting irritated with this fool's errand.

"There isn't a warehouse. He's just a bloody drunk, a liar and a murderer. I'm taking us back." Billy told Kerry.

"You will carry on driving until I get bored, not you. Take the next left," Kerry ordered, certain they had covered every inch of the road within two miles of Laxey.

They drove down a long stretch of road. A bank on one side was covered with trees, and the land on the other side was reasonably flat. Billy stared forward, unwilling to do any more than he had been ordered to as he acted like a scolded child. In the distance, she could just about make out the distinct slanted metal roof of a building. She sat up and focused on it. It certainly wasn't an old farmhouse. Another similar metal roof edged into view, and she felt confident this was it. She nudged Billy and pointed towards the structures. He barely mustered a nod as he continued along the road to the small complex.

As they came closer, the large wire fence that surrounded it became obvious. It wasn't suspicious that the owner may choose to defend their property, but the harsh industrial look didn't fit in well with the surrounding countryside. Their car pulled up to the locked gate. There was nobody there to greet them, and the site looked deserted. Kerry exited first, and Billy followed. She approached the locked gate and pulled on it, confirming it had been secured.

"Can you see anything that identifies who owns it?" Kerry squinted as she looked for any signs or markings that might help.

"Nothing. Local authority of Garff?" Billy offered as an answer.

"They wouldn't piss the money away. And if they had, something as posh as this would have a big shiny sign telling the world about it. This is private, and it's not a farmer," Kerry stated.

"It's hardly inconspicuous, is it?"

"It took us forty odd minutes to find it, so they're not doing too bad. This would have needed planning permission, that would be logged. When we get back to the office, you can spend some time on the government website and dig out all the planning documents."

"Is your laptop broken?" Billy asked, but instantly regretted it.

Kerry replied with a stare, until Billy looked away. "We're being watched." She pointed to a CCTV camera pointed directly at them.

As if on cue, a side door of the nearest warehouse swung open, and a man exited and began walking towards the gate. They didn't appear to be in any rush as they slowly sauntered towards the two detectives. The man was incapable of smiling. A permanent scowl on his worn, scarred face instantly informed anyone dealing with him he wasn't to be taken lightly. He reached the gate and stood behind it, not saying a word, waiting for the visitors to speak.

"I'm DC Hughes; this is DC Mulligan. We're conducting some enquiries and wonder if we could take a quick look around your warehouse." Kerry announced confidently.

"No." A thick northern accent answered.

"Look, it would be a great help for us. I promise we won't get in the way or be long." Kerry smiled, trying to come across more softly.

"I don't give a fuck if you promise to blow me. You and your man there can piss off." He didn't move an inch as he spoke.

"We can come back with a search warrant," Billy offered as an impotent threat.

"Go on then. I'll look forward to wiping my arse with it."

Kerry led Billy towards their car. "We're not getting in there, and we've got nothing for a warrant. But there isn't anything stopping us from going for a walk. Let's move the car down the road and we'll take a stroll."

***

They had taken nearly half an hour to walk around the compound, and their northern shadow had silently followed the whole time from inside the fence. The walk had yielded nothing interesting, only confirming the quality of the warehouse complex and the lack of any movement there. Not a single truck or van arrived, and besides the harsh man following them, they hadn't spotted another soul. When they had returned to their car, both instinctively checked their phones. Neither had any reception.

"So what was the point of that?" Billy asked.

"We know it exists, and we know it's shady. That's a start," Kerry answered, but was disappointed they had failed to spot anything that may help to get them a look inside.

"They could be stockpiling knock-off souvenirs ready for the TT for all we know."

"Yeah, they could. I'm sure when you've done some digging you'll have a few more answers, and I'll look forward to hearing them." Kerry replied.

Billy started the car and drove away. Kerry stared back at the warehouses and wondered what the hell was actually going on. As they carried on down the road, both their phones suddenly sprung into life as they hit a patch with reception. A symphony of pings and chimes signalled both had many missed calls and text messages. Kerry looked at her phone and her face dropped in disbelief.

"He's gone," Kerry said, shocked.

"What?" Billy quizzed, confused.

"Jim."

"He's dead?" Billy gasped.

"No, he didn't make it to the prison," Kerry replied, still stunned. "There was an ambush, and he was taken."

"Bloody hell. I guess this warehouse stuff is on hold then?"

Kerry stared at her phone as she flicked through the messages, each with an additional detail or shocked opinion from a colleague back at the station. She concentrated on the phone and ignored Billy. *'Car flipped, officers with minor injuries.'* That seems overly dramatic. *'Men with automatic weapons.'* These guys really are losing the plot. *'Walsh taken away in green hatchback.'* Not too many of those around. *'Correction: blue estate, make and model unknown.'* Probably a little more common.

"We heading back to the station?" Billy asked.

"Yes," she replied, eyes still glued to her small screen.

Billy put his foot down on the accelerator, pushing the car a little faster back towards headquarters and the flurry of activity that was no doubt awaiting them.

CHAPTER 30

J IM HADN'T DRIVEN FAR, but he already knew he'd have to find somewhere to hide the car sooner rather than later. The smell of petrol had terrified him on his brief journey. He was sodden with the combustible liquid, having sat himself in a pool of the stuff when he jumped into the car. He hadn't been confident that starting the engine wouldn't have sent the car up into a ball of flames, or a stray bullet may have had the same effect, but he knew he had no choice. His liberators had made it clear they weren't his friends, and he knew he had few left. Better to burn to death on his own terms than to be his tormentor's plaything. The thought of handing himself back to the police barely registered. They had their chance and weren't able to help. These people had killed and beaten those closest to him. Even with his life and reputation ruined, that wasn't enough. Still, these bastards wanted more, and he couldn't do anything about it if he stayed in custody. Their bumbled attempt at grabbing him gave him an opportunity to go on the attack, and he wasn't constrained by the rules anymore. He was covered

PAUL FORSTER

in petrol, handcuffed, and driving a car the police were hunting for, but he had a gun and the desire for revenge.

He drove another mile to an area he knew well, where there was an old, dilapidated farm off the beaten track. When he was last there, it had been in his official capacity as a police detective. Stolen farm equipment had been hidden there with a local troublemaker responsible. Not being the brightest, the young man had hidden everything on the old farm that he had inherited and let go to ruin. Despite his perfect large and muscular frame, he had no interest in becoming a farmer like his father and grandfather. He instead sold everything off and drank the proceeds. When that money ran out, he remembered how profitable selling farm equipment was and went about stealing from his neighbours and selling the equipment to other farmers on the island. The man hadn't counted on how small the community was, and they apprehended him quickly. The farm was now all but abandoned with the man in prison. Jim was banking on it being a good place to hide and regroup.

The approaching track was overgrown, and if he hadn't known it was there, he could very easily have missed the turning. As the car moved further down the track, it curled around a field that had been reclaimed as a wild meadow, with no attention given to it for the last few years. As the track headed down to the bottom of a small valley, the farm building came into view. The stone barn was in awful shape, the roof had partially collapsed, and the few glass windows had all fallen out of their rotten wooden frames. The doors were open, and the large opening enabled Jim to drive the car inside and leave it under what remained of the roof. He paused for a moment, hoping to enjoy a moment's peace to collect his thoughts, but the potent smell of petrol fumes and his wet bottom reminded him

176

it was best to get out of the car and as far away as soon as possible.

Inside the barn, the stolen machinery had all been returned to the rightful owners, but dozens of tools had remained, and a sorry looking red Nissan Sunny, covered in grime with four flat tyres, stood sadly under the wrecked roof. Random boxes of stolen tools had proven harder to identify and return, so what couldn't be identified had been left. Jim started looking through the piles for anything that may help get him out of the handcuffs. Hammers, chisels might have helped if he had someone to wield them for him, but on his own, they were as good as useless. Every bag or box he waded through had a similar assortment of rusty screwdrivers, miscellaneously sized wrenches and pieces of metal he couldn't have hoped to identify. Towards the back of the barn, a small workshop had been created, possibly decades ago. Like the rest of the barn, it had seen better days. The workbench had collapsed, but on the wall, there was a selection of larger tools. Pickaxes, sledgehammers, splitting mauls and hatchets, amongst many others. All of them were orange and brown with rust. He moved closer, and there were a set of large bolt cutters. The wooden handles gave away their old age, but they were big and might just work if he could figure out how to use them effectively with his hands bound. He pulled them from the wall and their weight gave him confidence he had the right tool for the job. He struggled, attempting to open them even the small distance the handcuffs would allow, but they were seized shut. In frustration, he smashed them repeatedly against the rotten workbench, levelling what remained of it. Feeling a little better, he tossed them onto the ground and they popped open, just a little. He picked them up and moved to the main farmhouse.

It was small and as rundown as the barn, but it looked mostly watertight from the outside. Jim set about rectifying that issue by using the bolt cutters to smash the small single pane of glass in the backdoor's window. Hampered by his cuffed hands, he still managed to reach inside and unlatch the door without cutting himself. A hefty shove with his shoulder opened it up and allowed him access. Inside, the smell hit him instantly. The smell of death was obvious. No doubt the place had remained untouched since they incarcerated the previous occupant who had himself neglected it for years. As he entered the kitchen, unwashed plates, opened packets of food and an endless trail of droppings. The local longtail population had probably found their new home very comfortable with a useful supply of food they probably dined like kings. Several half-eaten and decomposed vermin carcasses were obvious, and many more would certainly be hidden out of view. It would account for the smell.

Jim rifled through the kitchen cupboards and found what he was looking for. A large bottle of sunflower oil and a smaller one containing olive oil. It was hardly a purpose made lubricant, but it was all he had. He emptied the filth-stained dishes from the plastic washing-up bowl and placed the end of bolt cutters inside, and balanced the long handles against the side of the sink so that it was steady. He poured the oil over the neck and the blades of the cutters, emptying both bottles. The blades were mostly submerged, but the neck of the tool only maintained a light covering of the oil that had been poured over it. It would be enough if he worked the oil into the metal and made sure it had a chance to do its job.

A quick inventory of the kitchen produced four cans of sweetcorn, a tin of hot dogs, two tins of pineapples, and lots of spaghetti hoops. He hated sweetcorn. The pineapples would be nice, but the rest was junk, with barely any nutritional value. He wouldn't starve at least. The rest of the food was in packets and boxes, which the longtails had long since ruined. A quick scavenge of the rest of the house produced a box of shotgun shells, but no shotgun, a few changes of clothes that were better than the petrol soaked, poorly fitted outfit he was wearing, and a sealed bottle of tequila. He could easily have necked the entire bottle. It had been his first instinct to pour the entire thing down his throat, but he resisted. Drinking had helped get him into this mess. It would never get him out of it. There was a single room upstairs that wasn't wrecked. It was small but tidy and didn't smell nearly as bad as the rest of the house. He found a tin opener and took the tins of pineapples with him to the room to eat before he slept. It was several hours before the sun would set, but he was exhausted by the day's events. He'd let the bolt cutters soak whilst he rested and hoped they'd be usable when he woke later on.

With his hands cuffed, he could only remove his trousers, which he dumped on the landing outside of the room. The jumper and shirt would have to remain until he could free himself. Jim sat on the bed and opened the first tin of pineapples and scooped out a slice with his fingers. It was a few years out of date, but seemed to have survived well enough. In little time, he finished the rest and drank the juice out of the can. Even though nightfall was a long way off, the house was dark. Its position in the small valley robbed it of light most of the day. He laid back on the bed, placing the Skorpion machine pistol on his stomach, and allowed himself to drift off, feeling a bit safer and a lot more in control.

CHAPTER 31

K ERRY HAD BARELY BEEN back at her desk before they ordered her to visit the scene of Jim's jailbreak. She felt like the office junior again as she accompanied DC Ken Doolan. He had the authority of a GP, and a stern tone for anyone younger than himself, which within the constabulary was all but the most senior officers. Doolan was driving; he insisted on having the local radio playing in the background at a low volume.

"You know that he's been trouble since day one, but I didn't see this happening. Christ, who could? But he was always going to explode one day, and you have to make sure he's not going to drag you down." Doolan sounded like a man mounting his high horse.

"I'm doing okay for myself," Kerry replied, not wanting to get too involved with a conversation that could easily turn into a lecture.

"Yes, for now. But the trial won't be kind to you. It will hurt all of us, but you and Mulligan are especially vulnerable. You want to make your position crystal clear." His usual hard tone replaced with something more fatherly and caring.

"Billy, like me, will be fine. We brought him in. We've done everything by the book and continue to do so," she snapped.

"Everything?" Doolan whispered loudly enough for Kerry to hear, and leaving no doubt that he believed something was going on.

Kerry left that remark unanswered.

The rest of the car journey was awkwardly silent, and both officers were pleased to arrive at the scene and get out of the car. Kerry didn't wait for Doolan and made her way through the police tape and her uniformed colleagues to the damaged tractor. She kept a suitable distance as she looked at the smashed metal and pieces of broken glass as a woman dressed in white protective clothing inspected the farm equipment.

"Any idea who this belongs to?" Kerry asked the nearest officer in uniform.

"Not yet. There aren't any plates. Waiting for them to finish giving it the once over, then we'll take a look," they responded.

Kerry nodded and carried on towards the mangled car, carefully walking around pieces of broken glass and tyre marks. More officers in protective clothing examined the scene, every speck of blood, drip of oil and destroyed mobile phone. Several shell cases had been noted.

Doolan caught up and walked ahead of Kerry to arrive just before her. "What are we looking at?" he asked one of the forensic team.

"A mess," the nearest forensic expert bluntly responded.

"The casings, are they .25 ACP?" Kerry asked, looking at the small piece of brass from a few metres away.

"No, but something equally unusual in this part of the world, 7.65mm. Not something I've seen before in the flesh." The same forensic member answered with a little more enthusiasm. "We're going to be processing here for a while, but there's a second site a bit further down the road. Not as interesting to look at, but more blood and casings if you don't mind a walk."

"Thanks." Kerry began walking down the road, and Doolan followed.

Again, the silence was nearly painful, but both were too stubborn to start a conversation just to ease the discomfort, preferring to endure the ten-minute walk without acknowledging the others' presence. Further police activity ahead signalled the next crime scene. As they approached the gate, Kerry stopped and looked at a scratch on the tarmac exiting the field and carrying on down the road. She crouched down to inspect the markings. She couldn't tell if it was an hour old or a month old, but it was odd. Kerry was about to rise back to her feet when she took a deep inhale of air through her nostrils.

"Can you smell that? Is it petrol?" she asked, breaking the silence. She took another sniff. The odour was faint but distinctive.

"Maybe," Doolan replied, not being able to smell anything but not wanting his younger colleague to have one up on him.

They both walked into the field past another uniformed officer. Two more were taking photos of different areas in the field, not more than twenty yards apart. "You head over there. I'll see what is happening over here," Doolan ordered.

Kerry obliged and wandered over to the officer near a damp patch on the ground and some shell casings.

"Hell of a day, isn't it, Jenkins?" Kerry stated.

"Bloody hell of a few days," he replied.

"7.65mm shell casings?"

"That's a guess and half. Three of them, a small patch of blood, some tyre marks in the mud, and a piss load of petrol," Jenkins answered, impressed.

"Fuel tank damaged?" Kerry looked unconvinced by the slight stains on the ground.

"You'd have to ask one of the forensics, but it's splattered around a fair bit. So careful where you tread."

"How much blood is there? Are we looking for Jim dead or alive?" she pressed, eager for answers that poor Jenkins was struggling to deal with.

"Damned if I know Kerry. They just wanted me to take some more pictures and guard the scene," Jenkins answered, frustrated.

"Kerry," Doolan announced from behind her, placing his hand on her back.

"Bloody hell! I wish people would stop doing that to me!"

"We've got blood and some more shell casings."

"We've got the same here," Kerry stated, signalling to the evidence.

"Two groups want him? How bent was he?" Doolan replied, exasperated.

"Or he fought back and escaped. There's more going on here than any of us know. We're all so quick to be seen to make sure we punish one of our own that we're not looking at the bigger picture. Everything we have against him has been handed to us, and the press, on a plate. For a murderer, he would be seen as incompetent, but as an experienced police officer and detective, it's just utterly ridiculous the evidence we have. Sloppy and amateurish."

"You forget he's a drunk and a has-been," Doolan answered with anger.

"No, you forget he was a good copper once, and still better than most out there." Kerry stormed away to head back to the scene of the crash, but stopped at the gate.

She looked left to go back the way she came and right for the trail etched into the tarmac.

She passed the line of tape and gave a smile and nod to her colleague, protecting the integrity of the scene. "Many pissed-off motorists?"

"Nah, I think the Radio has been pretty good at telling people to stay clear."

"Any journalists?" she asked, noticing their absence.

"None."

Kerry again nodded and carried on walking, following the line on the tarmac. At every opportunity, the press had been on the scene, sometimes Patrick, but that scouse cow was always there. How come this didn't get her attention? It was a small island, and this was a big deal. News of the jailbreak would already have reached every corner of the Isle of Man. Yet she didn't come to look at the latest twist. *Why?*

It would soon be dark, and Kerry had been walking for long enough to know that she'd be hitching a ride back to the station with another colleague if she carried on. There was no way that Doolan would wait for her. As she had continued to walk, she had noticed small pieces of rubber near the line scraped into the road, giving her a little more confidence she wasn't just following the tracks of a damaged tractor from the previous year. The tracks turned off of the main road, and she continued to follow, becoming a little fed up with the task she had given herself.

Kerry walked a while longer, then stopped and looked ahead at a small trail of smoke drifting into the sky from a small wooded area not far away. She broke into a jog as she continued forward, heading off of the road towards the trees. Less than ten feet into the woods, she could see a blue van smouldering with a small trail of smoke emanating from inside of the cabin's open doors.

Suddenly, she felt very vulnerable. She was all alone, and the sun was setting. She had followed the trail that could have been left by multiple armed men, and now approaching a vehicle that they had likely used. Hours had already passed. It was highly unlikely she'd find anyone, but she knew she had to be prepared. A quick look around on the ground around her and she found a piece of broken slate slightly bigger than her hand. It was hardly a worthy replacement for a baton and definitely not a match for a firearm, but it was something that was definitely better than nothing.

Cautiously, she approached the open door, slate in hand, ready to strike. Both doors had been left open, and a half-arsed attempt to set the vehicle ablaze had been carried out. The fire-retardant material of the seats had mostly done its job. With the small amount of accelerant used, it had burned off and only scorched the fabric of the seats and mats. She looked inside, but the van was empty. A smear of blood on the inside of the open driver's door and across the dashboard to the front passenger seat was the only thing of interest. She took a step back and noticed the front wheel. Almost all the rubber from the tyre had gone and the metal rim was heavily damaged. Both of the number plates had been removed, snapped off in a hurry. The last digit of the rear plate remained. A solitary 'F' wouldn't yield many answers, but if the VIN number hadn't been removed, that might help track the owner down.

Kerry looked around again, but there were no obvious clues as to where the occupants had gone. She pulled out her phone and called Doolan. "We have another scene, an abandoned van. They tried to torch it, but it's mostly intact. Just follow the road down and look for a right turn. If you get to Sulby River, you've gone too far. I'll stay and protect the scene." After waiting for a response, she hung up the phone. Kerry looked around once again and could see the night drawing in and feel the temperature dropping. She hoped someone would get to her soon. She didn't fancy being stuck out there all night.

CHAPTER 32

J IM HAD ENDURED A few hours' sleep. His body and mind had been desperate for it, but neither allowed him to enjoy it. His body ached from everything he'd gone through since the nightmare began. He had several minor injuries, each aggravated by the botched attempt to kidnap him. His cuffed hands were sore, and every twist or turn caused the metal to rub on his raw wrists. His dreams were filled with anger and fear, much more than he had experienced sleeping in the cell. Ella's face flashed before him, as he could vividly imagine her murder and subsequent disposal. His brain made even the most horrid acts appear ten times worse, and the sound of Ella screaming and pleading for her life woke him. Whatever happened, he would always feel guilt for her murder and that of the poor girl they had killed to frame him. The best he could hope for was the chance to avenge them. He sat up and tried to adjust his eyes to the darkness. He wasn't sure how long he'd been asleep for, but it was now definitely the night. Jim rose to his feet and carefully navigated the room until he reached the wall and felt around until he could feel the light switch. Nothing happened when he tried to turn on the lights. He knew the likelihood of there being any power was remote and cursed himself for not looking for a lamp or torch before he slept. He soon found the wooden door and exited into the hallway.

The farmhouse was now pitch-black inside, and Jim slowly maneuvered through the hallway, his cuffed hands stretched out in front of him. When he made it to the top of the stairs, his caution grew, and he continued his careful journey to the kitchen. Even the moonlight failed to penetrate the house, its protection in the valley shielding it until the moon would be higher in the night's sky. In the darkness, he opened draws and cupboards until he found what he was looking for. A small torch. He flicked its power on, and the very dim light only offered a small amount of illumination. It had been sitting there for years, and he was lucky it worked at all. Using the little time he had, he found several candles, a lighter, and some matches. He had got them set up just as the torch gave out. The plastic lighter offered far more illumination than the torch had managed, and with the first of the candles lit, there became a useful amount of light in the kitchen.

With a candle placed near the bolt cutters, Jim examined them. The oil had removed some of the rust, and it floated in the washing-up bowl, but otherwise, they looked just as discoloured and stiff as they did before their soak in the cooking oil. He hopefully grabbed the handles and attempted to open them. Slowly, they moved a little, then a little more as he applied greater effort. He opened and closed them as far as his cuffed hands allowed until the oil penetrated further into the seized mechanism and he worked the handles with greater vigour until they felt as loose as they had been in years.

Jim looked around the dimly lit room. He had an idea of how he could use the cutters but had little confidence it would work. Two candles were placed on the floor next to the kitchen door, and Jim laid the bolt cutters next to them. He rested his back against the door frame and allowed himself a slow, steady descent until he was sitting on the floor in the middle of the doorway. He shifted his bottom to one side, then to the other, until Jim was satisfied with his position. Jim placed the bolt cutters between his legs, the handles facing away, and his left leg holding one handle in place against the wall. He pushed the other handle out until the two blades of the cutter were wide enough to fit the chain of the handcuffs inside. The blades were uncomfortably close to his testicles, but options were limited. Using his right foot, he slowly pushed the handle closed until the cutters firmly gripped the chain. He increased the pressure as the resistance grew. Jim struggled until the handle slipped beneath his foot, and the cutters jabbed him in his inside leg. The pain was sharp but only lasted a moment. His leg suffered a light scratch. A small trail of blood and broken skin confirmed the close call. A warning to be more careful. He looked at the chain and it had indeed warped under the pressure; he again lined up the cutters to take advantage of his previous effort, using his feet to slowly crush the metal links, aware that going too quickly might cause the most painful of vasectomies. Slowly, but powerfully, he crushed the chain until the pop of metal signalled success.

Jim held up his wrists. The set of handcuffs now turned into two individual bracelets with a short piece of chain hanging freely that glistened in the candlelight. A small victory, but now what? He was a fugitive on a small island where everyone knew his face. He wanted revenge, but against who? How he wished he'd been able to take one of his would-be kidnappers with him or to have had a little more time with them before he made his escape.

***

Jim hadn't managed any more sleep since he had freed himself. He spent the time sitting on the bed with just a single candle providing him with light. The small machine pistol was laid out in front of him. He had emptied the single magazine and placed the remaining small rounds of ammo next to it. The box of shotgun cartridges was also on the bed with a large carving knife. The cartridges were useless to him on their own, but the carving knife would be useful. He just had to find the people to use them on.

He knew where he was and that it would be quite the trek to get to civilisation. It was a level of protection from prying eyes, but it would mean he was isolated from striking out. The officers who had been transporting him to the prison could identify his car, but he might need to risk it. The old Nissan in the barn would never run again. It wouldn't even be able to roll down Snaefell if it was given a good shove at the top of the peak.

When the sun rose, he'd take another look around the house, fix himself something to eat, then decide upon his next step. However bad everything had become, for the first time, he felt like he wasn't being controlled by these people. They didn't know where he was; they didn't know what he was going to do, and they damn well didn't know what he was now capable of.

CHAPTER 33

T HE COTTAGE AND BARN had been a hive of activity the previous evening. The preparations for their expected guest had turned into a clean-up exercise with an angry Ian blasting orders at anyone in earshot. When the call came in to pick up his two men, both injured, with a crippled vehicle and without their target, he couldn't believe it. Everything had gone to plan until he had left the scene, and he was in no doubt who was to blame. The large tarpaulin set up in the barn had been destined to host Jim Walsh's last, extremely painful moments in this world. Now his own bloodied men sat in the center, both clutching their rudimentarily tended wounds, worrying about their own immediate future. This is what Ian had wanted from the start. Take Walsh, torture him, murder him and dump him where he'd never be found. But Johnson wanted him to suffer, and physical pain wasn't enough. He wanted his victim to lose everything, his reputation, those close to him and his sanity. He wanted him to know he was being played with and to degrade mentally until he was just a bitter husk, desperate for death.

The Irish and the Scots were pissed at the unnecessary attention the English were bringing to their joint enterprise. Posturing and threats had concluded with the Irish demanding their own men on the ground, a demand that Ian begrudgingly agreed to, hoping it would keep the peace, but he still tried to keep them out of the way. Ian just needed another day or two to end the Walsh situation himself. It pissed Johnson off Ian was now just going to kill Walsh, but sitting in his mansion across the Irish Sea, he knew it was the right thing to do. As far as Ian was concerned, Johnson would have his revenge, and they could move on with their multinational drug operation unhindered. Ian worked for Johnson, but he was the Isle of Man connection. Even when in Liverpool, they expected him to keep things running smoothly on the small rock. He had to keep all three parties happy, and when Ian had finally tried to put the whole thing to bed, his own men had gone and fucked it up. He stood over the injured men and glared at them.

"Give me a good reason why I shouldn't strangle you bastards, wrap you up in that tarp, and bury you in the hole we've already dug?"

"He caught us off guard," said the thug, nursing a head wound.

"Was he or was he not handcuffed?" Ian asked, his anger not fading.

Both men nodded.

"Did you both have guns?" Ian pulled a pistol from his own waistline and waved it at the men.

More nods.

Ian stood back, ready to lash out with his fists at the men, but kept a level of restraint that surprised even him. After walking away, he produced his phone from his pocket and called Johnson. He had bad news, and he would not take shit for it. He had long since given up being afraid of his boss.

"It's me. No, it's not done. There's been an issue, and he's in the wind." Ian listened. "No, this is on you. Your stupidity has put us where we are, not me, not my men." He pulled the phone back from his ear, the shouting on the other end of the line could be heard through the small speaker, but Ian wasn't taking it. "No, they're my fucking men. You just pay them. If we had done this my way from the beginning, it would have been done and dusted, and you would have had your revenge for your boy, but you had to be clever." More shouting from the other end of the line, but not as loud this time. "They don't know yet. I've got men out looking for him, but the police are everywhere, and we have a shipment being unloaded right now. I can't spare the manpower." He looked at the room, his two injured men and another two who had remained. The few other men he had at his disposal were at the warehouse or on their way. "It's a big shipment. We can't leave it unattended. Okay, I'll leave one man, but that means the Jocks will know something is off." He listened for another minute and didn't look impressed. Without saying another word, he hung up the phone.

He moved back towards the tarpaulin and the two injured men. Without giving a clue to his intentions, he punched one in the face with all his might and then kneed the other in the side of the head. Both men instantly shot back with the violent impact and braced themselves for more.

"Get them cleaned up, then we're heading out to find this bastard."

***

The small hotel room was in disarray. Pictures that had been secured to the wall had been ripped off, taking chunks of plasterboard with them. The table lamps launched as far as their wiring would allow, the tea and coffee facilities obliterated, and the television had been unceremoniously dumped onto the floor. Had the bed not been bolted to the floor, she'd have turned it over. Linda had a bottle of cheap rum that she took a swig from as knocks on the door disturbed her.

"What!" she screamed at the interruption.

"We've had complaints about the noise coming from your room. Are you okay?" the youthful male voice of the porter politely asked.

"I'm fine. Just leave me alone, now!" Linda shouted back between mouthfuls of rum.

A moment of silence and Linda was happy that the disruption to her drinking was over. Her phone rang, and before she looked at the screen, she half expected it to be the hotel management, but it wasn't. She answered the call and pressed the phone to her ear. "Dad, you promised! You fucking promised." Linda sobbed into the phone. "Is he dead already? Did you make him suffer?" Tears streamed down her face, and she battled to wipe them away. She paused and listened to her father. The tears stopped, and the anger returned. "What? That idiot couldn't even do that, right? Leon deserves better; he deserves the justice I had planned. That bloody arsehole detective needs to feel what I feel. I'll never get my brother back, and I have to live with that for the rest of my life. He needs to live with this!" Linda launched her phone across the room and into the wall before she collapsed onto the bed in floods of tears.

CHAPTER 34

M OST OF THE CLOTHES in the abandoned farmhouse were tatty, stained and had an off-putting odour. They were, however, a better fit and weren't stained with dried petrol like the clothes given to him at the station for his transfer. Whilst his new set of clothes reeked, at least they wouldn't be highly combustible. The blue jeans and work boots fitted nicely; the wool coat was long but irritated his skin where it made contact. He had to admit he quite liked the look, if not the actual clothes he was forced to wear. Ella had always tried to get him to change his wardrobe; the cheap suits and shirts for work or the tatty t-shirts and shorts he wore around the house did nothing for her. His lack of vanity had been endearing when they had first started dating, but many years later, his lack of effort had grated on his far more elegant wife. Jim knew Ella wouldn't have found his new outfit any better, but she would have at least appreciated him trying something different. The handcuffs remained on his wrists, but a roll of insulation tape prevented the irritating noise they made when Jim moved. His next task had been the car. In an ideal world, he would have had access to another working vehicle, but this was far from an ideal world. He had one car that was known to the police, or at least should be, and one which probably hadn't been driven in over a decade and was likely home to more than one family of longtails. The best he could do was to clean-up the number plates on the old car and fit them to his. It wouldn't do much good, but it might just confuse somebody enough not to bother with the car if they even knew what the number plate was to begin with. Procuring a new vehicle would be a priority, so would contacting Kerry.

It was early, and only when Jim turned the car radio on did he realise it wasn't even 5am yet. A quick breakfast of the tinned sweetcorn nearly made him throw-up, but as disgusting as he found it, he knew he needed something to help keep him going. He grabbed an old leather sports bag from the house that he had placed his gun, the shotgun cartridges, a few rusty tools and a carving knife inside of. He didn't want to drive too far and was on the lookout for a suitable target. A lone house or business would be ideal. It was early enough that any occupants would be asleep, but he'd need to be quiet and careful. Car keys and a mobile phone, and he'd be on his way without alarming his unfortunate victims.

The first house he came across looked ideal as he slowly approached in the car. A Range Rover and Volvo estate were parked in the driveway. Either would be fine for the single day he envisaged needed it for. Jim went past the house slowly, checking out his target, and then put his foot down before he parked up on a grass verge nearly half a mile away. He hoped the car would be far enough away and hidden well enough it wouldn't instantly be found, and then linked with the crime he was about to commit, but there weren't many options. Jim rooted around the bag and produced a long screwdriver and a stubby club hammer to check they were present before zipping up the bag and taking it with him. He had seen the results of enough burglaries in his career to have a rough idea of how to force a basic lock. He held the bag close to his body as he walked along the grass in the darkness, the collar of his jacket raised so he could hide his face behind it in case a car passed by.

The house was old, but not very big. Maybe two or three bedrooms, but it would have enjoyed a good size garden. The white render finish had recently been touched up to give the building a fresh, well-maintained look. Jim took a breath. Despite everything he had gone through, he wasn't comfortable with what he was about to do. He had been with the police for too long. He opened the half-height iron gate leading to the front garden and followed the path towards the house. Jim didn't make it any closer than five metres from the front door when a powerful LED light lit up the whole of the garden and Jim. He froze, unsure if the occupants had been alerted to his nefarious presence, but the light wasn't accompanied by any noise or flickers of activity within the house. He nearly took another step forward when he saw it. The smart doorbell stared back at him. It had probably already recorded his presence, his face. He could still break in, take the keys to one of the cars and be off, but then it wouldn't be a simple burglary for the police; it would be a sighting of a wanted man. Jim edged back slowly, and, once out of the garden, walked back towards his car briskly.

It was frustrating. Jim had been ready then had to stop, knowing the risk was too great. When he reached his car, he paused for a moment, unsure whether to climb back in or carry on walking. Surely another house had to be close. He looked out along the road, hoping to see something, but at this time of the morning, the street lights were off, and house lights were unlikely to be illuminated. He kicked the car twice with the bottom of his boots and walked away in frustration before turning back and cocking his leg backwards as if he was about to take another swing. Instead, he calmed briefly and popped off the set of number plates, ready to fix them to their third car of the day. If it took him an hour or even two, it would be worth walking and less risky than the car. It was dark enough still that any approaching car would be visible for nearly a mile in certain spots as its headlights would light up the countryside.

When he reached the next house, he was more observant. It wasn't as well cared for. Some of the render had cracked and fallen away. What remained was discoloured. Even in the dark, the green stains were obvious on the off-white finish. Of more interest to Jim was the single car in the driveway, an old Ford Focus. It was nothing special, almost perfect for his task of blending in and not calling attention to him as he drove through the island. No fancy lighting system or video doorbells were evident at this house, just a meagre wooden door and an oversized ornate knocker. As Jim carefully scoped out the rest of the house, he tried not to think of the victim, whose day was about to be ruined. He satisfied himself that there wasn't an angry farmer waiting inside of the house to take a potshot at him with a shotgun and eyed up the back door. The lock was ancient, and the surrounding wood was rotten with flecks of peeling paint. Jim wedged in a long screwdriver into the gap between the door and the frame, and without the hammer, could rock it backwards and forwards until the soft wood gave way and the door popped open.

It had been far easier than he had imagined, but the poor state of the outside of the house mirrored that of the inside. The major difference between this house and the one he had taken refuge in was little more than the number of vermin who had made it their home. Both were unloved, but judging by the loud snoring coming from an upstairs bedroom, this one was obviously occupied. Silently Jim searched the house, starting in the kitchen. On the kitchen counter, plugged into a wall socket, was an ancient mobile phone. There was nothing smart about this device. A basic phone, probably over ten years old. The small monochrome screen was badly scratched, the plastic case pitted with chips, and the numbers and letters on the buttons long worn away. Jim didn't believe for an instant that he'd find the latest overpriced piece of technology in this house, but he just hoped the battery on the ageing device would allow him to contact Kerry. He slipped the phone into his pocket and continued into the hallway. On a small side unit next to the front door, he saw the car keys amongst a stack of newspapers and leaflets advertising local businesses. Jim quickly swooped the keys up and made his way back to the kitchen. As he reached the open back door, he caught sight of a half-empty bottle of whiskey. He stopped and stared at the bottle. *Surely a sip wouldn't hurt?* He knew he couldn't drink, and with a deep breath, he was out of the house.

CHAPTER 35

T HE MANX TIMES OFFICE was a quiet place at this time of the morning. The first edition of the paper had already been sent to print and was currently being picked up and trucked to the island's newsagents and supermarkets. Besides a few members of the cleaning team wiping down desks and pushing a vacuum cleaner around, only Patrick was working at his desk. He'd written up a comprehensive report of the previous day's jailbreak, and a talented photographer had taken many dramatic pictures that made his write-up pop. The papers in the UK had cooled their interest in the murders. Even with the involvement of a senior detective and his subsequent escape, their interest in the story was minimal, and Patrick had to all but beg them to take his latest report. He was desperate for the exposure. This was his big chance. It was slowly slipping away and he couldn't fathom a greater twist than those which had already occurred that might reignite the buzz around the case.

Kerry walked through the office and pulled up a chair next to Patrick, who didn't even look up. "Pat, I need your help."

"Easy, Kerry, no time for small talk?" Patrick replied, then yawned.

"Not today. That scouse cow. She was pretty quiet yesterday. I've checked her rags website and not a sniff of the day's excitement. Is she still on the island?" Kerry made herself at home and rode her office chair closer to Patrick.

"Happy to help Kerry, but what have you got for me? I need something juicy." Patrick could tell the power had shifted to him.

"It's not the day."

"I'm dying on my arse here. No one seems to give a shit about your former boss. Another political scandal in Westminster is taking up all the interest and I'm left with this amazing story that only people on this bloody island care about. Maybe her paper found something better to write about, too." Patrick's frustration was getting the better of him.

"I'll see what I can do. I promise a little help now, and I'll get you something big, and soon. So she has gone back?" Kerry pressed.

"I didn't say that, did I? I heard she's been causing trouble in town. Surprised your lot hasn't been called out." Pat perked up at the vague promise of something coming his way, even if he didn't believe it would be groundbreaking.

"Trouble?"

"Apparently she's mistaken herself for some kind of rockstar and been smashing up her hotel room. One of our trainees does a few hours at the bar in McGill's hotel, and she is not too popular with her fellow residents or the staff." Pat smiled.

"When did she move into McGill's?" Kerry and Billy had tried every hotel on the island and had failed to find her. Neither could spare more time in finding a journalist, no matter how big a pain she had proved to be to them.

"She's been there since she arrived, checked in under her maiden name Linda Johnson."

Suddenly, it made a bit more sense to Kerry why they struggled to track Linda down. Kerry wasn't sure why the journalist bothered to take such a step, but at least now she knew where to confront her.

***

At some point, Kerry knew Patrick was going to call in a few of the many favours she owed him. She liked Pat. He was a nice guy, talented but ambitious. She had long ruled him out romantically as she couldn't see a future for herself anywhere but the island, whereas Pat couldn't wait to escape to whichever major city gave him the opportunity to first. If she could help him achieve that without jeopardising her own career, she would.

The McGills hotel was hard to find. Being buried within the backstreets of Douglas, it didn't enjoy views of the sea or easy access to the town's nightlife or tourist attractions. Most people who stayed at the McGills did so for business trips, as it was close to the town's financial area. It was clean, modern and reasonably priced. Only when the TT rolled around did the quiet hotel bar become raucous and lively. The morning breakfast service had just begun in the small dining area, with guests emerging from their rooms for their first meal of the day. Kerry approached the front desk with a smile.

"Hi, I'm looking for a Linda Jones, sorry, Linda Johnson. I understand she's staying with you?" Kerry asked softly, holding up her police identification to the receptionist.

The hotel manager was a few feet away and overheard the conversation. A tall and gaunt man in his late fifties, he quickly approached and stood next to the receptionist, making it clear to the young man that he was taking over. "Are you here about the damage and noise complaints?"

Kerry paused for a moment. "Yes, amongst a few other things. They have informed me she's been quite the handful."

"Rude, abusive and out of her mind. She will need to pay for the damage; otherwise, we will press charges," the manager stated.

"I'll have a word and see what we can do."

The manager stepped around the desk and beckoned Kerry to follow him to the hotel lifts. "You have to understand that we can tolerate certain behaviours during the racing, but this is a different crowd. We have many hardworking professionals staying with us who want a sanctuary after a hard day at work, a level of comfort to help them forget they're away on business. She'll need to pay for damages, but because of the complaints from our guests, she will need to leave the hotel today."

Kerry nodded, not really caring too much. She had bigger problems than a few bankers not being able to hear the sound of their pay-per-view porn because of a woman kicking off in a room further down the corridor.

They reached the room on the second floor and the manager approached and knocked loudly. Both he and Kerry stepped back, awaiting a response. After a moment, he repeated the knock, this time a little louder.

"Fuck off!" Linda screamed coarsely from inside the room.

"Miss Johnson, I have the police here to speak with you," the hotel manager proudly announced.

A fumble from inside the room could be heard before the door opened up to a crack. Linda looked worse for wear. She had worn little make-up, but what she had was smeared on her face, and she could barely open her eyes to more than a slit. "Oh, it's you," she said, acknowledging Kerry. "What do you want?"

"She's here about the damage and the noise. We are drawing up a bill at the moment and will charge your credit card accordingly. If there aren't the funds to compensate for your damage, our policy is to press charges," the manager told her, emboldened by his police escort.

"There's more than enough money to trash all your shitty rooms," Linda responded with a smirk.

"Linda, please, can I come in?" Kerry asked, caring little to continue in the petty dispute.

"Do you have a warrant?" Again, the smirk from Linda.

"I just want to talk."

"Well, since I'm up, you can talk to me whilst I'm having breakfast."

"Our dining facilities are no longer available to you," the manager announced.

"Look, just let her have some food. I'll talk with her and make sure she doesn't make any further fuss." Kerry waited until the manager nodded his head and walked away.

"Give me a minute." Linda shut the door, leaving Kerry on her own, waiting in the corridor.

When the door reopened, Linda looked little better than she had before. Smears of the previous day's make-up was now removed, but the hangover was gaining strength, and she felt a pressing need to counter it with a fried breakfast.

The pair approached the dining area and, without stopping to talk to the waiting staff, Linda went straight to the buffet area and filled a plate with large, unrealistic piles of bacon, sausages and fried potatoes. Kerry looked on with a degree of jealousy. A cooked breakfast would go down well about now. With a plate full of only the unhealthiest options, Linda sat down at the nearest free table. Kerry sat opposite her and watched with horror as Linda began shovelling in large handfuls of the fried feast into her mouth.

"Tea or coffee?" a young waitress asked.

"Coffee!" Linda spluttered out, sending small pieces of food in several directions.

The waitress tried not to look appalled before turning to face Kerry, who shook her head with an embarrassed smile.

"What is going on, Linda? I'm fed up with the bullshit. What aren't you telling me?" Kerry asked quietly.

Linda looked at Kerry and began chewing faster, eager to swallow the food she had crammed into her mouth. "Your friend Walsh is the reason my brother is dead. Leon was just a kid. He didn't deserve to go to prison, but your precious Jim wouldn't let it go. Twice he messed with my brother, and the second time, it was too much for him. He was a slight kid. There wasn't much to him but a big mouth that made you laugh and scream in equal measure, that and his childlike naivety. He wanted to be like our dad, to impress him. Impress anyone for a bit of clout."

"Your brother, he was the one who stabbed Jim?"

"He deserved it. The first time he was inside, they passed him around like some cheap slag. It only stopped when they found out who our dad was. When he was released, he was different, quiet. Dad did nothing for him on the outside. It embarrassed him what Leon had endured, as if it made him less of a man. Leon got worse, and when he saw that piece of shit detective drinking it up, having a lovely life, he snapped." Linda sliced into a sausage and put a much more reasonable piece of food in her mouth.

"He nearly killed him. Of course he was going to do some serious prison time. He tried to murder him." Kerry tried to respond with reason.

"When he went back inside, that was it. I think he had already decided to kill himself. If that drunk hadn't been in that bar, pissed off his head, my brother would never have seen him again, and maybe, with some time, he would have got on with his life." Tears formed in Linda's eyes.

"I don't understand how your brother's death brought this hell to the Isle of Man. What is going on?"

"My dad is Leonard Johnson. If you don't know who he is, your colleagues back on the mainland certainly do. This whole farce is his revenge," Linda stated, withholding the complete truth.

"My God, you're all fucking crazy. He did all of this, murder and hurt these people because your brother couldn't hack playing gangster? You played your dirty little role in this, feeding these stories to the public."

"I'm just a journalist. I'm not the major player in the criminal underworld. This is my dad's doing. This is all him and his band of merry fucking men." Tears flowed from Linda, and she didn't try to wipe them away.

"But you're involved, you're an accessory," Kerry informed Linda, seeing a chance to apply some pressure.

The waitress returned to the table and placed a small cafetiere next to Linda's down-turned cup.

"I just get fed information that I turn into stories. My hands are clean." Linda wiped the tears from her face and poured herself a coffee. "He deserves everything he's got coming to him, but I've not done anything more than my job."

"We'll see how well that does in court. People are dead." Kerry rose to her feet and reached for her handcuffs.

"Put them away, detective. You don't need to charge me. You need someone to clear that bastard's name. Not only that, I can deliver you one of the biggest drug rings in Europe. Imagine what that could do for your career."

Kerry paused for a moment, unsure how full of shit this woman was. She was obviously in the middle of a breakdown, but that didn't mean she wasn't telling the truth. "Why would I believe you would throw your own father under the bus?"

"He had his chance to make that cunt pay, and he blew it. I can never forgive him for this." Linda spat the words out with venom. She dumped her napkin on the plate, her appetite gone.

Kerry sat down, taken aback by the revelation. "Who is the man on the motorbike? Where can I find him?"

"I only know him as Ian, Ian the arsehole. He's a lackey who runs the operation here. The only other thing I know is my dad trusts him more than anyone. He's the only one who can give my father shit, and not end up in hospital."

"You're going to need to come to the station with me to make a statement." Kerry wanted to explode. This was it. She could clear Jim's name and bring these murderers to justice.

CHAPTER 36

J IM HAD DECIDED A wise move would be to take the stolen car and himself as far away from the scene of the crime as he could before traffic built up with people heading to work and parents ferrying children to schools. He drifted until he reached the car park at Ballaugh beach. It should have been quiet at this time of the day and a random car in the car park would be unlikely to raise suspicion, easily passed off as just another dog walker taking their hound for some exercise. Jim's body was fighting him. It ached and his head throbbed. It could have been the physical and mental trauma he had endured, or it could just be a drunk's body craving alcohol. Whatever the cause, it wouldn't stop him. It reminded him of how far he had fallen, how far they had gone to hurt him, and how far he would go to hurt them right back.

It was brisk on the exposed shoreline, the strong winds proving ideal for the single brave kite surfer who enjoyed having the stretch of beach all to themselves. The lone dog walker worked hard to walk into the wind following their unperturbed golden retriever, who pressed forward,

208

enjoying its morning walk. Jim stayed in the car as the wind gently rocked it. He had waited a short while, trying to work out what he should say. He knew he needed to be quick and that as much as he trusted Kerry, she was still a police officer, and he was still facing a murder charge and on the run. She was always an early starter, but he wanted to have the best chance of her being in when he called.

He pulled out the antiquated mobile phone and powered it on. The dim green display only featured a basic black text. It showed it had two bars of reception and offered only the most basic of functions. Jim only needed the one. He didn't know Kerry's mobile number, or her direct number, so he settled with what he knew; the station's switchboard number. Jim cleared his throat and tried to put on a Scottish accent. "Hello, can I talk to—" He stopped, not happy with his first practice attempt. "Hi, can I speak with a detective Hughes please?" That sounded more like it. His Scottish accent wasn't great, but it didn't need to be. He just needed to not sound like the island's most wanted fugitive.

He punched in the number and waited for a moment until the other end of the line picked up. "Hi, detective Hughes please." The accent was passable, but he felt he was too direct. "Peter Dalglish," he stated confidently, proud to name drop a combination of two of his footballing idols.

"DC Hughes," the voice on the other end of the line announced.

"Kerry, it's me." Even though they were talking on the phone and he was alone in his stolen car, he felt the need to lower his voice. "Do you see my number on your screen?"

"Yes," Kerry answered, confused.

"When I hang up, call me back on it from your mobile. If you don't call back within a minute, I won't answer, and

I'll bin the phone." Jim spoke quickly, and before Kerry responded, he hung up. He waited a moment nervously, unsure whether she would call back, or even if she did, if she would support him. Every second ticked by slower than the last. He nearly jumped out of his skin when the phone rang, but he quickly answered.

"Jesus, what the hell are you doing?" Kerry angrily demanded. Already, thoughts of what she should do raced through her mind.

"Can you talk?" Jim asked nervously.

"Not really. What are you doing phoning? Where are you?" Kerry demanded.

"I needed you to know I got away from them. I'm safe, but I need your help," Jim stated directly.

"Are you hurt?" she asked with concern in her voice.

"I'm fine. I need your help to get these bastards. When I make my move, I need you to buy me time," he pleaded.

"I can't help you like that. You know I can't. Come back in. We have a witness who can clear your name. We can get them, all of them." Kerry told him excitedly. She was outside of the headquarters but quietened down and checked she wasn't overheard by a passerby.

"It doesn't matter. There is nothing left for me. I barely had anything before this all started. I'm going to take care of it, and I'll deal with the fallout from my actions, not theirs," Jim said defiantly.

"Don't do it, Jim. You're a good detective, a good man. Come back, and we can take them down, piece by piece. It's bigger than just you. This is massive."

"Can you help me?" he asked again.

"Not like that. Come into the station, please. You don't know what they've been up to," Kerry pleaded.

"Take care, Kerry. You carry on doing what you're doing and don't take any shit from anyone." Jim hung up the phone and immediately popped off the back case and removed the battery. He opened the car door as the strong wind attempted to close it on him instantly. He forced his way out and took a lungful of air as he looked at the dismantled phone in his hands. Two litter bins were nearby, and he dropped the battery into one and the phone into the other. Back in the car, he glanced around to make sure he wasn't about to be greeted by a dog walker and opened up the small sports bag. He checked its contents, removing the small machine pistol, carving knife and a rusty hammer, readying them for action.

Kerry had remained silent after Jim's call. After making her way back to her desk, she played over her options in her head. She knew she should have gone straight to her superiors, but didn't want to face them. Before Jim's call, she felt ecstatic, finally having a witness who could clear his name and start righting all the recent wrongs. Because of her state, they had deemed Linda was in no shape to be interviewed. The duty doctor could smell the alcohol the moment she stepped into the room and refused to sign off on the interview until she was happy Linda wasn't intoxicated. Kerry had briefed DCI Ingham, and he wasn't as enthusiastic as her. He could see the potential problems and how it might all look to the outside world. As much as he hoped Walsh was innocent, the mountain of evidence against him would be hard to overturn with a potentially unreliable witness. They had assured Kerry she had the full support of the department, but to be careful. It was as good as she could have hoped for, and the only issue could be if Linda would be so open once the booze had left her system and reality reared its head.

"Kerry, you're needed!" Billy called out from a few feet away.

"What?" Kerry asked, agitated.

"There's a representative here for Linda Jones," he replied sheepishly.

"And? She can see her brief if she wants to," Kerry said, irritated but controlled.

"That's the thing, though. She doesn't want to see him. Said she never called and that he must work for her father. She doesn't want him anywhere near her." Billy's voice cracked, the confidence knocked out of him. Kerry was becoming more like his boss and less like his friend every day.

"Well, the lady has spoken. What's the problem?"

"He says she's intoxicated, being held without charge, and he is insisting on being given access."

"She said no. Tell him what the doctor told us. Try again in four hours."

"He's very insistent." Billy didn't want to argue with the man on his own. He knew he'd likely come off second best.

"Who is it?" Kerry asked. She knew a lot of the regular advocates and was surprised this one wouldn't happily wait in the station charging their client by the hour whilst drinking coffee and reading the paper.

"I don't know him. I think he's from Liverpool," Billy speculated.

Kerry rose to her feet. "Take me to him."

The pair left the CID office and made their way to the front desk. He was quite obvious. Tall and in his early forties, Kyle Lawrence wore an expensive suit and carried a luxury leather briefcase. Both put him at a level above what most of the local advocates might wear to attend the station to visit a client. Kerry approached, bearing a false smile. "How can I help?"

"You can help by getting me in front of my client," the man stated angrily.

"I'm sorry. Do you have any identification?" Kerry's fake smile grew.

The man placed his briefcase on the floor and pulled out his wallet, producing a UK driving licence, which he held out for Kerry.

"Mr Lawrence, this is a UK licence. Are you a resident on the Isle of Man?" The smile was now bursting with its insincerity.

"No," he stated with an accompanying glare.

"Are you allowed to practice law here?" Kerry asked, as if genuinely unsure.

"My client is a UK citizen. I'm here to represent her and protect her interests." Kyle wasn't used to being messed around by those he thought little more of than a village bobby.

"I understand, but I'm sure you appreciate that the Isle of Man is a separate legal jurisdiction, and that directly affects your standing here. I might be wrong, but I recommend you double-check your rights and if I am wrong, feel free to lodge a complaint against me." Kerry's face turned from a fake smile to an overenthusiastic frown.

"This is outrageous," Kyle protested, but no one was interested.

Kerry turned and led Billy away.

"Is that true?" Billy asked, unsure.

"Yes, I'm not sure how far we can go with it, but it will buy us some time for her to sober up. Jim's been in touch. We need to talk to Ingham."

CHAPTER 37

As HE DROVE TO the warehouse, he couldn't help but feel that every car he passed, or person he saw, might suddenly recognise him and alert the authorities. It was unlikely, but his face would have been all over the papers for days. Most of the island would recognise him if they gave him a second glance. As he approached the road leading to the site of where this all began, he could feel his heart racing. The car picked up speed as he put his foot down, working the old motor harder than it would have been worked in years. He didn't care if they recorded a video of him with their drone. He was beyond that, and so were they. As he approached the front gate, he turned the steering wheel towards it, smashing through the wired frame, sliding to a stop twenty feet away from the entrance.

Jim fumbled for the gun, certain he was about to be set upon by a goon from the security booth next to the now smashed gate. Nothing. *Had they been so careless to leave themselves unprotected?* He spent little time considering his options. He looked at the buildings. There was no movement. No hive of activity. *Had they already left*? Only a solitary 4x4 car was parked in front of the nearest building. Jim threw the car back into gear and headed towards it. A warehouse door swung open, and a blast of shotgun pellets peppered the car, smashing the windscreen and denting the metalwork but doing no terminal damage to the car or Jim. He turned the car, facing the driver's door away from the gunman, and threw himself out of the car and onto the ground.

He waited as another two shots rang out in quick succession and then scrambled to his feet, moving towards the door with the machine pistol outstretched in front of him and the hammer stuffed into the top of his jeans. The man again popped into the doorway, ready to fire but was too slow to spot Jim as he pulled the trigger, sending a stream of bullets towards the man, with one striking him in the shoulder and another on his thigh. He screamed in pain as he dropped the sawed-off shotgun and fell to the floor. He grabbed the grip and crawled backwards. Jim fired another burst as he ambled towards the injured man, the rounds striking the ground around him as he continued to scramble away. Another brief burst and the gun was empty, clicking every time Jim pulled the trigger.

The man on the floor laughed as he stopped moving backwards and looked at Jim, who was now only a few metres away and had clearly fired his last rounds. "You out? What are you going to do now?" He raised the short-barrelled shotgun and pointed it crudely at Jim.

Jim looked at the man as the two barrels raised up and, without wasting another second, he launched the now useless machine pistol towards the man, striking the shotgun, sending it pointing away just as he pulled the trigger. Both barrels emptied, and before he had a chance to even think of reloading, Jim was upon him with the hammer and struck the man's hand. The bones crunched as the rusted metal crushed the fingers against the wooden stock. He instantly released his grip on the gun and it fell to the floor. A second strike of the hammer struck the man's chest. The snapping of ribs echoed in the warehouse with the soft thud of the metal hitting the flesh and muscle protecting them. "Who are you?" he screamed at the man, holding the hammer above his head, ready to send it crashing towards the man's skull.

"I'm nobody. I'm just here to watch the warehouse," the guard whimpered as he squirmed, the pain and fear overtaking him.

"Who do you work for? Why did you murder my wife?" Jim's voice didn't lower.

"I don't know. I just do what I'm told. We all do!"

Jim slammed the hammer down onto the man's wounded shoulder, causing a deafening scream of pain. "Who do you work for?" Jim's face was red, sweat covered his brow and spit left his mouth as he screamed.

"I work for the English side. It's our turn to be here."

Jim looked at the guard, confused. "The English side? What the hell is all of this?" Jim raised his head and peered into the warehouse. They had stacked hundreds of crates and boxes up in the centre of the large room with several crates smashed open and the contents spilled onto the floor.

"The Irish, the Scots and us, the English," the man whimpered.

"Why are they after me?"

"They're not. You're just a project for the boss. I swear it's a personal thing for him, and he doesn't tell us shit. It's nothing to do with the Kings of Mann."

Kings of Mann. Jim tried to take the information in. What had they had dragged him into the middle of? "Who's the boss?" He grabbed the man by his neck and menacingly held the hammer, ready to strike.

The man shook his head and closed his eyes. "I can't."

"You know I have nothing to lose. I've already lost it all. Opening up your skull with this will not cause me any sleepless nights." Jim stretched back a little further, ready to bring the hammer down.

"Leo Johnson," the man muttered regretfully.

The hairs on the back of Jim's neck stood up. Surely the little scrote who had stabbed him when was in Liverpool wasn't in charge. "You mean Leon Johnson?"

"No, Leo, as in Leonard Johnson. Leon was his son, but he died."

This kid had tried to take his life, and now his dad had picked up the baton and was ruining it. *But why?* The kid was a criminal, a dealer who got caught and then progressed his criminal career from drugs to attempted murder. He knew it didn't matter what had got them to the point they were at now. Whether it was down to him getting a wannabe gangster sent down or he spilled someone's pint, it didn't matter. Their response was over the top, and his would be too. "What's in the boxes?"

The man shook his head, not wanting to talk. Jim smashed the hammer down into the concrete floor inches away from the man's skull and lifted it back again, ready to strike.

"What is in the boxes?" he repeated.

"Charlie. A quarter of a tonne," the man quietly replied. "It's brought in with the coffee, which is bagged and sold on, then all the coke is sent to the three partners."

Jim rose to his feet and dragged the injured guard across the room towards the boxes and crates. The smell of the coffee beans was strong, and he could only put it down to the adrenaline that he hadn't noticed it sooner. The open wooden crates contained a large foil lining and were filled to the brim with fresh coffee beans. They had set aside two bricks of cocaine, and another was poking through the beans in the crate, ready to be removed. Suddenly, any ideas he had of beating every single one of these arseholes to death left his head. This was a substantial amount of class A drugs; losing this would hurt them a lot.

Jim didn't know how much time he'd have, so he would have to act quickly. Within minutes, he had bound the injured guard to a radiator, using the man's own belt as a makeshift restraint. His own car wasn't up to the task. The light damage had been more than enough to make it stand out from the crowd, but the 4x4 outside would do. The guard quickly gave up the keys and Jim reversed the car up to the entrance of the warehouse and opened up the boot. He grabbed the bag from his car and reloaded the shotgun, keeping it close as he set about his new task. He found a fresh vigour as he began cracking open the crates and removing the bricks of cocaine.

Soon, a small pile had been created, and his feet crunched on the coffee beans that had spilled out. Every crate he opened, every package taken, increased the risk of discovery. He had kept a rough count going in his head, and by his reckoning, he had recovered over fifty bricks, and he was feeling it. Jim was still nursing several injuries, and his initial enthusiasm was now waning, resulting in every jerk and stretch to grab a crate, sending a bolt of pain through his body. He asked himself how many bricks were enough. A few bricks would be missed; a fifth of their product would hurt them. But not enough.

"Where are your friends staying?" Jim asked calmly, holding back the anger in case he was required to go up another gear again.

"You're going to get me killed," the man protested.

"You'll be safe, I promise. Safer than if you don't tell me." Jim raised the shotgun, not pointing it at the man but making sure they understood the implication.

"It's in the sat nav, under home," he sadly confessed, looking away.

Jim quickly began throwing the drugs into the back of the 4x4, leaving three bricks of drugs in plain view near the crates. When he'd finished, he slammed the boot door shut and walked over to the guard. The man was bleeding, but he'd live. The wounds would be treated when the police arrived. Jim picked up the landline phone and dialled 999. "I'm at a warehouse on a road off Creg Ny Baa, the back road. I heard gunshots." Jim raised the shotgun and fired into the crates. "Come quick. They're shooting at us!" He hung up the phone and smiled at the man.

"You bastard. You said I'd be safe," the wounded man shouted.

"The police will protect you and make sure you're patched up, ready for the trial," Jim said as he made his final move and reached around the man's pockets, producing first a wallet and then a mobile phone. Jim opened the wallet and flicked through it. He looked at the large wad of English banknotes and produced a solitary £20 note that he slid into one of his pockets and tossed the wallet onto the floor. He looked at the smartphone. It was big and expensive looking, no doubt the latest model that cost more than his first car. "What's the code?"

"1-2-3-4," the man sheepishly replied.

Jim looked at him in disbelief, but punched the code in, and, to his surprise, the phone unlocked. He quickly whizzed through the screens and, satisfied, slid it into his pocket as he walked towards the car. He fumbled with the built-in sat nav for a moment until he found the entry for home and set it as his destination.

CHAPTER 38

K ERRY HAD WALKED DOWN the promenade to get some much needed fresh air, thinking it better to look out to the Irish sea than stare at the clock back in her office. Even with the drizzle and the wind, it felt like the better option. Despite her efforts, she couldn't help but look at the screen of her phone every few moments to check the time or see if the station had called or messaged her. They were so close. Within hours, Jim could have been officially on his way to being cleared, but he was going to do something stupid, and she couldn't be part of it. She had reported everything to the DCI but held back a few details in the hope that she wouldn't incriminate Jim further, but she neglected to divulge anything further than Jim was investigating the perpetrators. She couldn't bring herself to say Jim was embarking on a suicide mission to get what he now deemed to be justice. Her only hope would be that Linda would give them the information they needed before Jim tracked down those responsible.

It had been two hours and thirty-seven minutes since they had been instructed to hold off interviewing Linda when Kerry's phone rang. It was already in her hand as she accepted the call and pressed the phone to her ear.

"Yes?" she eagerly answered. The voice on the other end continued for a moment, and her face dropped. "You're fucking joking? I'll be right there."

As the crow flies, she was less than a kilometre from the police headquarters. In reality, it would be closer to two kilometres and most of it uphill, but Kerry didn't waste any time regretting her decision to leave the station for a breath of fresh air. Kerry broke straight into a sprint across the road from her spot overlooking the sea, dodging cars coming from both directions. As she ran up the road, she slowed down. She was naturally fit, but she was far from her best condition. The last few days had taken much from her physically and mentally, but she pushed on. She picked up the pace. Her lungs were already on fire, and her legs were desperate to betray her, but she wouldn't let them. The ground flattened out, the strain on her body lessened, and she squeezed a bit more speed as the headquarters came into sight.

When she arrived at the entrance, Linda was walking out, accompanied by the English solicitor, Kyle Lawrence. He shot her a shit-eating grin as he stood between Kerry and Linda.

"You're making a mistake. Come back inside and talk to us. We can protect you," Kerry pleaded through desperate gulps of air, hoping for a spark of sympathy or a desire to do the right thing.

"I don't need protection, you silly bitch. I told you exactly what you wanted to hear, and you ate it up like the small-minded little islander you are." She spat the words like venom at Kerry and then continued to the waiting black Mercedes outside of the station entrance. Kyle held the car door open for her as she slipped into the rear passenger seat, then closed it behind her and entered the driver's door.

Kyle didn't waste any time in getting away. With the police headquarters still in his rearview mirror, he glanced at his passenger. "He's pissed, Linda, really pissed."

"Good. I am not happy myself," she replied quietly.

"What did you tell them?" Kyle pressed. He was the family solicitor, but her father was his client and where his loyalty was rewarded.

"Nothing."

"Linda, let's not mess around. We know you talked with the police at your hotel. You were far from discrete, and you were overheard," Kyle told her as they made eye contact in the rear-view mirror.

"What? I'm being watched? He has someone following me?" Linda accused Kyle, eager to change the direction of the conversation.

"Your father is worried. He wanted to make sure you were safe. We need to get a few things straight. Tell me everything you told them. It's okay. We just need to know." Kyle made sure he sounded sympathetic, but he was as annoyed with her as anyone else. She was the reason he had to leave his Liverpool office at short notice and spend the morning waiting in a police station.

"Fuck off, just take me back to the hotel. I'll be on the first plane, boat or dinghy back home. I promise," she replied angrily.

"I'm sorry. We need to make another pickup." Kyle had tried. Ultimately, she wouldn't tell him anything and he knew it, but he had to give it a go.

"Mini-cabbing now, are we?" Linda jibed.

The car pulled over on the promenade and waited a moment until the front and back passenger doors opened. Ian slipped into the front passenger seat, and another man made himself at home in the back next to Linda.

"What the hell is this?" Linda demanded.

"First of all, I don't care if he is your dad and you think you're protected. You ain't. You don't fucking talk to the bizzies, and you never talk about our business." Ian controlled his anger, but let the aggression poke through.

"Let me out here. I can walk to my hotel." Linda tried to hide her fear, but a hint of panic gleamed through.

"You're not going back to the hotel," Ian replied with a menacing smile.

"My dad won't like this." She struggled with her emotions. It took every ounce of strength she had to not scream out.

"You silly little girl. Your dad doesn't like any of this, and his partners like it even less. You are coming back with us, and I'll decide what happens with you once we've had a proper chat because I'll be honest with you. I don't have many men on the island, and they're hardly the best or brightest." Ian winked at his man in the back. "And the last thing I need is you out on the streets stirring up shit or getting cosy with the authorities. There is more at stake here than your bloody hurty feelings about your dead druggie brother."

Linda's face turned from fear to anger, and she lurched forward, grabbing Ian's face, digging in her nails and dragging them back, causing bloody scratches on each side. Ian's seatbelt and position prevented him from striking back, but his thug in the back happily obliged and struck the furious Linda square in the face with a powerful elbow. Her nose crunched from the impact, and her eyes rolled back in her head as she lost consciousness, her body slumped forward, and blood began gushing from her crumpled snout.

"Jesus, watch it. This is a rental!" Kyle screamed before looking at the bloodied Ian and thinking better of continuing with his moan.

Ian calmly removed a white handkerchief from his pocket and dabbed at the multiple scratches. "Get us back. Then you can give it a damn clean."

***

Jim had been watching the farm buildings for a few minutes and had seen no movement. Maybe it was empty. Maybe there were a dozen armed goons sitting in the dining room cleaning their weapons. He thought quickly and decided since he was in one of their cars, he'd drive up to the main house with the shotgun ready. If they challenged him, he'd respond with both barrels. He drove to the barn and stopped outside, beeping the car horn several times to see if it stirred anyone from within. Jim checked the car's mirrors for any movement, but there was none.

He double-checked the shotgun and reached into the back, producing a single brick of cocaine, and opened the car door. He held both the drugs and the gun under his coat as he approached the barn entrance. Two large panes of glass flanked a large double door. He tried the door, but it was locked. He stepped back and shot at one pane of glass. It shattered but didn't drop to the floor and create the opening he had imagined. He fired the other barrel, and this did more damage to the double-glazed piece of glass, and with a couple of hefty kicks, he had created an entrance he could use to get inside safely. He broke open the shotgun and carefully removed the two spent cartridges, popping them into his pocket and replacing them with two fresh ones. Loaded once again, he stepped inside, his shoes crushing the broken glass on the floor. He raised the barrels, waiting for an attack that didn't come.

Jim looked around the ground floor, maintaining his caution, but there was nothing out of the ordinary. It was just a nicely finished barn conversion; it was even tidy. Jim didn't know what he expected, but this wasn't it. He went back into the kitchen and pulled out the brick of cocaine, which he placed on the black marble worktop, and stared at it until something clicked in his head. He searched a few of the drawers until he found a small paring knife and used it to split open the brick. Even with his experience of drugs with the police, he was still expecting a mass of powder to gush from the package like emptying a bag of sugar. Instead, it was almost solid where it had been packed so tightly. Jim chipped away at it with the small blade and flakes popped off, not at all what he was hoping for but suggested the purity may be high. He returned to the kitchen drawer and pulled out a rolling pin, *perfect*. Jim hacked at the brick further until the pile for powder, flakes and chunks had grown and he lightly, repeatedly bashed it with the rolling pin until he was satisfied with the mostly powdered pile of coke in front of him. He spread it thinly across the black surface, and using his finger, he wrote in the pile.

I have the rest. Meet me at Mooragh park crazy golf 3pm.

Jim struggled to write his message in the space he had, but he completed it and was happy it was easily read. He had pushed his luck more than enough and quickly left the way he came in.

He broke into a jog across to his car and hopped in. With the door barely closed, he had the engine running and headed out of the farm's exit and onto the road. He was formulating a plan in his head, still unsure if he could do anything other than shoot these men, knowing that wouldn't be the justice they deserve. Death was too quick. Their drugs, whilst valuable, could be replaced. He had to take those in charge down, not just inconvenience them. This whole thing was much bigger than he could comprehend, and Jim wanted to destroy them all.

As he drove down the road, he passed a single black Mercedes heading in the opposite direction. Neither vehicle noticed the other, the occupants of both far too distracted by their own problems.

CHAPTER 39

E ACH OFFICER SHARED THE buzz of excitement at the warehouse. Never had such a large haul of drugs been discovered on the island. For the younger and more junior colleagues, they had seen more on the job in the last few weeks than their more experienced peers had in their entire careers. The Isle of Man had gone from reports of bottles of milk being stolen from doorsteps to murders and now international drug smuggling. DCI Ingham was in attendance, happy with a massive drugs find, but wary of how this would make the island look and how the government might react to the optics that the island was now being observed through.

They showed Ingham into the warehouse. The injured man was being treated by paramedics, with two uniformed officers standing over him. The constant clicking of cameras as they documented the scene was nearly irritating. DC Doolan approached and immediately got in close so that the pair could talk discreetly.

"Sir, there are no cameras here, but in talking to the injured man, I believe Jim Walsh did this and walked away with a substantial amount of drugs," Doolan stated in a sly tone.

"That's a stretch. An injured criminal, sitting on a huge stockpile of Class A drugs, tries to pin it on our rogue detective. That's a little convenient." Ingham stated. A murderous detective was one thing, but a drug kingpin was something he didn't want to think about or for the press to run with.

"I believe him. Somebody did this. And Jim doesn't have many options left, does he?" Doolan persevered.

Ingham stepped closer to the crates of coffee that had spilled onto the floor, instantly increasing his desire for a cup of the stuff to drink. He walked carefully, wary of disrupting the scene but able to see several bricks of cocaine on the floor and another poking out from inside of one of the open crates. He took a step back to do a quick count of the untouched crates still in the room. Even if each only contained a solitary pack of drugs, it would be a record.

Doolan didn't allow himself to be more than a few feet away from his superior. "Sir, I believe him. We have concrete evidence that Walsh has committed murder and lied to us. Being involved in drugs isn't a stretch. Who knows what contacts he cultivated during his time in Liverpool? He could be capable of anything."

"Kerry Hughes disagrees," Ingham replied, without looking away from the stash of drugs.

"With all due respect to Kerry, she's young and far too trusting. She knows Jim well, or she thinks she does. We all want him to be innocent, but I think she'll go further to prove it. That's what caused the mess with the reporter." Doolan's tone wasn't far off the one he liked to lecture younger colleagues with.

Ingham looked around the room as his colleagues worked tirelessly, processing everything with the resources provided to them. "You will take the lead with this and the other matter. You report directly to me, but you will utilise Hughes and Mulligan. I want nothing linking this to the murder case getting out to the press. As far as they're concerned, we're investigating this as a separate issue but maintaining an open mind." Ingham didn't want anyone talking to the press in an unofficial capacity and trusted that Doolan's reputation as a disciplinarian might stop the less experienced colleagues from feeding a few lines to a pretty reporter who batted their eyelids at them.

Kerry arrived and already knew this was Jim's handiwork. The injured man was being loaded into an ambulance, and armed police patrolled the area as everyone pored over the scene. A hand landed on her shoulder, and she swung around, expecting to give Billy another bollocking. Instead, Doolan stood before her.

"Still think he's innocent?" Doolan asked with a wry smile.

"Why wouldn't I? You think this is him? He swooped in here and shot up the place?" Kerry mocked, hoping Doolan would back off.

"That's exactly what I think. He has double-crossed his accomplices, those that intercepted him and came back here to rip them off. Had we not received a call about the gunfire, he'd have taken every ounce of drugs here," Doolan told her with absolute confidence.

"Do you know who called? Was it the gunshot victim?" Kerry asked, knowing it was unlikely a criminal would call the police, but keen to hear Doolan's wild theory.

Doolan looked at her with annoyance. "It wasn't Jim. He didn't call us."

"How do you know that?" Kerry protested. "Drug dealers are hardly known for calling the police on themselves."

"Ingham has placed me in charge, and I need you to canvass the area. Talk to the neighbours, see if there are any witnesses nearby."

"Neighbours? You drove here. There aren't any neighbours." Kerry's anger grew, and she struggled to remain respectful.

"Take a wander and find some." Doolan turned away sharply, heading away before Kerry could respond further.

Kerry left the inside of the warehouse and climbed back into her car, slamming the door behind her. Doolan had made his mind up, and it was hard to blame him to a certain extent. He hadn't been threatened or attacked. He hadn't seen Linda the way she had. For Doolan, it was unsavoury, but obvious that a fellow detective had committed these heinous murders, and to be involved with a major drug smuggling operation wasn't an enormous leap to take. Kerry was in two minds whether to appease Doolan and drive around aimlessly, hoping to find someone who would tell her they heard and saw nothing, or to head straight back to the office. She drove away from the warehouse and onto the main road towards the police cordon with a few journalists waiting for the first official statement and interested locals who had travelled to see the fallout of the latest major crime to befall the island.

Patrick spotted her car as it approached. They lifted the cordon up, and those standing on the other side parted to allow the car through, but Patrick wasn't as accommodating. He stood in front of the car, forcing it to stop, and lifted his hands, gesturing for help. A flick of Kerry's head and Patrick took the signal to get into the car beside her. "You kept that quiet, Kerry. I thought we had an arrangement?"

Kerry drove away and didn't say a word until they were well out of view, and then pulled over. "We don't have an arrangement, Patrick. We have an understanding. One which you've done well out of."

"Still, I heard them talking. There's a shitload of drugs in there." Patrick was excited.

"If that's what you heard, I wouldn't say it was wrong," Kerry said, deciding to be vague.

"Come on, off the record. What are we looking at?" He moved in closer, with a whisper, as if someone might overhear him.

Kerry looked at Patrick. She trusted him more than any other journalist, but that wasn't saying much. "Yes. Cocaine, potentially a massive amount."

"Any arrests?" he probed.

"Just one so far. Listen, your friends on Fleet Street might take some interest again, but I think what comes next will be just as intriguing."

"Walsh?" Patrick said with disdain.

"Keep your phone on. When it happens, I think you will find yourself very busy."

"You've got to give me more than that?" he pleaded. She could have laid the whole situation out, and he'd always want more.

"You should start jogging back. You wouldn't want to miss anything." Kerry smiled and signalled at the door.

Patrick knew better than to waste his time getting more out of her or begging for a lift back to the cordon and took the advice, exiting the car and rushing back to where the current story was. Kerry pondered what would happen next. Maybe Jim would get his revenge, maybe he'd disappear and Doolan would believe it proved him right. Whatever Jim's game plan was, they hadn't managed to kill him yet.

***

Ian couldn't control his anger anymore. He used his feet and fists to smash everything in sight except for the open brick of drugs. He didn't know what was happening at the warehouse at that exact moment, but the brick and the message left him with little doubt that the Kings of Mann had taken yet another hit. Ian would do whatever he could to recover every gram he could.

"Get everyone back here now! Anyone not in this fucking room in the next 15 minutes will have their heads smashed to a bloody pulp!"

The solicitor stood awkwardly in the corner. Kyle was already closer to the shitty end of the stick than he was used to and didn't wish to get his hands any dirtier. Ian turned to look at him, still seething with anger. He didn't say a word, but Kyle wisely made himself scarce. They had unceremoniously dumped Linda on the floor. She was regaining consciousness but could only whine in the small pool of blood that had gathered under her face. Ian briskly approached Linda and pulled his leg back, ready to send a forceful kick into her head, but he stopped as he looked at the door and a figure emerged. Ian stepped back and took a deep breath, straightening himself up.

"You had better start explaining yourself," the figure said as he walked into the wrecked kitchen. "Because if you put a finger on my daughter, I'll have your fucking balls!" Leonard Johnson was well into his sixties, but still a physically imposing hulk of a man. His shaven head, muscles and presence made gave him an air of violent authority, which had served him well on his way up the underworld ladder. The expensive suit didn't mask his obvious menace, but it and his wealth opened more doors to legitimate businesses to protect him from the law.

Ian turned to face Leonard. He wasn't afraid. He did this old man's dirty work for him, as he was no longer capable of doing it himself. In Liverpool, Johnson had plenty of loyalists, and Ian had been one of them for a long time, but on the Isle of Man, Ian had his own team, and the other kings had theirs. If Johnson thought he was going to come to the island to slap him down, he wouldn't like the response. "You shouldn't be here," Ian told him firmly.

"What happened to my daughter?" Leonard's voice grew harsher.

"She was talking to the bizzies." Ian replied with no emotion.

Leonard stepped forward towards his daughter, who had roused herself after hearing her father's voice. Gently, he crouched down. "Are you okay, sweetheart?"

Linda sat up, clutching her bloody nose, and winced with pain. "Dad, they hurt me. And they're incompetent. They let him get away."

Leonard helped her to her feet and turned back to Ian. "Who did it? Point the bastard out."

"I struck the stupid cow," Ian stated as he moved closer to Leonard with his chest sticking out. "And I will do it again if she flaps her trap to the police. I've told you from day bloody one that this is a stupid waste of time. We have a successful operation that you are putting in jeopardy for your childish revenge."

Leonard moved closer to Ian and saw the fresh scratches on his face. "You work for me!" He screamed at Ian.

"To protect your interests here, you've lost sight of that. Now we've been exposed, and the latest shipment looks to be gone." Ian pointed at the drugs and message on the kitchen worktop. "I don't know how much longer I can keep the other kings happy. This might be it. We could all find ourselves with our throats slashed by tomorrow. They're on the island, and they won't keep away any longer. I've done all I can."

Leonard took a moment to look at his bloodied daughter and then at the message written with his drugs. "Get it sorted," he ordered.

"Dad?" Linda protested.

"Get in my car."

"But dad?"

"Get in the fucking car!" Leonard grabbed Linda's arm and led her to the door. He turned to Ian. "You know where I'm staying. Let me know when it's done."

Ian tried to calm himself as Leonard exited the building, supporting his daughter. Ian slowed his pace and walked to one of his men and rested his hand on the man's shoulder. "We're going to be in the park at 3pm. You have until then to bring that woman copper."

"How am I going to find her?" the man asked, aware the task would prove difficult.

"Kyle, you posh prick, get your arse back in here!" Ian shouted with menace.

The solicitor appeared nervously. "Yes?" he answered quietly.

"Call the woman detective. Tell her Linda wants to meet and arrange somewhere close to Ramsey. Then, give the address to this big man and you can fuck off back to wherever. Okay?"

The solicitor nodded and set about his task, eager to complete it and get away.

CHAPTER 40

HAVING FOUND JUST A solitary house over half a mile away and on another road entirely, Kerry had asked the elderly owners if they may have witnessed any comings or goings to the warehouse. The response was predictably confused, and Kerry couldn't blame them. She saw little reason to continue the busy work Doolan had assigned her just to keep her out of the way and was already heading back to Douglas. Her phone rang, and the number was withheld. Kerry paused for a moment, then fumbled to answer it.

"Yes?" Kerry asked, unsure of who it might be. She listened for a moment; her face changed from confusion to excitement. "Where?" Kerry paused to let the voice on the other side speak. "Is she okay? Does she need anything?" Kerry hoicked the car over to the side of the road and nodded to herself as the caller finished up. As soon as the call was over, Kerry called Billy and put the speaker on. She didn't wait for him to answer as she turned the car around and continued on towards Ramsey.

After a few more rings, he picked up, and before he had the chance to speak, Kerry started. "Billy, Linda wants to talk. It doesn't feel right, but I've got to check it out. I need you to back me up," Kerry said in short, excited bursts.

"I'm just at the warehouse. Can it wait?" Billy asked, slightly disappointed at the request. The warehouse was where the action was, and Billy didn't want to miss out.

"No, it can't bloody wait! I'm heading over there. She wants to meet at the football stadium in Ramsey now. Make an excuse with Doolan, then come over, okay?" Kerry ordered.

"Okay, I'll make my way over. Wait for me, and don't do anything stupid," Billy answered, frustrated.

"I'll leave that to you. Thanks Billy," Kerry replied, glad she had Billy to depend upon. She didn't know whether Linda was looking for protection or if she wanted to abuse her again. The solicitor sounded worried when he briefly spoke to her, and Kerry tried to figure out what his story was. Obviously, he didn't work for her directly, so why would he arrange a meeting with the police so Linda could betray his actual paying clients? Kerry reached over and popped open the glove box and began searching blindly with her hand until she found what she was looking for. She pulled a set of handcuffs and a baton out and placed them on the passenger seat. She hadn't carried her baton since she was in uniform. Its small size hid how hard it could strike in the right, trained hands. Kerry was glad she had kept it in the car rather than locked up in her desk. It wasn't a match for a gun, but it was better than nothing.

***

Mid-afternoon on a weekday, the stadium would normally have been closed, with a heavy padlocked chain securing the gates, but today it was absent. The players, coaches and other staff of the club would likely be at their day jobs, and no one would have been in the small stadium until training that evening. Kerry had parked up on the side road and slipped her baton and handcuffs into her jacket pockets. She looked around, and the street appeared quiet. At best, Billy would be a few minutes away. If Doolan made it difficult and he couldn't easily slip away, he could be much longer. Kerry called Billy on her phone, but there was no answer.

She stepped out of her car and walked across to the open gates, and looked through. The ground was tiny, a standard sized football pitch and a small, well-used concrete stand stood to one side of the playing area. It was empty. No Linda, no English solicitor. Kerry looked up and down the street and saw no signs of anything unusual. She strode back to her car and again tried to call Billy, but again there was no answer. Kerry looked at her watch. She had made good time, roaring over the mountain roads, and couldn't think Linda had already left. Maybe she was inside, keeping herself out of sight until Kerry bound into the stadium, and then she would reveal herself. Another glance at her watch, and it was 2:55pm. A look up and down the street, and she boldly walked to the gates. Scanning again inside, she couldn't see any movement. She paused and took a deep breath before she cautiously crossed the threshold.

Kerry's heart pounded in her chest as she walked towards the stand. Looking left and right for Linda, or possibly an attacker, she carried on further into the stadium. She began wishing that she had waited for Billy. Another pair of eyes would have eased her nerves and boosted her confidence. As she approached the concrete stand, she already knew it was empty. Her fear of an ambush or hope that Linda was going to make everything better both drained from her. Just a wild-goose chase. Linda was a bitch, but this was just unnecessarily mean.

A hand came down on her shoulder.

"Damn it, Billy!" Kerry shouted as she whipped round.

The man standing behind her was a behemoth and certainly wasn't Billy. A toothless grin and a pistol confirmed Kerry's worst fears were true.

"You're gonna come with me," he said menacingly, raising the pistol to emphasise his point.

Without wasting a moment, Kerry caught the man by surprise and pushed the handgun away, sending it flying to the floor. She followed up with a kick to his knee, sending the man buckling to the ground. Kerry stepped back to give herself some space as the man rose back to his feet, with his fists raised in front of him, ready to attack. Kerry reached for her baton and flicked it to the side, extending it to its full length. Her attacker remained unimpressed.

The man charged her, throwing a fist in her direction that Kerry skillfully dodged, following up with a strike of the baton to the man's legs. Forcing him to the ground again. Before he could rise to his feet, Kerry struck him across the face with the baton, and this time, he stayed down. Kerry stood over the man, waiting to hit him again if he tried to climb back to his feet, but he didn't move.

"Kerry!" Billy called out as he ran through the stadium towards her.

"Billy!" Kerry shouted back, pleased that he had arrived to support her.

"Are you okay?" he asked, looking down at the man and the nearby pistol.

Kerry already had her set of handcuffs out and was securing the unconscious man on the ground. "I'm fine."

"Linda?" Billy asked, trying to figure out what he had missed.

"No, I don't think she was ever coming. They wanted me."

Billy had his phone to his ear and looked around the stadium to confirm the situation. "This is DC Billy Mulligan. We have an armed man in custody at the football stadium in Ramsey. Requesting firearms support immediately and an ambulance." He looked at Kerry. "Is he alone?"

"I don't know," she replied, unsure.

"I'm securing the scene. Be advised, there may be further armed threats," Billy responded before listening to the response.

Kerry started searching the man's pockets. Two magazines of ammo for the pistol, a wallet and a set of car keys. She looked at the keys and walked away towards the stadium gates.

Billy looked towards her. "Hang on, one minute." Billy spoke into his phone before he pushed it into his shoulder. "Kerry, I'm the idiot, not you. Stay here until support arrives." He put the phone back to his ear and continued with the call.

Kerry looked at the man, the gun, and the keys. She knew Billy was right and set about helping to secure the scene. She wished she hadn't knocked the thug out. He could have told her what was going on; why they wanted her. Even wide awake, Kerry was aware these were professional villains, and not likely to roll over with vague threats of jail time. They had their chance and blew it. She worried about Jim once more. They were obviously getting desperate. If they were willing to kidnap a serving police detective in the middle of the day, they were capable of nearly anything.

CHAPTER 41

I T WAS EARLY AFTERNOON. Soon, the local schools would empty for the day. School children looking for a kick around, a friendly BMX race or an ice cream on the crazy golf course would join the odd dog walker or visitor to the park. Jim had little time when he reached the park to put his rushed plan into action. He put the car in the attached car park and opened up the boot, looking around to confirm he wasn't being watched. The bricks were everywhere. None had split open, but they had all moved freely during their unsecured journey. He picked up the nearest one and placed it under his jacket, struggling to hold it in place. It fell to the ground, and he groaned in frustration. Jim loosened his belt and shoved it inside the top of his trousers. A few awkward steps confirmed it wouldn't budge, and also how uncomfortable it was for him as it rubbed against his gut. Jim looked next at the shotgun. He reached for it, then stopped himself. It was one thing going into these bastards' home or warehouse toting a gun, but this was a public park. The risk was too great that an innocent passerby would be hurt. Indeed, he'd picked the park to keep it public and reduce the risk of violence, knowing they wouldn't want to draw attention to themselves with so many witnesses. His own blood lust had subsided, and he wanted them all in prison, their names and faces all over the media. He locked the car and walked through the park, checking the clock on the smartphone. It was nearly time. Jim searched through the installed apps and found the recording app he'd installed, set it to record, and stuffed the device into a pocket.

Jim didn't for a moment expect them to turn up at 3pm on the dot. They might already be there or possibly hadn't even seen his dramatic message. His eyes shot around, looking at every person who came into his view, looking for someone who didn't fit in. A heavy, like those he'd seen already, should stick out amongst the mothers with prams and pensioners taking their Westies for a walk. Everything was normal, and Jim's heart sank. If they didn't turn up, what would he do then? He had a car full of drugs and his face was better known than any member of the Bee Gees; Jim wouldn't enjoy freedom for long if he stayed in the open. He was counting on being recognised. He wanted the police to come, but only after he'd got the evidence he wanted. If they arrived before his tormentors, they would only catch him with a car full of Class A drugs to bury him deeper. It was a gamble; he knew that.

Jim recognised the man instantly. The last time he had seen him, Jim was bashing the back of his head in, using his cuffed hands, but he was definitely one of his attempted kidnappers. The man's eyes had already locked on to Jim, who looked around and saw a second, then a third likely member of the team. Each stared at their target, but none of them looked like the boss. They were large units, more than capable of looking after themselves, but even from a distance, none enjoyed an air of authority. Jim moved towards the crazy golf course, opting against entering the area, and instead waiting on the nearby grass verge, his three shadows keeping a respectful, menacing distance.

"Fancy a game?" a voice boomed from the crazy golf course.

Jim looked up at the man. Ian stood with his arm outstretched towards Jim. A well-used putter and a scarred orange golf ball were in his grasp and being offered to him.

"Come on Jim, let's get started, shall we?" Ian stated.

Jim looked around and noted the thugs had kept their positions and were unlikely to make an immediate move.

"Do you want your drugs?" Jim asked, suddenly uncertain.

"Hold it there, big boy. I thought you wanted to play?" Ian slowly walked over to Jim and made sure the golf club and ball were received.

"I don't want to play bloody crazy golf."

"Then why are we here?" Ian placed his ball down and took a shot on the first hole, failing to get near the flag.

"You've ruined my life, and I've got your drugs." Jim seethed.

"Drugs? I heard there was a bust on the island. Sounds terrible. Sounds like they confiscated an awful lot of drugs. I'd say whoever they belonged to would be pretty pissed. Blind fucking fury, I'd imagine." Ian stared at Jim, leaving him with little doubt of his mood.

Jim stared at Ian as he cued up his second shot and put the ball in the hole. "You came after me. You decided I was worth bothering with, and I bothered back. I have enough drugs left to at least hold off the other Kings, buy you enough time to replace what the police now have."

Ian looked up with genuine surprise that Jim had mentioned the Kings. "I'm listening."

"Give me Johnson and leave me the hell alone, and you get everything I grabbed from your warehouse," Jim offered.

"Give you Johnson? Hand over my boss? No bloody chance." Ian lined up a shot on the next hole, about to take his shot. Jim tossed his club in front of Ian's ball and followed it with the brick of cocaine. Ian looked up. His anger grew, but he tried to conceal it and any reaction.

"You were dead the moment you met that girl. You were dead the moment he decided it," Ian told him flatly.

"Do the other Kings feel that way? You killed my wife and that poor girl. Did your Irish and Scottish friends sign off on risking everything because you and your boss are morons?" Jim said with a smile.

"They're dead because of you. We just did the dirty work. You pissing off the wrong person made it happen," Ian bitterly answered in response. "You drove our car here with our drugs in it. Who's the moron? I was expecting more from you as you tried to beg for your life, but I guess you're just a stupid Manx detective who couldn't make it on the mainland. You have nothing we need now. So, I'll make you an offer. Come with us quietly, and Johnson will kill you himself, quick and painless. If you make us have to wrestle you into the back of a car, I promise your death will take days." Ian dropped his putter to the floor and looked at his watch. "You know I'm not alone, and there's no point in running. Don't be silly. Just come with me now."

"Leonard Johnson blames me for his kid killing himself, and he's risked everything to get to me. He's put you in the way and will sacrifice you to get me. You don't owe him anything," Jim pleaded.

"You know nothing about me, but I can tell you one thing. If you believe I'll choose you over him, you've lost your mind."

"Give him up!" Jim screamed at the top of his lungs, catching Ian off-guard. Jim needed the police and needed to draw attention to himself. He had as close a confession as he was going to get and now needed help. He hoped the police had already been called and that they would turn up at any moment and that the firearms unit would put the thugs on their knees at the end of a 9mm carbine. But there was nothing. A few school kids on bikes cycled through the park. The first and the fastest out of the school gates had made their way straight to the park, leaving the next wave on foot to follow behind in the next few minutes. Jim had the evidence of his innocence on his phone, but what good was that if he couldn't get it into the right hands? Maybe he should have brought the shotgun after all.

"You need to calm down. A very painful death is still on the cards. Come quietly, without a problem, and I'll promise you it'll be quick." Ian looked around to see if Jim's outburst had caused attention to be shown their way.

"How do you want to do this?" Jim asked, resigned to his fate.

"We'll just walk to the car, you get in and we'll drive to the boss. You do anything silly and I'll put a knife in your leg."

"Can I relieve myself first?" Jim asked.

"You're joking, right?" Ian asked in disbelief.

"I'm coming quietly. What am I going to do, make a swim for it?" Jim answered sarcastically, gesturing towards the lake in the middle of the park.

"You can piss against that palm tree," Ian responded, pointing to a tree just off of the small course.

Jim nodded and walked to the tree. Facing away from Ian, he skillfully produced the phone without letting Ian see and held it in his hands as he unzipped his trouser fly. He slid the handset into the front of his trousers and into his left leg, where he let the phone slide down until it popped out from the bottom of his trouser leg and lay next to the tree in the grass. Jim positioned the phone with his foot, hoping a passerby would discover it and not his tormentors. He zipped his trousers back up and walked back to Ian. "I'm ready."

Ian picked up the drugs from the crazy golf course and shoved them into his jacket before walking with Jim, signalling to his men as he led the disgraced detective away.

Jim no longer felt the need to comply. They said it themselves. He was dead anyway. The park wasn't too busy, but in the next few minutes it would fill with children. It was now or never.

The tarmac was smooth and blemish free, but Jim was convincing as he feigned a trip, allowing himself to stumble a few feet, then stop to compose himself. Ian stopped beside him, and with a clenched fist, Jim swung at Ian, connecting cleanly with the man's chin, catching him by surprise. Ian spun to the ground and scrambled to get back to his feet as Jim punched him again, knocking him back to the tarmac. Jim didn't wait for the others to jump him and ran off as fast as he could.

Anger overtook Ian's surprise, and he pulled out a 9mm handgun from under his coat and fired two unaimed shots at Jim. Both pinged past him and harmlessly into the ground ahead. Jim slowed to a stop with his hands up. He couldn't risk a member of the public being hurt. He turned slowly as Ian approached with fire in his eyes. Ian landed a solid punch into Jim's gut, causing Jim to collapse to his knees, the wind taken out of him. Ian placed the barrel of the pistol against Jim's head.

"You had to do it, didn't you?" Ian screamed as he kicked Jim to the ground. "You stupid bloody prick!" Ian looked around and could see the mix of witnesses, some frozen in place, others running for their lives and several pointing their smartphones at the altercation recording the action. "Come on!" Ian grabbed Jim's collar and tried to drag him back to his feet, but Jim was unwilling and mostly unable to comply. "Get up, you piece of shit!" Ian bellowed at Jim and shoved the pistol into the back of his head. "Get moving now!"

Ian's men rushed to the pair and pulled Jim to his feet. Jim let himself go limp. His enormous frame made him a deadweight that the men couldn't easily manoeuvre. They dragged him forward; his feet bumped along the ground as Jim waited for his next chance. Each of the men now looked panicked as they struggled to get their man across the park and back to their waiting vehicles. All of them were aware of the scene that was in progress and the witnesses who were now recording them. Only their loyalty to Ian had kept them onside this long, but as the first man let go of Jim and ran, the second, then third followed, leaving Jim on his knees with Ian anxiously standing over him as sirens sounded in the distance.

"You're all on film, probably live on the internet right now. Give it up, give him up," pleaded Jim as he slowly rose to his feet.

Ian paced around and pushed the gun into Jim's chest. "Maybe it is over, so why shouldn't I just finish you here and now? It's not like you're all armed over here. I can slot you and get away."

The sirens grew louder. Jim looked at Ian, and the gun pointed at him. "You're loyal, but you're not stupid. This is an island. The only way off for you will be a bloody jet ski back to England, and then what? Your face will be everywhere. What little freedom you have left will be spent looking over your shoulder or trying to barter your way onto a ship to some non-extradition country. And that's if he doesn't take care of your first."

Ian looked around him and calmed. He could see his men nearly at the van and car, and just like him, their actions were captured on a plethora of phones. Ian lowered the gun and handed it over to Jim. "You know, she screamed. God, she screamed a lot. Of course, she was in a lot of pain. I made sure of that."

Jim quivered. He didn't realise he had raised the pistol and had it pointing at Ian.

"The lads wanted a go on her. I thought about letting them, but I actually think she wanted that. You could tell she hadn't had a good seeing to for quite some time," goaded Ian.

Police were shouting in the distance at Ian's men. Two more were now in sight, running towards Jim and Ian.

Jim gently squeezed the trigger until it was nearly fully depressed, then he stopped himself and took a deep breath. Carefully, he removed his finger from the trigger and placed it on the trigger guard. He looked Ian in the eyes and, without warning, smashed the pistol across his face. "I don't think anyone will begrudge me that."

Ian staggered backwards and fell to the floor. Jim placed the pistol on the ground and stepped back, dropping to his knees with his hands on the back of his head. As the two officers cautiously approached, he laid down on the ground with his arms and legs spread out.

He was done.

CHAPTER 42

Despite the relatively calm waters, the small fishing vessel bobbed up and down as it drew to a complete stop in the middle of the Irish Sea. The boat had made it far enough out that the island was barely visible on the horizon. Four men stood in pairs over two hooded figures that were on their knees on the deck, a broad man and a smaller woman, their hands bound behind their backs. They greeted any movement or sound from the pair with a swift kick to put them back in their place. The four men waited patiently until one member of each pair signalled the other. They quickly whipped the hoods off, and Leonard and Linda Johnson adjusted their eyes to the light.

Leonard looked at his daughter, and his face dropped. He turned to the men. "You're all dead. Do you know who I am?"

The four men looked at each other and smirked.

One stepped forward and produced a small hatchet. "Yeah, we know who you are. You're the English bastard who lost us a lot of money. The English fecker who did his best to destroy a profitable business. The English gobshite who risked everything and got nothing." He had a thick Irish accent and a curious smile.

"I can get the money. The Kings will be whole, and I'll take the loss."

"The Kings will be whole? That's very kind, Leo. But this isn't just about money, not anymore. You put us all at risk. Aidan isn't happy. He thinks you put him and his family in harm's way for your revenge." The Irishman walked slowly behind Leonard.

"Aye, and you should have seen Fraser. He was very displeased with these events." A Scottish accent belonging to one man in the other pair.

"I know. I went too far, and I shouldn't have involved the other Kings. It should have been dealt with differently. I'll pay for the next two shipments and take a quarter of the profits." Leonard knew how serious this situation was. He was completely vulnerable. They could kill him and dump him in the bottom of sea and no one would ever know who had done it or that it had even happened.

"You are a kind and generous man," the Irishman smiled. "But they have already come to an agreement. Just one more thing and you're good."

The two non-speakers stepped forward and picked up Linda, grabbing her arms and dragging her to the edge of the boat. Leonard squirmed, sensing where this would go.

"Daddy!" Linda cried out, tears streaming down her face.

"It'll be okay, sweetheart, it'll be okay!" Leonard tried to reassure his daughter. "Please don't," he pleaded. Leonard was a hard man, but his eyes watered as he fought back the tears.

They hoisted Linda onto her feet and began rooting through a nearby storage box. One man lifted an old rust-covered anchor from the box and dropped it to the floor behind Linda with an audible thud that made her flinch. The anchor wasn't big, but it was solid, and a short piece of discoloured rope had already been attached.

"Please don't!" Leonard shouted.

The Irishman put his finger to his own lips. "Shhh."

They carefully tied the anchor to Linda's legs, pulling the rope until it was uncomfortably tight and secure.

"Daddy, please don't let them!" Linda screamed desperately.

Leonard turned away, unable to look at Linda as they lifted her to the edge of the boat. The Scotsman grabbed Leonard roughly by the side of his head and forced him to watch the murder that was about to be committed. Linda screamed desperately as she looked into the dark sea beneath her. The horrible sound filled the air, and with a single splash, silence was restored.

"Now, Leo. I know this hurts. That is on you. If you have a problem, you can join your girl, but if you're smart. You'll draw a line underneath this. That stupid shit you pulled when your son topped himself, no repeats. We're not some noddy copper who you can target. We're stronger than you are, and can take you apart." The Irishman spoke quietly, but roughly, emphasising the end of each word.

"You bastards," Leonard sobbed.

"Now, now, don't be like that. This is over. Do you understand?" the Irishman stated firmly. Leonard stared at him but didn't say a word. The Irishman turned to one of the other men and nodded. The man produced another small anchor from the storage box and dropped it on the floor in front of Leonard. "It's your choice."

"I understand," Leonard confirmed through gritted teeth. "Take me back, now."

"You heard the man. Let's head back to port. If you don't mind, we'll keep the restraints on until we get back. Give you a little time to compose yourself." The Irishman signalled to the small pilothouse, and the engine roared back into life.

CHAPTER 43

T HREE MONTHS LATER.

It was a typical Saturday afternoon in the Nelson. Live rugby was showing on the screens dotted around the bar area, and the occasional request to put the football scores on was met with groans. Jim was sitting at the bar with an empty barstool next to him. A hand came down on his shoulder and made him jolt.

"Jesus, don't sneak up on a man," Jim replied with a smile.

Kerry responded with a smile of her own. "Can I get you a drink?"

"Orange juice and lemonade, please."

Kerry nodded and signalled to the barman that she was waiting. "An orange juice and lemonade, and a small white wine."

"Careful, that's how it starts," Jim joked.

"I think I'll be okay. Anyway, I'm not on duty. This is a social visit." Kerry sat down on the empty barstool.

"That's Daz's seat. You can keep it warm until he gets back from the little boy's room. If he ever gets back." Jim looked anxiously at the small staircase leading up to the toilets.

Kerry looked too, but saw nothing. "Bloody hell, Jim, didn't you think to help him?"

"He survived on the mountains overnight, half beaten to death. I'm sure he can handle a slightly awkward set of stairs to take a piss."

Kerry sat down next to Jim and enjoyed a few moments without speaking, soaking up the atmosphere of the afternoon in the pub and how normal life was slowly returning. "When are you coming back?"

Jim stared ahead, not looking at Kerry. "I don't think I'm wanted back."

"You were innocent. They cleared you," Kerry said. In her mind, it should be that simple.

"Of the murders, yes. But I didn't come out smelling of roses. I didn't behave in a manner, becoming of a member of the constabulary. I'm lucky I'm not being charged and facing a prison term of my own."

"That's bollocks," Kerry replied.

The barman brought over the drinks, and Kerry handed him a banknote.

"That's the law, Kerry. I can't complain about what the Command Team chooses to do with me. I regret nothing I did. Maybe I regret not doing a few things. I still wonder if I should have just shot the bastard, but I am where I am because of the decisions I made," Jim said, looking at the nearest TV screen but not paying it any attention.

"And if you didn't make those decisions, you'd be on trial now, or dead. You have to fight it, surely?" Kerry wanted Jim back. Now that he was sober, she knew he could teach her even more.

"Well, on the bright side, with me out of the picture, you've got yourself a promotion." Jim smiled and raised his glass in her direction.

"Not yet. Doolan has managed to get his foot in the door. They're giving him six months in the hot seat, but they have assured me I'll get my turn." Kerry stated sarcastically. Already deciding she had missed her chance.

Jim had a genuine look of shock on his face. "He's stepping away from the coroner's office?"

"The lure of DS is too great. Maybe he feels you're not a hard act to follow," Kerry answered, taking a sip of her wine.

"They're fools if they don't give it to you."

"Thanks, but for some reason, they've been really careful with the appointment. I can't think why." Kerry winked at Jim. They both knew exactly why anyone looking to take the detective sergeant role would now be heavily scrutinised.

"Just keep doing what you've been doing. You'll do well. And now, you'll find out just how much of a pussycat I really was," Jim said confidently.

"So what now for you?" Kerry asked, hoping to shift the focus away from herself.

"I'm on compassionate leave. I guess that's a friendlier way of putting it rather than a suspension. After the trial is all taken care of, I expect I'll be quietly let go," he said sadly.

"It's not fair."

"After what happened with Cassie, Ella, Daz, and even to you? Me losing my job is hardly the greatest injustice. I'm not in a place where I can just get back to it even if I wanted to. I'm sorry."

Daz slowly appeared on the from the doorway leading to the stairs. He walked awkwardly, unable to hide the discomfort of every step as he limped towards the bar. Kerry instinctively rose to her feet to give him back his seat. Jim stood and placed his hand on her shoulder and shook his head. She sat back down, and Jim offered his seat to his friend.

"You come here to arrest him?" Daz asked with a touch of aggression.

"Not today. I'm just saying hello," Kerry replied, not sure if he was joking or not.

"Well, now you can say goodbye," Daz replied with a snarl.

"It's okay, mate. We're just going to head outside for some fresh air. I'll be back in five." Jim grabbed his coat from a hook under the bar and signalled for Kerry to join him in heading outside.

They crossed the road toward the harbour and to the water. A few small vessels were secured, but the low tide only made them visible if standing directly over the water and mud.

"Daz is still in a bad way?" Kerry asked.

"Yeah, I don't think he'll ever get back to who he was. Not just physically, but mentally. Don't take it personally. He doesn't feel he can be angry with me. He knows those who tortured him were just lackeys, and he's bitter."

"We couldn't build a case against Leonard Johnson. The recording was good, but it wasn't enough compared to what we had on the others. Johnson was a name on a recording. There were no other ties. He's too far removed from the criminal activity, and he's not stepped back on the island in months. That smug bastard Ian Harrison isn't saying a word, and his men haven't budged an inch either. If Linda resurfaces, maybe she'll talk again, but I think it's over. No more international drugs ring, just back to people stealing their neighbours' milk and the odd post pub fight that goes too far," Kerry said, relieved life could return to how it used to be.

"It's not over, Kerry. Not for me or Daz. But it's not over for them either. Whether it's three months or three years.

They'll be back, causing misery. You have little idea how they got the drugs in, how they got them out. Just coffee crates on a ship that appeared from nowhere. All we know is they were moving a fortune in cocaine and were doing very well for themselves." Jim looked at one of the larger vessels unloading its catch of scallops at the far end of the harbour. He squinted to see better, almost as if he expected to see large crates of coffee being unloaded.

"All the more reason to fight for your job. If you really think they'll be back; you need to be at the forefront," Kerry pleaded.

"If my experience of going rogue has taught me anything, it's that not being bound by the rules can yield results. I'll be waiting for them," Jim answered calmly.

"So just like that, you're giving up on the police, on being a detective?"

"I'm still a detective." Jim fumbled in his pockets and pulled out a small stack of business cards. He took the top one and handed it to Kerry.

"Jim Walsh, Private Detective, JW Investigations Ltd, The Manx Detective," she read. "Is this a joke? You're going to be looking for missing cats and tracing long-lost relatives now?" Kerry asked in disbelief.

"There are an awful lot of wealthy financial institutions on the island. They need experienced investigators all the time and don't discount the rich people who run them. I'm a name now. I'm not Jim Walsh, the nobody. I'm not Jim Walsh, the murderer. Now I'm Jim Walsh, the man who cleared himself and stopped a multi-million-pound drug ring. I already have a client cued up, and as soon as I'm discharged, I can start working again."

Kerry rubbed Jim on the back, comforting him as if he'd just given her bad news. "Good luck Jim. Try not to bend too many laws. I really don't want to arrest you again," she said with sadness in her voice. Kerry was losing a colleague, a mentor. And no matter how bad he was at times, he had taught her a lot.

"Next time, I'll be ready for them. I'll get to Johnson and wreck his life. He'll pay for his sins. I swear he will." Jim's voice broke as he spoke.

Both looked across the harbour and watched the ship being unloaded, hypnotised by the task. Kerry hoped the criminals never returned, and that Johnson stayed in Liverpool. If they came back, there would only be more bloodshed, and next time, Jim might not survive.

About Author

I have so many memories of the Isle of Man and have a great affection for the island.

When I first visited the Isle of Man, I'm pretty sure I was in Junior School, maybe 8 or 9 years old. My parents had divorced, and after a few years in London and the surrounding areas, my dad had moved to the Isle of Man to continue his career in finance. My mum would have driven me and my brother to Heathrow airport, where she checked us in and stayed with us until we had to go through the gates. I remember getting the little VIP wallet that hung from our necks, identifying us as children travelling without an adult, and carrying such little things like our plane tickets. The Manx Airlines planes were smaller than I had ever been on before. Sometimes you might get a jet engine, but I think I remember sometimes it would be a prop plane. I remember the props were especially loud on my young ears and never enjoyed them. I also remember the bowl of boiled sweets the cabin crew would walk down the aisle with prior to takeoff and getting a Coke once in the air. Both were my favourite part of the flight experience. It seemed like every time we flew out to the island it was in the evening, so there was nothing to see, even if I beat my brother to the window seat.

I was always a bit of a nervous flyer. Maybe it was being so young on a plane with just my brother, who is only a couple of years older. Maybe it was because I was about to see my dad and we could go months or even years without seeing one another. Once there, we were always entertained. My dad would arrange activities for us, take us out to dinner and buy us things we couldn't normally afford. Every day he'd give us a little money, so when we strolled around Ramsey or took the bus to Douglas, we had something to spend. We'd normally spend it on rubbish, or spend hours in the arcade on the Douglas sea front, but we had fun. Something we always liked was the pound notes. For a couple of kids who normally didn't have a great deal of money, we aimed to get as many £1 notes as possible until we had a good size wad of cash. In truth, it was never more than £20 or £30 pounds, but that was a lot to a kid in early nineties, and we'd enjoy carrying it until dad dropped us back at the airport and he would then exchange the Manx banknotes for English ones which we could more easily spend back home. We were still flush, but it didn't feel the same.

I remember the time my dad's house was in (at the time) Andreas; it was close to Christmas, and somebody pulled a prank who apparently believed someone else lived at the house. They expertly switched over all of his expensive white light bulbs from his external Christmas lights with the much cheaper multi-coloured ones from the local school. I say expertly, what I mean is they broke less than they swapped. We spent a chilly morning unscrewing the bulbs and swapping them back with those at the school. My dad didn't find it all that funny. I also seem to remember I preferred the colourful bulbs.

One time we were visiting, and it was around fireworks night, and my dad duly obliged to put a mini display on for us at his house. We sat on the step of the sliding patio door as, a few feet away, my dad let off the small rockets from a little box of fireworks sold in one of the local shops. Rocket after rocket whizzed into the air, giving a small, yet delightful, explosion above. That is, until one rocket didn't. It fizzed, but didn't budge from where it had been stabbed into the flowerbed launchpad and exploded on the ground. The only injuries suffered were to my favourite shell suit (it was the early nineties, I was very young and I assure you it was the fashion); it was peppered with holes where the outer material had melted as the sparks had struck it. A near miss, but like any true showman, my dad didn't let a little thing like a near death experience ruin the performance and the display continued until there were no more fireworks to nearly kill his kids with. After promises of mothers back in Kent not being told, and replacement shell suits to be purchased we didn't think of it again (I didn't get a replacement to my beloved shell suit, and it was the first thing I told my mum when we returned home).

As we got older, our activities changed a little. My dad arranged for activities such as going bunny hunting with some of his friends. I remember the car trip with a scouse lad and a true Irish gentleman, picking up a dog on the way to help flush out the rabbits and driving to some piece of land somewhere on the island to bag a few bunnies. A 14-year-old with a 12 Gauge Browning shotgun is not necessarily the recipe for success. The first rustle of bushes, a confused command to shoot, saw me blast the shotgun into the undergrowth only for our dog to come bounding out seconds later. "He shot the fucking dog!"

was the shout from the big Irishman. Thankfully, he was wrong. The dog was unscathed and my nerves were the only thing that had been shot. We spent a few more cold hours outside, not seeing a single rabbit, and I can't say I was too disappointed. My first and last hunting experience had been set up by my dad, and I was grateful for that. It wasn't his thing, but he made it happen. Turns out it wasn't my thing either, but it was an enlightening experience. The pub factored a lot, but not in a bad way. My dad might work whilst we were there visiting, so spent much of the day in his office, but he would take us for lunch in a local pub. Or it might be the weekend and we'd go to watch the football. When we reached legal drinking age was about the time he probably spent less time in the pub, with us at least. I wish we could have enjoyed a few pints together, just him, myself, my brother, and our sister. But I never seem to remember it happening.

Whether it was staying up until the early hours watching some questionable Steven Seagal films, going to Jurby Junk or having a drink in the Traf, when I think of the Isle of Man, I think of my dad. He loved the island and never had a desire to move back to England. For a boy from the East End of London, he found his home on a small island in the Irish Sea. I miss him, and I miss the excuse to visit the island. I hope to get back there soon, as the world now returns to something approaching normal. Maybe with my brother and sister, or even my wife and children. Because the island meant so much to my dad, it will always mean a lot to me too.

If you enjoyed "Fall of Man", I hope you'll perform a genre swap and look at my other titles, "Deadweight", "The Last Bite: Deadweight Part II" and "Thornhurst: A Deadweight Novella"–my zombie apocalypse series set in the UK.

The Manx Detective will return, if you'd like to keep up to date with what's happening, or check out my other books, head on over to https://www.paulforsterauthor.comto take a look around, and maybe even sign-up for my mailing list, and as a thankyou you will receive a free short story.

ALSO BY PAUL FORSTER

Deadweight

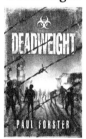

They hailed it as the answer to the obesity epidemic; a pill that allows you to eat anything you like and still lose weight. The promise of a leaner, fitter body attracted millions, but there was a fatal and unforeseen flaw in this new panacea.A tiny microbe, lurking within, slowly infects the users. In turn they pass the infection to others with a sneeze, a cough or a simple kiss, and before long tens of millions are infected and turned into mindless, shambling wrecks, with the sole purpose of existing to eat. The virus is rampant, reaching into every corner of the globe. Governments collapse and shut down, unable to contain the outbreak, while the army works hard against the unending assault in a desperate bid to stop the dead from achieving total victory. But there are even greater dangers to be faced. A few unfortunate souls suffer with the hunger of the dead but the mind of the living. They are neither dead nor alive, but something in between; something far more dangerous to the surviving humans. And amidst this carnage of the end of the world, in the south east of England, a small group of survivors are fighting on, against all the odds, as they try to stay one step in front of the dead, trying to avoid being the next item on the menu. The question is, in a world now claimed by the dead, what will they have to do to survive?

The Last Bite: Deadweight Part II

The promised cure for obesity turned out to be the catalyst that made the Black Death look like a quiet Sunday stroll. It infected hundreds, then thousands, then millions, until the world was all but consumed by the ravenous hordes it created. They found their way into every safe haven and fortress and massacred the few remaining survivors at will. Nowhere was safe. Nobody was immune. Nothing was sacred.
And yet some resilient survivors remained.
As a few clung on in small groups, somehow evading

the death that was all around them, they were hoping against hope for salvation. Then, a chance to save the world emerges with the hunt for an enigmatic scientist who may hold the key for a cure.

But even this piece of good news may have come too late. In the English Channel, a flotilla of ships keeps the new Prime Minister, her closest advisors, and thousands of desperate survivors away from the madness that is unfolding on land. And here, protected by what remains of the military, the Prime Minister is prepared to do whatever is necessary to maintain her iron grip on power. Even if it means sacrificing those who remain to new and emerging subspecies of feeders that are becoming ever more dangerous.

Can a cure be found before the last remaining survivors are overwhelmed? Or is it already too late?

Thornhurst: A Deadweight Novella

When the feeders started to rise, the small English village of Thornhurst believed it was immune to the problems of the towns and cities. The news of civil disobedience, rioting and violent attacks didn't initially seem a concern for a small and traditional place such as Thornhurst. They had a peaceful existence; the old village pub and tea shop being the most lively part of village life.

Then the dead came. Former neighbours and wandering

strangers only had one thing on their primitive minds, to feast upon the living.

The simple invention of a weight loss drug had changed the world forever. Fighting off the dead, raiders and dealing with an overstretched army, the villagers of Thornhurst were ill-prepared for this new dead world. This is the story of what happened to Thornhurst, and those that called it home.

A standalone story from the Deadweight universe.

Printed in Great Britain
by Amazon